MR. INSIDE

A Novel

MR. INSIDE

A Novel

L. Frank James

The Salt Works

Roseville, CA

The Lost & Found International Series

ISBN 13: 978-1934080016

Library of Congress Control Number: 2007934526

Creative director: Robert Brekke

Cover design: Chuck Donald

The Salt Works

a division of
Publishers Design Group, Inc.
P.O. Box 37
Roseville, CA 95678
916.784.0500
www.publishersdesign.com

In memory of my mother,

Jeanette Clerye Fitzgerald James, 1921 - 1975

Two men looked out
From prison bars...
One saw mud,
The other saw stars...

—ANONYMOUS

But we had to celebrate and rejoice, for this brother of yours was
dead and has begun to live, and was lost and has been found.

—LUKE 15:32

A human life is like a single letter of the alphabet. It can be
meaningless or it can be part of a great meaning...

—ANNE LAMOTT

CONTENTS

Continued on next page

THE CAST

Dear Reader,

Deep, profound, and intimate tragedy has a way of either softening one's heart or hardening it—oftentimes making us cynical and self-protective.

For eighteen years I have worked in church ministry, the past four as a Care Pastor, and I have found such circumstances to be all too common, virtually universal. We can all point to the disappointments and suffering that have defied our ability to overcome doubt. Our reaction to such adversity is often paralyzing.

The characters in this novel are, in essence, real—I have met hundreds of them, both inside and outside the church. The issue always seems to be the same: *If God is good, if God cares, how could he allow this or that to happen?*

For most unbelievers, this issue is admittedly a pivotal one, at least on a subconscious level, and they have no problem expressing their thinking when asked. For most believers, this issue is also prevalent, although it tends to be camouflaged by the trappings of prosperity, religion, and ritual. It is only when dire circumstances upset us that we become aware that deep inside, we have something in common with unbelievers—the existence of those gnawing, unsettling, pivotal questions: *Is God good, loving, and just? Does he really care?*

In my first novel, *An Opened Grave: Sherlock Holmes Investigates His Ultimate Case*, the arguments for belief and unbelief were handled logically; Holmes and Watson were the perfect characters for the debate and counter-debate.

However, *Mr. Inside* approaches the arguments for belief from the heart, the center of that protected core where doubt, anger, and fear lurk. I found it much easier to argue with agnosticism in the first book; I could keep my distance while I wrote.

Writing *Mr. Inside* was an emotional rollercoaster. It made me think about the many people I love—family and friends, believers and unbelievers—who really would like to settle the issue about God's goodness and why he lets things happen.

In *Mr. Inside*, through the plot, the characters, and the circumstances, I hope to demonstrate that the answer is simple—not easy, but simple and freeing.

—L. Frank James
Roseville, CA 2007

CHAPTER 1

Fairfield, Missouri – 1947

I will never forget a particular Sunday afternoon when I was twelve and a half years old.

"...forty-seven, forty-eight, forty-nine, fifty! Ready or not, here I come!" I yelled out confidently. I was a master finder. There was no one like me. In most hide-and-seek games, the term "It" meant you had to do the seeking. Most folks believed that being pursued was more enjoyable than being the pursuer. Not me.

I'm Gus, formally Gustov, which is the family name of my long-departed great-grandfather Gustov who, along with my great-granduncle Werner, immigrated from the old country some eighty-five years earlier.

I turned to survey the panorama. Home base was an old telephone pole converted into an electric wire pole. I paused for a second, taking great pride in being undefeated in the finding department. No one could elude me, not my younger brother Andy, not Ted, Virgil, or any of the guys, not Alice, or any of the girls for that matter. I was the king of finding things.

Andy no doubt was hiding behind the old combine in the shed next door. Ted, attempting to be tricky, had buried himself inside a haystack by the Johnson place at the end of the lane. Virgil, always trying to outmaneuver me, had cleverly found an empty fifty-five gallon drum that he turned over on top of himself in the vacant lot. The girls had probably stuck together and selected the tree house, thinking that it had not been used for a while and therefore was exempt

1

from suspicion. I knew they knew that and so, of course, it was high on the list of possible target sites.

I quickly prioritized the best route to flush out the hiders. I estimated their individual foot speeds, their relative locations to the proximity of home base, their access to firm footing and time, and the distance and their desire to reach their maximum rate of speed over the untilled farmland. Taking all the variables into consideration, I laid out a plan. Knowing that most of the kids could outrun me, I had to rely on my wits.

"Ready or not, here I come!" I gave the required warning.

I deftly sneaked up and captured the attention of the girls first, Virgil next, then Ted, and finally Andy, easily beating them all to home base. Once again victorious, I was the master. It was another successful game with not one person uttering *ollie ollie oxen free*. For me, it was a cinch—just another day at the office.

"How do you do that, Gus?" Alice wanted to know.

"What?"

"Find everybody so fast all the time."

I pointed to my head and asserted, "I read in a book that most people use only eleven percent of their brain. I'm using twelve."

I didn't really like the moniker Gus. I liked Gustov even less. It was a traditional name. I wanted to be referred to as Buzz. I asked my family and friends to call me Buzz, but no one did. They all called me Gus. You can't come up with your own nickname. One of the guys has to give you a nickname, like Pee-wee or Eight-ball, and it has to have a reason that's farfetched or unflattering, like you're oversized—Slats—or you're clumsy—Butterfingers—or something. But no one could make the Buzz connection with me. I couldn't either, really, I just liked the name Buzz. It sounded like a tobacco-chewing, home-run-hitting baseball player. I hadn't made up my mind about the tobacco-chewing, but I liked the home-run-hitting baseball player part.

The church bell rang.

"Come on, gang, let's go," Virgil yelled. "Lunch!"

I followed the older boys, and Andy tagged behind me to the field beside the church. Every year the Andersons opened up their fresh-cut alfalfa patch to the Baptist church for the annual summer picnic. It was always on Anniversary Sunday.

Food overflowed the tables that were set up in orderly rows on the grass not too far from the wood-framed sanctuary built by the townsfolk some thirty years earlier. It was a real potluck cornucopia; all the ladies brought their favorite dishes with pride of family specialties passed down through generations. It was a beautiful day: clear, not too hot. Every Anniversary Sunday was a beautiful one, as far back as I remembered. Maybe God made it that way just for me.

The families gathered around the tables as my father began with a prayer. My dad was the minister, Dr. Werner Miller, named after his granduncle. Actually, he was a medical doctor turned pastor.

After the opening prayer, the mixed quartet sang the national anthem and then led the congregation in the a cappella hymn, "Higher Ground." Everyone stood at the tables in family groups. We all knew the words by heart. I sang along with the crowd. I loved my church. I loved my family. Life was good.

My mother, Edith, wanted me to learn a musical instrument. She thought it a necessity for a well-rounded education. She pushed the trombone on me with no luck. She then switched to piano lessons, which were even worse. She finally gave up and told me to go outside and play. I wore her down. I liked music, but I had no personal musical acumen. All I wanted to do was play baseball or dig up buried treasure.

In the summertime, I was fanatic about getting in on a pick-up game with the gang on a homemade baseball diamond on the vacant lot. When that option was unavailable, I would take a shovel from the shed and go out into the country all day just to see what I could dig up. I'd take my finds to the local public library. The librarians would roll their eyes when they saw me coming because they knew I wanted them to help me research something impossible. During the school year, I loved to learn and read—a real bookworm, they called me. None of the other kids read the books I took out of the library. Many of them were so old, I might just as well have dug them up, too. Some of the kids even called me Poindexter. If I couldn't be Buzz, I sure didn't want to be Poindexter.

The preliminaries concluded and the potluck line opened. The kids were allowed to muscle into line right behind the old folks, who always got the right of way. The trick was to jockey your way into position in order to arrive at the dessert table before Mr. Elmquist's cherry cobbler was gone. Eventually, everyone settled down to the annual focus of Baptist community and food.

Much of the talk and laughter that day centered on the practical joke that Andrew Miller had pulled. Yes, my brother, eleven-year-old Andy, had done himself rather proud.

It seems that he had given to Alice Menton, under the guise of a 4H project, some little chicks to raise. Alice was a sweet, naive, slight ten-year-old who lived in town and was unfamiliar with the growth rate of poultry. Anyhow, Andy gave Alice several newborn chicks with the warning that she must be conscientious to feed them and mother them to adulthood. Alice took this admonition very seriously. She mothered them as only a serious mother would do. After all, she would someday be a real mother and this, she told herself, was the testing ground. She had a lot invested in their potential for full-blown chicken-hood.

Alice carefully kept the little chicks in a safe coop she made herself in her own backyard in town. She was a responsible girl and didn't need any help from her parents or anyone. By all accounts, the chicks should have thrived. Unbeknownst to Alice, however, Andy periodically sneaked into that same backyard in the middle of the night and replaced the neophyte chickens with a fresh batch of newborns. Alice's chicks never seemed to grow at all. You really can't tell the difference, one chick from another. Alice fed them and watered them, but they remained the same—or she thought. This pattern went on for weeks. Andy would replace, and Alice would experience increased concern. Every morning Alice went out to tend to her chicks, and every morning they seemed to be the same. This lack of progress began to prey upon poor Alice's self-worth. What kind of a mother was she? Where had she failed? She altered their ration of food. She changed brands of chickenfeed. She lost sleep. Nothing helped; they remained small chicks. She dreaded scurrying out every morning to see if there was any growth, while there was none.

Finally, out of frustration and resignation, she threw herself on her bed and cried her eyes out, swearing she would never be a mother. Her parents were dismayed. The pastor was, naturally, consulted for wisdom. Experts were brought in. Andy finally confessed the truth, and Alice was humiliated—and a little relieved. Eventually she got over it.

Andy was publicly admonished and punished, but privately praised and admired—by most.

My younger brother Andy adopted practical joking as a lifestyle. He would take the newcomers to our country school snipe hunting on a summer's eve. He left many a new kid out in the fields all night. It was sort of a rite of passage in this small town.

"Oh, yeah, I went snipe hunting with Andy last summer; caught five of 'em in one night. It was a hoot!" some second-years would boast.

And on April 1, Andy would tip cows and put salt in the sugar bowl and sugar in the salt shaker. He did all the stuff that the family came to expect but liked just the same. We were even a little disappointed when he didn't do such things. But the ever-loving lulu of all time was when Andy somehow swapped gallons of whitewash paint for some fresh milk at the Goodman Dairy.

There was also the time when my brother and I found dead the puma that had been killing chickens and causing quite a little stir in our small rural town. The local farmers were in an uproar for something to be done to eliminate this scourge. So, naturally, Andy secretly cut off the foot of the huge cat, buried the carcass and, with the leg, laid down some pretty convincing big-cat tracks all over the place. He had Sheriff Bender and a volunteer posse tracking an already-dead, notoriously troublesome mountain lion over half the county for a six-week period. I was mortified; Andy was gleeful. My brother was indeed calculating for an eleven-year-old PK.

Did I mention that my dad's workplace was that little Baptist church where he served faithfully for years? I guess I did. And I also suspect I'm repeating myself when I say my dad was actually an educated physician who willingly left the medical field shortly after his certification because he felt the call of God to be a pastor. I suppose I was proud of that. Anyway, Andy and I were known as PKs (preacher's kids).

My dad, being the senior pastor of the only Southern Baptist church in Fairfield, Missouri, was usually the center of attention. On a previous Anniversary Sunday when I was six, one of the elders, thinking himself to be funny, threw a coconut cream pie in my dad's face. Everyone laughed, and so did my kind-spirited daddy. I remember crying my eyes out and burying my head in my mother's dress.

On this particular annual-church-picnic Sunday, after most the people had gone home, my father sat the family down to make an announcement.

Dad loosened his belt, leaned back, and cleared his throat. He spoke in his slow, gentle way.

"Boys, your mother and I have been talking and praying about something very important to us." He paused.

Andy leaned forward and widened his eyes. I furrowed my forehead and crossed my arms. I knew this was big.

"We're leaving our church in order to take up another calling from God."

Uh-oh..., I thought. I already didn't like where this was going.

"Mom and I for a long time have been burdened with the continuing need for the Gospel in Africa, and we have decided to accept this leading to be missionaries to Kenya and Tanzania." My father hesitated and glanced at us to test the effect of his most recent statement. We just sat there.

"So, in a few weeks we will say goodbye to our friendly town here and have ourselves a little adventure in another part of the world."

Our mouths dropped open.

"What do you think?"

Finally, I piped up and turned to my mother. I asked, "Mom, what do you think about this?" She was my last hope of reprieve, however remote.

She responded quite predictably. "Your father and I have prayed and talked it over, and we both think it's the right thing to do, for the sake of the lost and needy. We feel called to do this."

"Well, I don't feel called," I said adamantly.

"We must be responsive to the will of God, Gustov."

"God, God, God! Why does God always have to be in charge of things?"

My mother paused and looked at me gently. She said winsomely yet firmly, "Hush now, son. We must have none of that irreverent tone about our Savior's will. We have not raised you that way."

I immediately knew that if my parents were on board and armed with a call from God, there was no way to dissuade them. We were going to Africa, whether we liked it or not.

I glanced at Andy for confirmation. We exchanged little else but a look of silent resignation.

❖

CHAPTER 2

Southwest Kenya – 1947

I didn't want to go to Kenya to be a missionary. I wanted to play baseball for the St. Louis Cardinals. I logically went down the checklist to assess my chances of making it in the big leagues. I had to admit that I didn't have a great arm. I also had to confess to myself that since I couldn't throw the ball very well that's probably why the name Buzz never stuck. I was also slow of foot. On the positive side, though, I could hit just like Stan "The Man" Musial. But was that enough? I couldn't say, but I wanted to find out. I wanted to play Little League and high school ball. Going to Kenya was not in the plan.

Andy didn't know what he wanted to be but, like me, it certainly wasn't a missionary. Maybe it was a professional prankster, if you could get paid for that kind of stuff. But our parents obviously felt a calling of some kind that we boys didn't fully understand. We had to go along, however reluctantly.

The southwest border of Kenya contours the shape of the great inland lake of Africa. Named after the queen of the British Empire during the nineteenth century, Lake Victoria is one of the world's largest inland bodies of water. Just to the east of this vast water basin lies Masai land.

The Masai are an ancient, indigenous tribe of proud nomadic warriors. Living off their herds of cattle and little home gardens, historically and periodically the tribal family units would migrate and set up tiny homesteads on any land available.

The Masai Mara is a huge tract of flat land spotted with acacia trees, waist deep in sandy-tan grass, and rife with wildlife. Lions, leopards, elephants, rhinoceros, and herds of zebra roamed freely, coexisting with the land and the tribesmen.

Today, transecting the plains of the Masai Mara is a national border, south of which is Tanzania and north of which is Kenya. Both of these nations, at the time of this story, were British colonies: Kenya and Tanganyika. The indigenous people, designated Masai in Kenya and Massai in Tanzania, could not understand why an imaginary line should separate their clansmen from one another. Standing high on the bluff of Olempito, one could see the Masai Mara stretched out to the splayed horizon.

The Masai were not the only tribe in the area. There were the Kisii, the Luo, the Kikuyu, and others. Being a British colony, Kenya's official language was English; African Swahili and the particular tribal languages were also spoken.

These were the people that my mom and dad wanted to reach with the Gospel. Coming from the Midwest, armed with a purpose, my family sailed from New York to England. Commissioned under the auspices of the African Inland Mission, we made it by steamer around the Cape of Good Hope, up the eastern side of Africa, landing at Mombasa. Taking the night train west through Nairobi, the Kenyan capital, to Kisumu on Lake Victoria, we aimed to be missionaries to the Masai. Or at least my parents did.

Upon arriving in the southwestern town of Migori, Kenya, we settled into a crude hostel in order to acclimate ourselves to the culture. The hostel was fit for traveling dignitaries: plaster wall sleeping chambers, a crude kitchen-dining room area, and a pit around back in the bushes—very luxurious.

To begin with, we took day trips, traveling by van or on foot out into the bush, accompanied by white church representatives and local black pastors. Everywhere my folks looked, they were not disappointed in what they saw. As they had heard, there was a pressing need for medical services as well as teaching facilities. The British government encouraged representatives from western aid groups to help in the betterment of the locals. We also saw a great need for agriculture assistance and education.

My dad found the greatest destitution among the indigenous Masai was the urgency for mobile medical clinics. There were people out in the bush who could never—or would never—go into Kisumu for medical care due to either their lack of money or their abundance of fear.

It was a risky way of life for a typical tribesman. One of the Masai rites of passage was a solo pilgrimage out onto the Mara with nothing but a few cakes made from a cornmeal mush called ugali, an urungu cudgel weapon, a loincloth, and a bright red, thick fabric wrapping for protection from the elements, both animal and climatic. If he survived the ordeal, at this time a Masai man could establish his identity and find his place in the universe. He was then expected to come back to the group and settle down and raise a family. He would more often than not acquire multiple wives and inevitably practice such rituals as male and female circumcision.

There were, of course, the local medical practitioners referred to by western types as witch doctors who, in order to maintain a living, required the native clientele to remain unhealthy, unsafe, and dependent on their services. Besides universal circumcision, some of the therapies prescribed by the local witch doctors were shocking to my parents.

"I've never seen anything like it," Dad volunteered one night around an open fire.

"What's that?" Mom asked.

"I saw a man today with an application of ox dung mashed together with a red plant dye and applied to an open wound, then bound over with a less-than-antiseptic bandage. Apparently this 'remedy' was prescribed by a local witch doctor," Dad said.

I winced.

"Needless to say, germ theory is high on the list of educational topics. The demand to impress upon these folks the necessity for clean, uncontaminated drinking water is also high on that list."

Mom and Dad were interested, as well, in the spiritual well-being of the people. The local tribe members believed in spirits. According to them, the spirits were everywhere and influential.

When talking about another person in their village, tribesmen would, at night, refer to that someone only by a nickname, believing that the spirits could overhear the proper name of that fellow villager and possibly do the person harm. Some of the tribes believed in night runners, who supposedly would climb up into trees and urinate on passersby.

Upon examining one ailing child, my dad inquired, "What's this?"

He had noticed three scars on the young boy's lower arms.

A local practitioner called a *doctari* responded, "That witch doctor medicine. He come into village last year and do that to stop evil spirits."

"What?" Daddy asked.

"Evil spirit not enter through here." The doctari continued pointing at the scars. "That keep child from wicked ghosts."

"You don't believe in such things, do you?"

"You can't be too careful. Western medicine good, but got to use old ways, too. Why not do both, just in case?"

My father learned that in many cases a local witch doctor would be hired to enter a household and "inoculate" a child against evil spirits by making three cuts at the base of the neck, the wrists, and the ankles—naturally leaving scars. This belief that evil spirits could not enter the body at these points because of the scars, coupled with the practice of wearing black bracelets to ward off the malevolent specters, was extremely vexing to my parents.

Despite the discouragements that faced us, we Miller boys soon began to make the best of things. *Mzungu* was the Masai name for "white man." We made friends rather easily with some local young men who found Andy and me to be interesting *mzungu*.

One of the native boys, Henry, said, "You ever play rock game?"

I asked, "Rock game?" Maybe if I learned to play their game, they would let me teach them baseball.

Some of the kids chattered in their tribal language, then, smiling, Henry said, "Come with us."

We trekked for some distance out onto a rolling plain with random acacia trees and knee-high brown grass.

"Got to find sleeping rhino."

I looked at Andy. I was worried; Andy seemed intrigued. That was just like him.

"Wait here," Henry said.

We and most of the Masai adolescents stood still as Henry and one other boy did some reconnoitering.

When the Masai boys slunk back, I noticed that they both gripped a couple of hand-sized rocks. Henry whispered to me, "If you want to be Masai, you got to put rock on rhino."

"What rhino?" I swallowed hard.

"Follow me."

Around a large bush and down in a shallow valley, we came upon a sleeping behemoth: a single large black rhinoceros snoozed in the grass.

Henry handed me a rock and jerked his head in the direction of the dozing beast.

I dropped the rock and wordlessly stepped back.

One of the African boys took another rock and slowly advanced on the animal. Deftly he placed the stone on its right foreleg. He sneaked back and was silently congratulated by all. Eyes turned back to us, the American boys.

Henry whispered, "You put rock on sleeping rhino."

I shook my head. But Andy picked up the stone that I had dropped and anxiously moved forward.

"It's okay, rhinos don't eat people, just leaves and twigs," Henry said. "They can't see too good either. Still got to be careful."

Andy crept close enough to the animal and in a death-defying move, he lightly placed his rock on the right rear leg of the sleeping goliath and quietly retreated.

The rhino snorted in its sleep and ticked a bit.

Each boy, save me, took his turn, but it was Henry's rock that finally woke the rhino. The snorting animal shot up and was after us like a Brahma bull out of the shoot. I speculated that the rhino's anger was engendered by embarrassment at being taunted as much as anything, so the beast ran hard at first until finally giving up the chase. He sleepily snorted and turned back to his bed. We outran the armored animal—with me, of course, being the slowest.

This was just one among the many activities into which we enjoyed being initiated. The winner, it turned out, was the one who placed the last rock before the hulk awoke. Henry had won. A dangerous game, one would say, if one were merely minimizing the pastime.

We would have mock battles where groups of boys would team up and play at war games with spears, shields, and urungu clubs. A special high honor was placed upon a young man if others witnessed him holding aloft the tail of a lion, the acquisition of which was another dangerous practice.

I almost had a cardiac arrest one evening while I was strolling across the sullen savannah. On my way, a lion roared in my ear from behind a clump of acacia trees just off to my left. The moon was full above the horizon. I'd never heard such a menacing sound, the deep guttural sigh of a man-eating beast who had his supper in sight.

I froze; beads of sweat formed on my forehead. Finally, I broke into a cold run. My usually leaden legs churned faster than I'd ever thought possible, steaming into camp with my side splitting in pain, only to find Andy rolling in the dust, laughing. Resting my hands on my knees, bent over from frantic panting, I wondered how different my future would be if I could ever run from first to third that fast.

"Just trying to help you on the baseball diamond," Andy grinned, tear-streaked dirt staining his smiling face.

My brother, true to form, had hired a group of Masai boys to make lion sounds in the dusk. Another triumphant practical joke.

I laughed afterward to myself. Maybe Africa wasn't so bad after all. If only I could interest the boys in baseball.

The whole family moved from the hostel and temporarily stayed in an outlying village at the home of Henry's father, a Masai elder named Ole Katembe. Ole was a very wealthy man. He had over two hundred head of cattle, four huts, three wives, and seven children—in that order of importance. Yes, indeed, Ole was a man of means who also considered himself to be progressive and interested in helping to establish our family in the area. You see, my dad wanted to start a clinic to attend to the health needs of the village. He also wanted to work with the local Christians to found a church in the area.

I would never forget my first night in a Masai hut.

Henry was Ole's oldest son. He had been educated in Migori and was versed in English.

"Karibu."

"Karibu," I responded, returning the welcome.

"So, what is it like in the United States?" Henry wanted to know one day. "Do you live in a big mansion?"

"No," I said, "we lived in a house with three bedrooms and two bathrooms. Not a mansion at all."

"Bathrooms inside the house and not a mansion?" Henry said, as if expecting more of an explanation.

"Well, not compared to some homes I know of."

"Is it made of mud?"

"No," I said, "it is made of wood, lath, and plaster."

"What is lath?" he inquired.

"Wood strips that reinforce the walls."

"Ah, I see. We have sticks packed with mud that make the walls of our homes," he said.

"Sort of the same thing with us, only we call it plaster instead of mud."

Each hut in the village was approximately twenty feet in diameter, a round single-story mud structure with wood stick reinforcement and a thatch roof. Our hut was divided into three compartments. One room was the combination entrance and sheep pen, to keep the animals safe at night from the roaming carnivores. The next room was a common area with a fire pit in the middle. And the third space was a sleeping chamber with raised cots on crude wooden stilts for sleeping two people. Andy and I slept in the common room, while Mom and Dad slept on the raised cots.

That evening, we all stood under the stars—an amazing view.

"Which one is that?" I asked, pointing at something I didn't recognize.

"That's the Southern Cross," Dad responded. "You can't see it north of the equator."

"You can't see it north of the equator," Andy echoed.

I regarded Andy. "I heard him."

Dad said, "The cross of Christ."

Mom nodded and sighed.

It was a still, hot night, so Andy turned to Henry. "Can we sleep out under the stars tonight?" he inquired.

Henry laughed. "Bad for your health. If the hyenas don't get you, the lions will."

We stepped over a foot-tall threshold into the sheep pen and bolted the door behind us with a wood plank hasp. The thick wooden door was almost airtight, allowing for no ventilation. It was stifling. I could not get any shut-eye. I was afraid to sleep uncovered due to the possibility of bugs and varmints. So I covered myself with my army surplus sleeping bag and consequently was way too hot to get any rest. I lay there all night long, imagining crawling bugs and yearning for circulating air.

The next morning, Andy and I got up with the first break of dawn and hustled outside to catch some fresh air. We witnessed one of the wives milking a cow, producing a small skin vat of yellow-white liquid, fresh from the source. Just minutes later, in the main hut, we were offered morning tea with fresh milk in it. I watched my father tilt his head to the host, who looked expectantly at the white visitors. I hesitantly took a little sip of the beverage and immediately felt sick to my stomach. *What vile, disease-ridden matter is in it?*

Andy and I would accompany our father to the makeshift clinics set up in the bush. Henry, serving as our interpreter, went as well. The *doctaris* would tag along and occasionally a local black pastor or colonial representative accompanied the clinicians. Mom usually stayed in the village and developed relationships with the local women. This pattern went on for weeks.

A word about *doctaris*: they were locally certified medical practitioners who had passed a six-month course of study at "medical school" in Kisumu. They cared for many poor patients who would not normally receive any medical attention, but the level of care was extremely deficient by occidental standards.

One morning an entourage of Masai elders, including Ole, went with us and our company. This particular morning, Mom had decided to join the crew.

"Where are we going this morning?" my dad asked.

"To a little village on the edge of Masai land," responded Henry. "We heard last week there has been trouble in this particular place."

"What kind of trouble?"

"Land dispute between Masai and Kisii," Henry stated curtly.

"Is that why your father and the other elders have brought along their machetes?"

"Yes."

"Do they intend on using them," Dad asked after a pause, "on the Kisii?"

Henry laughed. "Not as weapons, I don't think. Maybe just as, how you call it in Britain, negotiating tools."

"We are not British, we are Americans."

"All the same."

"We want to help with medicine and spiritual guidance," Dad added.

"All the same," Henry said.

"How far is this village?"

"Not far. Eighteen kilometers," Henry stated calmly, as he flipped a small black snake out of the path with his staff. "Asp, very dangerous."

The vehicle was ready, so we got in. We traveled African style, which meant eighteen to a van, carrying with us our own water that had been carefully boiled the night before. It was still warm, but it was water. The sun was already high in the sky when our group came upon this little provisional village. A long line of gentlefolk was already queued up to receive medical care.

"Some of these people have traveled overnight to be here for the medicine," Henry said. "Most of them have never seen a doctor—or a white man, for that matter."

"What tribe are they from?" Dad asked.

"Mostly Masai, some Kisii."

Andy and I went over to some young children waiting in line and offered a hand of friendship. Several little kids squealed and hid behind their parents. A few adults gawked at the white Americans.

A couple of the local official-looking types stood at the beginning of the line and took a small amount of money from each patient.

"I don't want to collect any money from these people," my father said firmly. "I want to render this medical service freely."

"Got to," Henry said. "Keeps out the riff-raff. If you don't make them pay something, people from miles around just stand in line to stand in line. Nothing else to do."

"Who gets the money?" Dad wanted to know.

"The elders."

"I want to help them for free."

"Don't make trouble. This is the way it works." Henry shook his head.

This specific day, I could clearly read as never before the concern on my father's countenance. I was, vicariously through my father's distress, intensely sensitive to the great need for which my family had come to this part of the world. There were lepers, people with horrific medical needs, untreated tumors, open neglected sores, untended broken bones, skin diseases run amok that required ardent medical care. The results of dung-covered wounds were now evident. A little baby had a severe burn on the top of her head that had been ignored and was now a gaping infection exposing the skull while oozing pus. Goiters, skin lesions, scabies—my dad sat a man down, without anesthetic, and pulled several rotten teeth that were infected and had caused his jaw and cheek to swell up like a balloon. On another individual, cancer lesions left unattended had eaten through to the bone, which was exposed and quite painful, I am sure. Malaria, typhoid, yellow fever, dengue fever—the list went on and on, as did the line. I recoiled at this parade of afflictions as my father and the local *doctaris* did what they could with limited resources. I remember being thoroughly impressed with my father, my kind, gentle dad, and his calm resolution to aid the sick and dying. I wanted to be like him. I wanted to be good.

The morning conversation was helpful. Through Henry, we had learned that there was, indeed, tribal trouble. The Kisii were at odds with several of the Masai over boundary issues. The Kisii used their land for agriculture; the Masai, for grazing.

The Masai elders were going to walk to the nearby Kisii hamlet to try and negotiate an agreement. Ole asked us if we would like to join their party. My father declined, seeing the long line of patients.

Midway into the afternoon, a local Kisii witch doctor showed up. He began to rant and rave to the elders of the village. Several henchmen with machetes backed him up.

"This is not good," Henry said.

We paused in our ministry and sidled over while the crowd listened in. Henry muttered a broken translation to us.

Henry cocked his head. "Kisii witch doctor, Uru, want to know what's going on. Why are some of his people over here in this village seeing white doctor? You," Henry said, looking at Dad, "taking his business away from him. He is much angry at elders and you."

"I thought this was Masai land," Dad responded.

"Some say Masai, some say Kisii."

"We certainly don't want to get involved in a tribal dispute. All we want to do is help these people," Dad said.

"Witch doctor Uru say you not help people, but bring poison to people and invite evil spirits to rest on village." Henry looked squarely at Dad and asked, "Is that true?"

"Of course not, Henry. You know I just want to help. I bring with me a message of hope and health."

"Witch doctor say white doctor and Masai make trouble for Kisii."

"We don't want trouble."

At this point, the witch doctor looked directly at my father and uttered something fierce in his direction.

Mom closed her eyes. She appeared to be praying. My dad stood his ground. Andy and I were stock-still. I was terrified.

The witch doctor ranted and spat, brandishing his machete and advancing threateningly toward us, while spewing a venomous tirade in Dad's direction. Uru's cronies backed him up with similar histrionics. They pounded their chests and jumped up and down, flailing their arms and legs. Their banshee cries coupled with machete blades slicing ferociously through the air sent shivers through my body.

Everyone turned to look with wide eyes at the western doctor.

My father remained placid and immovable.

The witch doctor and his henchmen gave a final lambasting and stormed off into the bush, unsatisfied with the encounter.

At first, everyone stood frozen in silence. Then after much discussion and grumbling, some people left the line of potential patients, but most of the crowd continued to wait for medical assistance. Dad dismissed the incident and went back to the line of needy people.

About forty minutes later, a jeep carrying three well-armed British soldiers pulled up. Dad had met these soldiers once before in Migori and he was familiar with them.

"What is it?" he asked.

"Trouble down the road," one of the soldiers said. He pointed in the direction that the Masai elders had gone earlier.

"What kind of trouble?"

"Tribal squabbles, nothing new."

Another soldier said, "Best keep a low profile in this part of the Mara, Doctor. Stay to the east, where it's safer."

Dad scanned the line of pathetic clientele in need, and said, "Thank you." He turned back to his work.

Mom said, "We'll stay."

The soldiers shrugged and drove off in the opposite direction from which they came, leaving a trail of dust.

That day, instead of dwindling, the line grew even longer. Mom, Dad, and the *doctaris* worked into the early evening. The line was still long when Dad decided to quit for the night. The elders of the village came up to him and begged him to stay for another day. After a brief discussion among the physicians, they all decided to spend the night and work again the following day. It was too late, anyhow, to journey back to where we were living, so we agreed to stay in the huts of the local elders.

In the dark of the evening, the local elders issued small chits of paper with numbers on them to hold the places in line for the sick people. After a long day, the evening meal by the open fire was a welcome respite.

Ole and the Masai elders returned late with worried, silent demeanors. They chatted with no one.

Andy and I, along with Henry, bunked down in one of the elders' huts while my parents stayed in another.

It rained that night, hard. The rain was actually welcome, but as usual, when it rained it poured; too much rain or not enough. The rigors of the day made my sleep deep. The rain on the thatch was a soothing background.

In the morning, Andy and I were awakened by loud shouts coming from outside. Henry was not in the hut.

"Don't go outside," Henry said, rushing in. "It's plenty bad." Henry dashed out again waving his hands wildly.

There was screaming and wailing, feet stomping in the dirt outside our hut. We rubbed the sleep from our eyes and rushed outside to investigate.

We were immediately drawn to a crowd in the center of the village clearing shaded by a large acacia tree. Hanging from a thick branch of the tree were two bodies. I elbowed my way through the crowd and strained to make out who they were, but their skin had been stripped off, leaving bloody, undistinguishable corpses dangled in the morning breeze. Blood dripped onto the piles of flesh lying under their stubs. Swarms of flies maneuvering for position buzzed furiously around the mounds of human skin that matted the muddy dirt.

I stood frozen. I touched my own face to test the solidity of the moment. Was this a real event or was it just a nightmare? I did not understand why the villagers were backing away from me in wide-eyed revulsion. The macabre scene struck me as being beyond grotesque. "I wonder who these wretched people are," I said to Andy. "We need to get Dad out here to help them." I couldn't tell whether these poor unfortunate souls were hanging upside down or not. Villagers skittered around in babbling horror. Jabbering elders threw handfuls of mud onto the ground in disgusted gyrations. Imprecations and accusations spewed from their mouths. The womenfolk were on their knees in the wet dirt, keening back and forth and moaning an appalling drone. The pitch of the screaming noise grew to the level of my having to clap my hands over my ears for my own sanity: wailing and gnashing of teeth.

I looked around and thought, *Where are my folks? Surely they're awakened by all this commotion.* A frigid shock ran through me. I looked around again. Why weren't my parents coming? The townsfolk were pawing at me and my brother with gestures of quivering apology. *What does it all mean?* I thought. *Are these dangling things Mom and Dad? It can't be!* I ran to the hut where I knew they had slept. It was empty.

The realization swept over me like an icy tidal wave. I shuddered. Those bloody masses hanging up there were my parents! The village was in an uproar of deploring lamentation. Yelling and turmoil back and forth among the villagers rattled down the chain of creation: first the cosmic universe, then the tribal hamlet, and finally my own personal realm.

"Kisii medicine man, Uru, they say…bad business…very bad business," Henry said, shaking his head.

My own Mom and Dad were slaughtered at the hands of the people they were trying to help! I stood in open-mouthed horror, captivated by the sight of the suspended corpses. A feeling gradually overcame me, emanating from deep down in

19

the remoteness of my lower being, one of desperate isolation. I thought they were invincible. This couldn't happen, not to them. It was impossible. I was petrified with inaction. Henry tried to drag me back into the hut.

But both Andy and I were immovable.

"Are these our parents?" Andy asked blankly.

"Yes," Henry said, "Kisii witch doctor, Uru, came last night with men from Kisii village to butcher white doctor and wife. Bad business…bad business…very, very bad."

I stood there for a time, contemplating what to do. I did nothing. It could have been hours. I didn't know. All at once, I turned and ran back inside the hut. I fought to breathe, my chest refusing to inflate. Once I finally drew air, I howled from sheer terror. My screaming and shaking drew Andy back into the hut.

I curled up in the corner of the hut, intermittently sobbing uncontrollably. Henry hurried into the crude hovel after us and attempted to offer comfort. It was no use.

I reflexively threw up several times. Between the bouts of heaving, I raged, "Mom and Dad came to these people in the name of Jesus—and Jesus dumped them." I felt like my heart would burst with abandoned fury. "What kind of God would let this happen? Where is Jesus? Is he not here? Is he careless? Is he helpless?" Andy cried while I rambled, my anger rising. "God, why? Why Mom and Dad?"

After a while, I caught my breath and looked out the open door through bleary eyes at the mud, thick and impassable, at the ugly mud mixed with blood. It was dangerous and godless outside.

Flies continued to buzz in relentless swarms as the villagers worked quickly to remove the bodies. What was left of Mom and Dad fell to the ground with a dull thud. That very day some local pastors improvised a Christian memorial service, and my parents were hurriedly buried on the Masai Mara.

Andy dragged me out of the hut to stand me up by their graveside. I saw myself standing there: me, Gustov Miller, standing beside that hole in the ground, seeing nothing but blackness. Although my heart, mangled with hatred, confusion, and profound dismay, was churning inside like a helpless soul being ground beneath the wheel, there was nothing on the outside. Andy wept. I was too overwhelmed to even cry.

The Kisii witch doctor was never punished.

That day, someplace deep inside, my spirit congealed, like a large block of ice that refuses to thaw in the middle of summer. It was thereafter bitterly bereft of joy, peace, and comfort.

Some place deep inside me, the unfathomable place I thought of as my soul, froze solid that day. It became a place I could never go to for comfort, for peace, for joy. This hideous event destroyed something at the core of me. I resolved in covered silence, right then, to be by myself, alone forever. I pledged to never let go of this dreadfully unfair incident, to hold on to it for all it was worth; to do otherwise would be to betray the memory of Mom and Dad.

That very day, I made a vow against the outside. I would trust no one, least of all God. This was God's fault. I would build a safe fortress for myself. I closed my heart to the outside world and to God, and determined to find comfort in my own interior.

Andy couldn't help but notice an immediate and convincing change in my demeanor. He was unable to extract any conversation from me.

I overheard Andy's observation, "He's changed, Henry, different."

Henry said, "You get over it in time. You will see."

In my enveloping shell, a thousand secluded thoughts raced through my brain. I thought of the Robinson Crusoe narrative. I had believed the author intended that the shipwrecked victim be pitied because of his misfortune at being isolated and all alone on that spot of land in the middle of ocean; the story depended on it. But now, to my way of thinking, Robinson Crusoe was to be envied. What a release it would be to be alone and inside and shielded from civilization on my own little private island.

Andy and I went silently back to the United States. We lived with our aunt and uncle, Eugene and Constance Miller, in St. Louis, Missouri. I began to torpidly nurture and cultivate my hatred for God, whom I perceived as the cause of my perdition. I regarded my Bible, the one given to me by my parents on my twelfth birthday, as a pariah. I turned my back on that Bible, literally refusing to touch it. Andy and I went through high school together, but I was always alone. He went out with friends, and I stayed home in our room. I was quiet and studious, staying to myself. I lost all desire to play baseball; sports required other people and being outside of myself. I followed the Cardinals from afar and went to an occasional game, but I knew I would never throw a baseball again. Andy gave me a baseball for my birthday one year. I put it in a drawer.

Some things in life were dependable and safe; some things were not. I learned to count on nothing but my own knowledge and my own efforts. Everything else was of no use to me. Andy and I, at the behest of our aunt, went to a local community college; I grew further apart from my brother, enjoying my own introspection and isolation in growing amounts. By the time we transferred to four-year colleges, we had gone our separate ways.

❖

CHAPTER 3

Cairo, Egypt – 1971

No!" James Morrison stood to his full height. With a clenched fist, he clouted way too hard on the wooden slab that separated him from the fat Egyptian. He thought at the time the pounding of the table was a nice touch. It encouraged him to keep going. "That's not what you said you were going to do, and it's not good enough!"

"Things change. That was then, and this is now!" Hassan mimicked Jim by standing up on his side of the bargaining table; the only difference was that it took the stout Egyptian outfitter a little less time to reach his full height, considering his five-foot-four, two-hundred-fifty-pound frame contrasted to Jim's lean six-foot-two, one-hundred-seventy-five pound version.

There was a long, silent, eyeball-to-eyeball, Mexican-style standoff, only instead of south of the border it was deep in the shadows of a backroom rug shop in the lower intestines of the seedy section of the Kasbah. The air smelled of incense and dung, sweet and sour.

While standing locked in position, Jim Morrison reflected on the advice his boss had given on how to deal with these Middle Eastern horse-trader types.

"If they pound the table with their fist," the Chief had said, "you pound yours twice as hard. If they yell at you, you yell back even louder. They threaten you? You threaten them. Haggling and blustering is a way of life in that culture. More than half the fun of a successful negotiation is the journey. Focus on the process, not the result, and you'll do fine, James," the Chief told him.

After some internal contemplation, Jim decided to go for it. "You're trying to cheat me of my deposit, and I'm not going to stand for it!"

"What did you say?" Hassan said, gritting his brown teeth. The Egyptian knew English very well. He had told Jim he was educated by British nuns in a North African Catholic school. He didn't like the nuns, especially when they whacked his knuckles with his own wooden ruler. His parents wanted him to be western-trained, but it was all the same to him. He pretended to be ignorant of English when it was convenient to be so. But he always kept detailed tabs in his head; his mental account ledger was long, and Jim knew it.

"You heard me!" Jim shot back.

"What are you going to do about it, you spineless American?"

"I'll show you what I'm gonna do, you liar!" Morrison drew his hunting knife and waved it in the direction of his adversary. *Attitude is everything*, he thought.

This move might have seemed a bit rash, considering the size and quantity of Hassan's henchmen standing behind the fat Egyptian. No less than eight well-armed thugs glared at Jim as he stood alone. At the brandishing of the knife, the backups did not budge. Not an iota of expression changed. They stood motionless, glowering at Jim the same way their leader did.

"Saving face and showing bravado is everything to these people, James. Don't back down, and don't give in!" The Chief had assured Jim.

Hassan spoke calmly. "Over here, you know, it's not polite to insult a man in his own house." The Egyptian snapped his sausage-sized fingers and the backup chorus removed their formidable daggers in order to clearly outmatch Jim's.

"Who says you're a man? A man doesn't go back on his word!" Jim expressed himself vehemently, wondering where that came from. He thought maybe that last statement was a little too much, considering the odds.

"Nine against one does not portend a good outcome for you, my friend," the Egyptian said. "What if I order my men, right now, to jump you and cut you to pieces? You wouldn't stand a chance."

"The question is, could they get to me before I get to you?" Jim aped the Arab's calm demeanor.

An eternity plodded by while Jim considered what Hassan would do next, and vice versa.

"I could order my men to cut off your hands," Hassan snorted, "or worse."

"It would be your last command. I could gut you like a pig faster than they could get to me!" Jim sneered. "What say let's give it a go, eh, Hassan?"

Another long pause ensued while the sun beat down on the roof, high overhead on its perpetual course. It was just about lunchtime and the pig comment started to work on the fat outfitter's appetite.

The other shoe dropped, as the tension was finally broken.

"Ha, ha, ha," the Cairo businessman laughed, "I like you. You are not such a typical American. You have courage and a spirit that is almost as good as an Egyptian—but not quite. Let us sit down and negotiate over a meal fit for the likes of you and me." He clapped twice, and the men behind him relaxed, sheathed their weapons, and filtered out the back door.

Jim put away his knife and followed Hassan out the same door as the Arab beckoned him with his hand over his shoulder.

In a lush tent behind the back room, the food was lavishly served and the large Hassan ate everything that was brought within arm's length.

I'd hate to stand between that guy and a pot roast at suppertime, Jim laughed to himself.

After a good long meeting of the minds, it was all settled. The outfitter was to provide supplies, transportation, camels, expert guides, and so on for the agreed-upon price. The price was a little more than initially proposed, but the Chief had anticipated even this and given Jim adequate resources to cover the venture and then some.

Even though Dr. Gustov Miller predictably stayed home and never accompanied Jim on any assignments, the Chief always seemed to foresee every little detail of the mission. During their partnership, Jim grew to realize the importance of the preparation his boss always did in order to guarantee the success of each case. He quickly learned to rely heavily on the advice and counsel of the Chief. Even though he was back home, inside his study, thousands of miles away, the Chief was continually involved in the quest. This was not the first time, nor the last, that the Chief would be proven correct.

The following day, the caravan started out east, into the wilderness of the Sinai Peninsula.

"Where to?" the lead guide wanted to know.

"That way," Morrison pointed to the rising sun.

The guide, Mohammad, shrugged his shoulders and went that way. The corpulent Hassan was conspicuous by his absence. "Perhaps I would kill one of my own camels with my weight, you know, my fat belly and all. My wives like me this way!" Then he laughed loudly at his own joke as he gestured goodbye.

Jim had the Chief's meticulous maps and directions tucked away in his back pocket. The company he worked for was called Lost and Found International, better known as LFI, or Dr. Gustov Miller: finder of lost treasure. It was a regular two-man show, but not a rinky-dink outfit. The Chief was known worldwide for being able to locate almost anything, old or new. He had a reputation, a good one. He was the brains, Jim was the brawn, and Beatrix Peeters (*ah…Beatrix*) was the heart and soul. LFI was a small, agile, efficient machine, well oiled and nimble.

Jim settled in on top of the camel swaying gently back and forth, knowing that it would be a long trip across the desolate plains to the object destination.

His boss had told him to write his memoirs of this case for posterity. Jim did not consider himself much of a writer—or reader, for that matter—but he used the slow, bumpy ride to record his thoughts and experiences.

Jim always loved being outdoors. Under the open skies was the only place for him. He loved his work—adventure, discovery, the ancient, the new, the unexpected. He loved going into the badlands and thinking fast on his feet, riding shotgun. The solitude of the trip and the danger of the journey were their own reward. He felt invincible, especially with the Chief doing the prep work.

He thought about Dr. Gustov Miller.

Observing his own dromedary, he mused, *I'd like to see the Chief up on top of one of these hump-backed camels.* He especially relished the part that the Chief told him about *Zarathustra* meaning "lover of camels." He laughed out loud at the thought.

The Chief wouldn't last three minutes on one of these long-necked desert beasts of transportation, he thought. *I could just see him swaying on top of one of these things, with his bow tie and his three-piece suit and his well manicured goatee.*

The Chief hated the outdoors with a passion. He'd much rather be reading some dusty old book in his office than out in his own backyard looking at the stars.

Jim was the opposite: nothing like fresh air and plenty of elbow room for James Morrison, adventurer, stargazer. No one was going to tie him down to a desk.

When he was twelve years old, his foster mom made him take violin and piano lessons. She could afford it; his foster dad had a good shipyard job. All of his friends were out in the vacant lot down the street playing football. Jim couldn't stand the thought of them having fun and him missing out on all the bone-cracking action. He would squirm and whine, trying every angle he could think of to wangle out of taking piano lessons. But his foster mother was resolute—up to a point. Eventually, Jim's will was stronger than hers. She threw up her hands at last, and said in exasperation, "I give up! Go out and play stupid football. But you'll be sorry some day, James Morrison, that you didn't take piano! Mark my words!"

He was never sorry. What a waste of time, banging away inside on some old keyboard. He was rough and ready for the outside job. At least that's the way he liked to view himself: as a self-made man of the world, young but wise, with street smarts. He didn't need any help from anybody, except maybe the Chief and Beatrix. *Ah...Beatrix.*

Morrison was literally hot on the trail, there under the desert sun. He was after the Amulet of Zoroaster. He'd thought it was a lot of bunk when he'd heard about it, but if some people were willing to pay the tab, Jim was willing to do the search.

After the novelty of the camel-back journey wore off, the way eastward grew boring. Jim knew he had to make it to the ancient land of the Persians. The goal was the Mesopotamia valley, and the amulet was the prize.

"It is true, James," he remembered the Chief saying, "the devoted followers of Zoroaster know of the foretelling of the Avesta and of Sosiosh the Victorious shining in the brightness of the mighty. The last and the greatest, the very Amulet of Zoroaster—that is the prize that the Raja seeks, and that is the prize he is willing to pay handsomely for. That is your job, James. Find that prize!"

"Do you believe in all this amulet mumbo-jumbo?" Jim had asked him.

"It is only important that the Raja does. He's paying the bills, James," Dr. Gustov Miller concluded.

Dr. Miller had given Jim the layout of the immediate area where the cave of Zarathustra was supposed to be: somewhere between the two great rivers, the Tigris and the Euphrates, surrounded by a deep rift, spotted on either side of the sheer-walled gorge with countless caves that held treasure and artifacts of priceless value and, of course, the amulet itself. But Jim would have to discover the whereabouts of the specific gorge. There might be a hundred such land formations in that part of the world that fit that description.

Miles and miles of wilderness, that's what it was: a big sand pit. As Jim went along, the sameness of the topography dulled his mind. But he still thought it was better than being stuck in some moldy old library, like the Chief.

After seemingly endless tracks of dunes and scrub brush, the entourage came to the Gaza. Pressing on, they skirted the valley of Megiddo, desolate and arid. Jim liked the starkness of the journey. They purposefully avoided the Israeli cities and Palestinian groups, choosing to pose as a nomadic caravan in order to minimize contact. Dr. Miller had advised Jim to avoid the possibility of political entanglement. This was an area of the world where turmoil was always fomenting under the surface. Since the caravan was just passing through, the locals ignored them.

Day after day, they went on through a land swept by wind and ancient erosion. Was this indeed the birthplace of the human race? Was it once the Garden of Eden, now sheared walls of dry sandstone? They traveled vast plains of wilderness and dust, a world of mystery and secrets, on to the valley of Mesopotamia.

Some dead carcasses strewn nearby caused Mohammad, the guide, to veer slightly to the right. Jim could not tell if they were human or animal. They were covered with carrion birds, vultures and ravens, picking away.

"You've got to be on your guard, you see," Mohammad stated. "Roving bands of thieves will cut your throat, ear to ear, just for the camel you're on, if nothing else." He then laughed and added, "And especially you, because you are an infidel, an American. This is a very dangerous territory, filled with lawless gangs of bandits!" He laughed again.

Jim failed to find the humor. He continued to keep a wary eye on the horizon and his guide, trusting neither.

Mohammad's prediction was, unfortunately, to be proven true. The very next day, Jim was gently sleeping while swaying back and forth on his plodding camel. He'd gotten very little sleep the previous night due to the watchful nature of his concern. Suddenly he realized he was surrounded on all sides by muggers. Instinctively reaching for his sidearm brought a stiff belt of his hand from a blunt cudgel that numbed his whole side from the elbow down. There were too many of them, too fast. He tried to fight them off, but it was no good. Before he knew it he was dragged away, blindfolded, gagged, and tied, helpless.

Hauled like a sack of potatoes for what felt like days, Jim lost track of time. He was hoisted over the back of his camel and finally thrown down, without sympathy, onto the dirt floor of a rough, enclosed tent—alone and abused. He worked his blindfold off so he could see out of one eye. Such as they were, his accommodations were not good. Jim heard nothing but the sounds of the desert and mumbling of men's voices outside. There was no sign of his guide. In fact, he saw no one. Secured to the center pole of the canvas canopy, he couldn't move.

The tent was small. This made him nervous. He hated tight places. They always reminded him of his upbringing.

At age seven, he was abandoned by his mother, who was a single mom, and given up as a ward of the court. Jim never knew his real father. He was a typical squirmy boy at that age and was moved through a few households within the system. Finally, at age twelve, he settled into a rigid, strict foster care home with a set of parents who were determined to straighten him out. If he made the slightest false step, which was inevitable, his foster parents would lock him in the downstairs closet as a punishment. This happened more than once. As a consequence, Jim hated cramped, enclosed places.

Jim squirmed and wrenched desperately to free himself from the bonds and the feeling that the tent walls were closing in on him. His imagination ran wild. He couldn't loosen his bindings, and he couldn't overcome the feeling of entrapment. Jim simply closed his eyes and gritted through the anxiety.

He distracted himself with fantasy. What a mess. If only the Chief were here to give him some badly needed help and advice. If only Bea were here to loosen his constraints and free him. She would be his heroine, his rescuer. If only he could see Beatrix again. *Ah, Beatrix.* Somehow, someway, Jim had to get back to the Chief and Beatrix.

The next morning, Jim was brought to consciousness by the brisk pulse of a piercing hot wind. His shelter was gone, and so were the thieves, his guide, all his things, and the feelings of claustrophobia. He felt again for his absent knife, which he normally kept on his belt loop. The only thing he had were the notes the Chief had given him and the memoirs he'd been writing.

Lying there bound and gagged in the middle of the desert, left for dead, encouraged him to speculate that the gang hadn't felt it was necessary to waste a bullet on him when the desert would do the same thing over time. After all, bullets were expensive.

Jim's well-honed survival skills kicked in. Getting to his knees and working his bindings slowly loose, he maneuvered his wrists under his butt and with his hands in front of him removed the gag. It felt good to breathe through his mouth and smack his lips. With his teeth he worked the knot on his hands free and then loosed his feet.

Taking the time to look around and evaluate, Jim was left with very little hope. He was all alone without water or food, on foot, in the middle of the desert. He spied a walled canyon a good two miles to his left. He would go there for shade from the midday sun.

Due to the mistreatment he had endured at the hands of his captors, he was already in want of the basics of life. He needed to satisfy his body, to quench his crushing thirst and feed his system with food. As he reached the craggy sandstone wall, Jim noticed a rift at its base. That would offer some small level of protection against all the dire elements—natural, animal, and human.

Jim struggled along parallel to the base of the rock face, moving in what he thought to be an eastward direction. Fortunately, he had a pretty good sense of direction, rarely getting lost.

On he went. As the hot day wore on, the shade left him and the heat of the afternoon was almost unbearable. Jim removed his shirt and put it over his head like one of the locals. He now fully appreciated the fashion statement of choice when it came to native headgear.

The night was cold and merciless.

The next day Jim pressed on without stopping. Feeling himself getting weaker by the hour drove him onward. He needed moisture and food urgently. He moved forward not of his own strength, but as if on autopilot. There was nothing else to do. He dreamed of Beatrix and refused to give up.

Jim moved in the mornings as long as he had shadows and then again half the night under a full moon, resting in the afternoons and early predawn hours among the rocks. The next day was the same. The rift got more impassable; his movements, harder. Desperate, Jim was barely able to creep forward.

An overhead noise captured his attention. Large black birds circled in the zenith. Vultures? Buzzards? No, they were huge black ravens, carrion birds for sure. No doubt they were waiting for him to fall and squeak out his last breath. The scavengers would then descend and vie to be the first to rip open his dead flesh. The cadaver's eyeballs were considered a delicacy and would be, of course, the priority feasting target.

Morbidly, Jim wondered if the circling birds had dibs on him. He wondered if there was an honor system among scavengers. It was a very competitive field of endeavor for the various scavengers on the wilderness floor. Any advantage that a creature could exploit was welcome. The airborne scavengers had a bit of an edge on the grounded type. The former would start on the project and the latter would finish things up.

Picturing himself as a raven feast jarred Jim back into motion. He paced himself as hard as he was able along the rift floor that seemed to be getting deeper as he went eastward. He looked out over the desert plateau and saw a pool of water, beautiful liquid water, refreshing and cooling. He deliriously ran out away from the rift to dive into the dust and sand of the unrelenting dessert mirage. Spitting out the sand drove him back to the shade of the canyon rift. Numbly he continued eastward.

Finally succumbing to the inevitable, he fell, at the end of his strength. Jim lay on a rock bed, facing upward, with parched and puffy lips.

The birds overhead had seemed to lose altitude, sensing the imminent feast. James Morrison closed his eyes, thinking about Dr. Gustov Miller, and how he had let him down. He thought about the Amulet of Zoroaster and what it was supposed to look like. He thought about Beatrix Peeters. *Ah...Beatrix.* He regretted that he would never see her again. Jim knew that sometimes Bea prayed for him. She told him that. She prayed to her Lord Jesus for him. He usually felt uncomfortable at the notion that someone was praying for him. Religion was a crutch he didn't need.

Under the circumstances, however, perhaps he could use a good prayer.

Oh, the things he would tell Bea if he could. Why had he not reached out for her when he had the chance? He extended his hand upward to the sky, to a vision of Bea reaching down to him. Jim smiled.

The vision left.

The birds were gone, as well. He heard something to his left. With his near-to-last ounce of strength, Jim rolled his head to see a big black raven standing not a yard from him. Bird and man stared at each other. The raven cocked its head to one side. Jim noticed something in the bird's mouth, wiggling. It looked like a cigar. *Yeah, that's right,* he thought, *it's a small pale cigar wiggling in the mouth of a raven.* He blinked. The raven hopped closer to a nearby rock. Jim blinked again. It wasn't a cigar, it was a big fat worm or grub or something. The bird put the grub on the rock and hopped away. Jim managed a dry laugh. Was the bird feeding him? He moved toward the wiggling thing and without thinking popped it in his mouth and ate it up. Slimy and bitter, it was actually better tasting than a cigar, but not by much. In spite of his weak state, Jim felt fortunate to have dulled taste buds.

Jim was immediately refreshed, mind and body. What was that story Bea had told him once, a raven feeding a prophet? The bird, knowingly, hopped away and took flight. Jim thanked the raven in a parched whisper.

He lay there for a while until he found the energy to get up and stagger on.

Later that same day, the raven caught Jim's eye again by circling overhead. He noticed something else in its mouth. The bird dropped the object and Jim actually had the presence of mind to catch it—another fresh grub. He fought the gag reflex and quickly downed the moist, fat nourishment. *Ah…Beatrix.* Maybe someone was praying for him.

Maybe someone was watching him.

The gorge deepened, and Jim looked overhead for his buddy, the raven. No sign of it.

The very next day he was awakened early by the bird skittering on a rock beside him, as if the creature knew of his plight. The bird had in its mouth this time not a fine looking grub, but instead a large chunk of bread. *Where had it acquired bread?* Jim wondered. And wiggling on the rock in front of him were two more grubs. Weird. The strangeness of this idea had already run its course in his mind as far as he was concerned. Even though the newness had worn off, he was eagerly aware that the chewy moist grubs would at least keep him alive. The bread made the wigglers almost palatable. The bird once again cocked its head and flew off after making its delivery.

The canyon made a slight turn to the north. Jim heard something. Was it the sound of rushing water? Was this another hallucination? He scurried around the next bend to discover a beautiful river. Was it real or was it another mirage? It looked real. He shook his head and blinked his eyes to look again. It was still there. It was muddy and turbulent for sure, but wet nonetheless. Jim ran and plunged himself into the liquid. He was tossed around by the water, but he didn't care. Every pore of his being soaked it in. He gulped it down. *Ahhh.*

When Jim came up for air, he noticed that several veiled women doing their wash in a serene pool on the far bank were watching him. Mercifully, they noticed his state of distress. In his broken Arabic and their broken English, they somehow managed to communicate. They led him to a small nomadic encampment where they introduced him to the menfolk, then fed him and treated him like an honored guest. After a restful night, he woke up refreshed. Having anything to eat other than grubs made Jim extremely grateful to his hosts. He poured out praises on them, which they lapped up.

Jim pulled out from his back pocket the wet map that the Chief had given him. When he effectively described the area he was seeking to find, the leader of the Bedouin tribe and his host, with a big smile on his face, held his hands up to indicate that it was all around. Running outside the tent, he looked around to behold in front of him a deep gully in the ground surrounded by vertical cliff walls spotted with caves. Why hadn't he seen it? Apparently he had plunged himself into the Euphrates River, and this was the very location he sought. He looked again at the Chief's documents only to confirm the notion. This must be the place.

Donning the indigenous dress and promising great riches to repay his bene-factors, Jim borrowed a guide and pack animal. He soon found himself and his scout, Achmed, at the base of the rock wall. Upon close inspection he perceived a small pathway etched in the face of the cliff—just enough of a foothold to traverse his way up to the caves that spotted the vertical wall. Scouring the many caverns might take weeks.

Referring to the Chief's notes, Jim pondered the need for access and speed. He surveyed the scene and pointed to the area where he would begin. They started their climb, taking what they needed on their backs. They searched for a few days, spending nights in random caves.

On the fourth day of the quest, Jim noticed some strange markings on the rear wall of a particular cavity in the rock face. Achmed waved it off as useless graffiti, but Jim was not so sure. The pictograph was of a man with a holy aura being driven off by celestial beings, as if being exiled, a symbol he recognized. Pulling out the Chief's papers, Jim discovered a drawing almost exactly like the one on the wall.

Jim excitedly tapped on the wall and found a hollow spot directly behind the symbol. Taking up a rock and smashing at the hollow spot, he discovered it to be made of a sort of terra cotta material—man-made. Creating a hole big enough to crawl through led Jim and Achmed to a vault behind the rear cavern wall. The chamber was small. Jim felt sick to his stomach. The room closed in around him as he fought the claustrophobia. He flashed back on a time when he was young and his foster dad had locked him in the closet to correct his behavior. He had attempted to steal a pack of baseball cards. He didn't really collect the cards—he gave them away to his friends—but he really liked the gum. The store manager had caught him. His parents were called in and Jim had to make ten times the restitution to the store and spend a night in the closet. He found himself trembling, terrified and exhilarated at the same time.

"Let's work fast," he said to Achmed.

He noticed the faint outline of what appeared to be a shrine with golden images placed in a concave area on the back wall of the grotto. There was just enough ambient light. Underneath the shrine was a stone, box-like coffin, roughly the size to accommodate a small human being. He increased the size of the hole they had crawled through, allowing more light to be shed on the inner room. This seemed to help relieve his closed-in feeling. Jim's excitement grew as he and Achmed strained to remove the lid of the rough-hewn stone box.

Like the lifting of an age-old treasure intended to live on for eternity, the timeless mystery was made here and now. There he was in his entire splendor, forever in his final resting place: Zoroaster, or at least his remains—the sixth century B.C. Persian prophet, bones and all.

Zoroaster was apparently trying to take his treasure with him, for the coffin contained scattered pieces of gold and gems. But around the neck of the gentleman was the prize that Jim sought. There it was, the Amulet of Zoroaster! A beautiful, large, deep blue stone encircled by handmade golden detail, attached to a sparkling chain sporting encrusted gems of many types that lined the loop of gold around the fellow's neck. Jim, much relieved and without manners, grabbed the treasure, and ran outside to the edge of the cliff. He extended his hands to the vast wasteland and the ancient river that stretched out in front of him, and let out a primitive yell of exaltation that shattered the sky.

Jim raised his face to the heavens. He felt great—he could do no wrong. A black bird circled high overhead—the raven, his raven! Jim thought for a moment. Was this raven still watching over him? Or was it trying to correct him—like his foster parents? He felt a fleeting moment of judgment, but it rapidly vanished. It was hard for him to know the source of such a sensation.

He stood there, outside, until the stars came out and he breathed fully again. He was king of his world. He needed no one, except maybe Dr. Gustov Miller and Beatrix Peeters. Glowing in triumph, he thought about Bea.

Ah...Beatrix.

❖

CHAPTER 4

St. Louis – 1971

found I had an acumen for the ancient. I was smart. Planning strategically for my future career, I went to university on scholarship to study history, archeology, world religions, and related fields. I kept to the lab, textbooks, and the library, cloistered, living alone. I made my own decisions, alone. I became a man of the world without ever actually seeing any of it. I loved books. They were my only form of connection to the past and the outside world. The process of research was invigorating. I plumbed the depths and set myself up in my fortress of aloneness, constructing the framework of my life in line with my increasingly unaware bitterness, which I ignorantly allowed to grow. I watered it and fertilized it with my own solitude, in my own little ivory tower.

My brother, Andy, would write letters, and I would throw them away unanswered. My only brother would drop by, and I would refuse to see him. Andy finally gave up and moved on. I refused to see anyone.

During the early sixties, I avoided the military by cleverly making myself invaluable to the U.S. government in the international research division. I buried my nose in studies of North Africa, the Middle East, and Southeast Asia. I mapped and charted the lands and the cultures all from the vast research libraries the State Department made available to me. I loved it. I was safe. I provided much needed information to the War Department as a behind-the-scenes kind of guy. During the early part of the Vietnam War, I drew a draft deferment. What a relief that was; I never would have made it in uniform.

I then left governmental research and set up shop in good old St. Louis, Missouri, doing what I excelled at. My careful planning had come to fruition.

Through a mutual acquaintance, I met my outside man, James Morrison, an orphan, a foster kid. I suppose, just like Stan needed Ollie, Gracie needed George, and Sacco needed Vanzetti, I needed the adventurer James Morrison.

I meticulously set up my life free from the outside chaos. Like a reclusive owl huddled down in the hollow of an ancient tree, I was alone and protected—or so I thought. Developing a unique clientele, I found my niche in the acquisition of things past and present. Where does one go to pick up a long-lost two-thousand-year-old artifact? Say one was in want of an ancient manuscript, a stone tablet, or some sort of treasure misplaced in the obscure long ago, one would go to Lost and Found International, or me, Dr. Gustov Miller, Inc. I liked the sound of that. I would do the research, and then James Morrison would actually go out and get the thing.

What if one lost a family heirloom, something irreplaceable? LFI. What if one somehow misplaced a few million dollars in negotiable bonds, needed them found, and didn't want the press or the police or anyone to know about it? LFI.

How did LFI obtain its clientele? We received a lot of word-of-mouth referrals. You know, a couple of people are milling about at a cocktail party and start talking.

Marsha says, "Liv! I haven't seen you for ages. Where have you been keeping yourself?"

Liv says, "Our villa, Marshain San Tropae. It's such a dreadful bore this time of year. I don't know why Mal insists on making that trek every year. It's always the same. Marsha, darling, you look absolutely fabulous."

"Thank you, darling."

"Have you had some work done?"

"You are so sweet. No, nothing like that, just got back from a fabulous spa in Thailand, the Winston. I feel a full ten years younger."

Liv says, "You look it! It's been so long since I've seen you. You look fabulous."

Marsha says, "How long's it been, now?"

Liv says, "Well, at least a year, darling. What's new in your neck of the woods?"

Marsha says, "Oh, you wouldn't believe it. We had a terrible tragedy happen to us."

"What is it, darling?"

Marsha says, "You know how absentminded Gerald can be."

"Husbands! They're only good for one thing."

"You're absolutely, right, darling!"

"Of course I am."

"Well, anyway, he goes to the downstairs safe and discovers that one of the Rembrandts is missing."

"Which one?"

Marsha says, "Oh, I don't know, the one with the father embracing the long lost son or something like that, but anyhow, Gerald is beside himself with anguish."

Liv says, "Well, of course. You don't misplace a Rembrandt like that every day, darling."

Marsha says, "It goes without saying. So anyway, Gerald gets a referral from the insurance company and hires this absolutely fabulous man, a genius, Dr. Miller or some such thing, who runs a business called Lost and Found, something or other. Anyway, the man's a genius. Did I mention that already? Well, he finds the painting in a black market shop in Hong Kong of all places, and we get it back in a matter of weeks."

Liv asks, "What happened?"

Marsha answers, "Well, apparently, while we were down at our place in Trinidad, a thief broke in, averting the security system, cracked the safe, and covered his tracks on the way out. It was a master burglary. But thank God the thing was recovered. Gerald was extremely pleased, as was the insurance company, of course."

Liv says, "What a relief."

Marsha says, "Oh, you have no idea."

"Darling, what did you say this man's name was? Dr. Miller?"

"Yes, darling, Dr. Miller, Lost and Found something or other."

"You must give me the man's phone number. I have been at my wits' end for days."

Marsha says, "What is it, darling?"

Liv explains, "I simply cannot find that set of jewels passed down in our family for generations."

"Oh, no."

"They're a family heirloom! Irreplaceable! I've been sick with worry. If my sister finds out they're missing, I am persona non grata at all the family events, an outcast!"

Marsha says, "Not to worry, darling. I'll have Gerald call Mal with all the Dr. Miller information. You'll have the family jewels back in no time." Marsha, realizing her own joke, laughs. Liv joins in.

Liv says, "Oh, you are so wicked. I feel better already."

Case closed.

So Marsha passes LFI's name and number on to Liv, and the ball keeps rolling. And as we all know, success breeds confidence, and confidence breeds success.

There might not be a large quantity of business in this area, but the clientele is wealthy: priceless one-of-a-kind items, an artifact here and a treasure there. Money is no object. It's not like you can pull something like this off the shelf to replace a misplaced masterpiece or something.

I love the mystery of the past, revealing the unknown from the safety of my own study, like a magician. James loves his part of the job, outside on location. It is a natural fit, a mutually beneficial arrangement.

But the lovely Beatrix Peeters, she has told me more than once, isn't so sure about her current role at Lost and Found International. James and I are big-picture guys. We have vision aplenty. But what about the details, the business needs? Who is going to handle that? Who is going to be the administration behind the scenes at this vital organization, the crosser of the *t*s and the dotter of the *i*s?

Stepping to center stage is Beatrix Peeters, professional Girl Friday, as I like to call her: intelligent, capable, and beautiful, as well. She has it all, gorgeous inside and out. Organized, assertive (which is good), and a dream to work with. I sometimes have an inkling that James is secretly in love with her, and I myself would be telling less than the truth if I denied I am privately attracted to her. At thirty-six years of age, I am a bit older than she, but at twenty-four, James is far too young. Age, however, doesn't matter—only true admiration! I will not make out of this situation more than it warrants.

Bea is more than competent. She runs the household. I work out of my study–library in my own home, a stately mid-American mansion built by an industrialist in keeping with the spirit of innovation demonstrated at the 1904 World's Fair in St. Louis. She actually runs the business. She keeps the books. She hires and fires the staff. She answers the phone. She makes the appointments. She designs the meals. She handles the payroll. She sets the schedules. You get the idea. She does it all and more, a one-woman work force.

She is a whiz, and she comes by it honestly.

She doesn't wear any jewelry. She doesn't need any embellishments. The Star of India would look like a dime store rhinestone trinket on her. She is all woman and all business at the same time. There's so much woman oozing out of her, if you will allow, she should be continued on the next woman.

Her face is perfectly symmetrical. Her piercing green eyes sparkle with activity and vitality, framed by an abundance of chestnut hair. No makeup. Anything that dared to cover up her chiseled features and classic beauty would be a step down in attractiveness. She has it all.

❖

CHAPTER 5

An Army Brat

Beatrix's father was a decorated WWII hero in the Army Corps of Engineers. When Patton needed a quick bridge built in order to streak over a river with a few dozen tanks, her dad, Captain Peeters—heavy on the Captain—was there in a hurry to build the thing. Beatrix got her father's brains and her mother's good looks, a scintillating, excellent combination. It's a good thing it wasn't the other way around. Her father's nickname was Dog-Puss Peeters, and her mother, the blonde bombshell, did not graduate Phi Beta Kappa. In fact, she couldn't even wave at it from a distance.

Bea had nothing but wonderful memories of growing up as an only child. When she was born after the war, her father stayed in the Army as a lifer. Her family moved from post to post at the whim of the military. But wherever the Peeters family lighted, they made sure to find a good church. Her father insisted upon that, and he got no objection from her mother. His death-defying experiences in the war led him to a heartfelt relationship with Jesus, and he wanted to cultivate that acquaintanceship in his own household.

As a young girl, Beatrix felt intently touched by the simplicity and truth of the Gospel. One of the first verses from the Bible she memorized, at the urging of her Sunday School teacher, was from the Gospel of Matthew 19:14: "Jesus said, 'Suffer little children, and forbid them not, to come unto me: for of such is the kingdom of heaven.'" She embraced that sentiment, and it was an unforgettable day for her dad when she asked if she could be baptized.

She thought about it for some time and even witnessed a couple of baptismal services before she asked, "Daddy?"

"Yes, sweetheart," the rugged captain said tenderly to his precious daughter.

"Does Jesus love me, this I know?"

"Yes he does."

"Am I a child of the King?"

"Yes, you are."

Little Bea displayed a thoughtful pause.

"Daddy, what does the minister actually wear when he baptizes people?"

Her father said, "Well, he'll wear a bathing suit under the robe."

"How long will he hold me under the water?"

"Not very long. You can close your eyes and pinch your nose so the water won't trickle into your throat, sweetheart."

"How much does it cost?"

"No money, just your sincere devotion to the Lord."

"I've been praying about this…"

"Yes?"

"…and I want to be baptized."

"I'll talk to the pastor."

"I love you, Daddy."

"I love you too, Sweetie."

Beatrix's proud and doting parents cried authentic tears of joy at the ceremony. For Bea, a lifetime of devotion to the Lord was set in motion.

Time passed and her depth of spirituality slowly increased. There were ups and downs along the way, but God was faithful. Beatrix found great solace in reading Scripture and much joy in communing with God through prayer. She also felt a fervent tug toward alleviating the desperate needs of the lost and destitute.

Through a friend of a friend, she applied for the job at LFI, and Dr. Miller hired her on the spot. The more she learned about the operation, the more she liked it. She reorganized the whole enterprise, and the Chief seemed to genuinely appreciate it. She tried to be a bright light in a sometimes cloudy concern.

But she didn't want to stay a Girl Friday for LFI. She wanted to be in the field, see the world, experience adventure. She truly believed she would be a wonderful missionary wife and serve the Lord, help others and see the world at the same time.

The day before the big soiree for the Raja and Rani, she wrote this passage in her diary:

Dear Diary: I'm pretty sure I've got everything lined up for tomorrow—the food, the Indian atmosphere, the works. It was a lot of stress, but it will be worth it. I just want everything to go like clockwork. Jim should be back by tomorrow night. I can hardly wait to see him. I am not going to make a big deal over him when he comes back. He's got a big enough ego as it is. But I hope he missed me, and I hope he notices me. I've got to go now and get some sleep. The next couple of days are going to be really busy. I hope things go as planned.

Prayer Journal: I don't really know what to pray for. I guess, thank you, Lord, for your watch-care over me, Jim, and the Chief. I pray for courage, Lord. I am so angry with myself for my own lack of faith. I pray that your Spirit will touch the Chief's heart. I know he is bitter about what has happened to him in the past and callous to your voice. But, Lord, I pray that your Spirit will somehow touch his spirit. And Jim, Lord, I pray for his salvation. Give him the desire of his heart and mind, draw him to you. To be honest with you, God, I pray and hope that it is your will for Jim and me to get together. If it is wrong to want Jim, I am willing to be changed. Why would you give me the desire for him if it was not your will? Give me clarity, Jesus; give me you. May you be in this whole thing coming up, and make me authentic and convincing, for your glory, Jesus. Amen. Good night.

❖

CHAPTER 6

The Set-Up

The next evening came quickly. "All right, you guys, the Raja and his entourage will be here in two hours. We've got to make this place look like a New Delhi five-star restaurant." Beatrix shot out the orders.

She went with the smart, dark-gray pinstriped business outfit, wanting to exude all work and no play. Low heels—black—ivory-white blouse buttoned at the top, with a bright red power scarf around her neck, tied in a precise knot.

"I am a pert five-foot-seven and possess luxuriously long, enviable, chestnut hair with natural auburn highlights," Bea said to herself to bolster her mood. "I do not need any makeup."

She had her hair up. That always made her feel spunky.

"Where do you want the pillows, Miss Peeters?" one of the movers sheepishly wanted to know.

"I told you already, in the dining room and make it snappy."

"And how's about these luxurious oriental appointments?" inquired one rather large, dull-looking fellow holding a brace of delicate, priceless Chinese vases.

"Same place, and be careful. We only rented them for one night."

At this point, the hired chef (the internationally known Depak Batt) swept into the hallway and demanded to know, "Where are my assistants? I told you I needed three sous-chefs to do justice to this meal fit for a king and his party!"

"Look, Batt, for the money we're paying you, you could feed the population of Calcutta for a week. Get into the kitchen and start rustling up some grub?"

"I have never worked under such conditions!"

"You're working under them now." Bea stood firm, knowing the budget for the evening to the penny.

"This is intolerable!"

"Your sous-chefs will be here in plenty of time," Bea spouted. "Don't sweat the small stuff. Get into that kitchen and make some magic, Batt!"

"Oh!" Batt pivoted and stormed off into the kitchen.

"Come on, people, we've got to make this place radiate India. I want all of this furniture out of here and the oriental rugs moved in *toot sweet!*"

The large, dull mover was hoisting in an ornate, hand-woven Persian rug with the help of a smallish, weak-eyed laborer.

Large one said, "Over here."

Small one said, "She wants it over there."

"I said, over here!"

"She told us over there!"

"Put it here!"

"No, over there!"

It was a mental tug of war with very little rope.

Bea shot up a quick prayer and then strode right up to the big one and faced him off nose to nose. "Look, why don't you do us all a favor and shut up, the both of you, and put it over there, like I said!"

The large one blinked first. They put it over there.

Bea reiterated to all within earshot, "Opulence and exotic rich fabrics, incense and elephants, palm fronds, Taj Mahals, that's what I want, the whole nine yards."

"Elephants?" one of the eager movers queried nervously.

She looked at the go-getter with a flat expression. "Not actual elephants, people, I want the feel of real Indian elephants without any real Indian elephants. I want to make the Raja and the Rani feel at home. It was Mr. Idaja's request, and he's paying the bills. Let's step to it!"

Beatrix felt good, on top of her game. She walked around directing traffic with a clipboard in her hand and a pencil behind each ear.

Everything was perfect. The invitations were beautiful. The dining room was festooned with luxurious Indian fabric rented for the occasion. Chairs were abandoned for huge oriental pillows thrown about on the floor.

Two hours later, the guests of honor arrived at the precisely scheduled moment, the Chief descended the stairs, and the festivities began. The meal was of the eight-course variety and, literally, fit for a king. The Raja, the Rani, the Rajpoot, and their entourage were stuffed to the gills with the best-tasting Indian food they had ever had. Toward the end of the seventh course, the Raja himself ran into the kitchen and kissed the chef. It was a triumph of culinary superlatives.

It was a triumph and she knew it. So did the Chief. Bea could see it on his face. She excused herself from the room; her work was done for the evening.

Dr. Miller took over.

❖

CHAPTER 7

The Celebration Dinner

The dinner was a complete success. I had dressed carefully for the occasion, as always. On my five-foot, ten-inch frame, I wore my three-piece tweed suit with a dark-brown bow tie—not one of those clip-on types, but a real silk number that I actually know how to tie. My stiff white shirt boasted French cuffs and the black pearl cuff links I had received from a particularly grateful client. Under my dark-brown wingtip shoes were calf-length, dark-brown socks with leg garters to hold them up. I wore both suspenders and a belt; I was careful that way— always had a backup system in place.

My short brown hair was well maintained, and I was pleased with a full but neatly trimmed reddish-brown beard. My brown eyes would someday in the not-too-distant future need reading glasses.

Sitting across from me during dinner, Mr. Idaja, the Raja's right-hand man, did all the talking for the monarch. He would speak English and translate into Hindi when needed. The Raja did nothing but grunt, and the Rani didn't even do that.

The royal secretary, Mr. Idaja, was of a medium-height wiry build. He had a very dark skin tone and fine, sharp features. He wore a large white turban that covered most of his head. His face was decorated with a voluminous black beard, and his eyes were mostly obscured by strong-tinted prescription glasses. He wore sandals, all-white pants, and a suit with a white Nauru jacket.

"So, so, so, all in all, I would say, Dr. Miller, that it was a most successful adventure on your part," Mr. Idaja summed up.

The other Indians were by this time sitting closed-eyed and cross-legged as if in some meditative state, completely in their own private worlds. Maybe it was a sort of after-supper ritual. It made me curious. It didn't bother Mr. Idaja at all. He just went right on.

"Dr. Miller?"

"Oh, I'm sorry," I said. "I am not familiar with this custom." I tilted my head in the direction of the sleeping royals. "Is it usual to meditate after a big meal?"

"Only for the Raja. He feels it helps him digest his food. And as you can see, what the Raja does, so does the entourage."

"I see. What was the question?"

"A successful adventure, Dr. Miller."

"Yes, well, I do believe that my staff and I did put forth one of our best efforts," I replied. "It was actually quite a little interesting project." I glanced at the Raja. "Can he hear us?

"Yes, but no matter, he cannot understand. I do the translating," Idaja rejoined.

I studied his face, what little I could see of it beneath the turban and behind the large glasses. I had the feeling he was not entirely forthcoming.

"Tell me, Dr. Miller," Idaja said, "how did you find our country this time of year? I am most interested to find out how well-off Americans find India."

"I did not actually go there," I explained. "I have assistants for that, very capable people, too, good in the field. I do the brain work, the research, and they do the leg work."

"I see," Idaja nodded.

"Besides, my man did not go to India. He found the amulet in the Mesopotamia, as I knew he would. One can find almost anything with the right research."

"Ah, I see. Most fortunate." Mr. Idaja leaned forward to pick up a small gold box perched all alone on one of the large satin pillows that adorned the floor. He opened the box to reveal the amulet. He held it up by its chain as it twirled and glistened in the amber candlelight.

"So beautiful, blue and unique," he said. "One could almost get lost in it. But look at it, over two thousand years old. To the eye of the unbeliever, a mere trinket, but to us and those who are deeply concerned, a priceless religious artifact."

"Well, not totally without price," I pointed out, "considering my finder's fee and the generous bonus authorized by the royal family." I pointed my chin in the direction of the meditative Raja. "May I?" I added, holding out my hand, palm up, under the swaying amulet.

Mr. Idaja dropped the treasure in my hand.

"The Amulet of Zoroaster," I asked, "other than what we know of it, what does religious tradition say? Did he really wear the thing around his neck to ward off Ahriman?"

"It is shrouded in time. Nobody actually knows where fact leaves off and legend begins. But the belief is strong," Idaja said.

"Of course," I said, "that is the important thing, for in the eyes of the beholder is truth." After a pause, "I suppose that I would have even gone after it just for the sake of the hunt itself."

"This is quite a confession." Idaja raised his eyebrows.

"Just for the chance to lay my eyes on such a piece of rare antiquity."

"I wish you had told me that sooner," Idaja said. "I would have suggested to the Raja to reduce your recovery fee. I shall make a memory to me just in case it should get lost again." Idaja laughed at his own witty comeback.

"I should take steps to see that that eventuality never occurs." I handed the artifact gingerly back to Mr. Idaja.

Replacing the amulet back in the box, Mr. Idaja looked up quickly to ask, "Tell me, Doctor, if I may pry, why is this particular type of article so fascinating to a man of your sort?"

"It has, of course, some interest for me on a scholarly level. Its archeological and historical significance can scarcely be overrated. And of course, there is the mystery of it all, hidden for two thousand years, totally unique. As well as the amount of money someone might be willing to part with to possess it." I smiled.

The telephone in the other room rang, and Idaja turned his head slightly.

"Bea will get it," I said.

"But I am sure you have taken more than one degree from some impressive universities, have you not?" Idaja asked.

I raised an eyebrow and moved my head up and down in affirmation.

"So worldly wise and yet you are still not so old," Idaja stated.

"I have dedicated myself to the studies of philosophy, anthropology, history, archeology, and comparative religions, as well as other disciplines. I suppose I took advantage of a curious nature and a sound intellect." I leaned back on my pillow, pleased with myself.

"I believe this can be a very bad thing. To what religion do you belong?"

"Well, I don't personally adhere to any organized religion. I think that objectivity and reason are best in my line of work."

"You do believe, do you not, in the God of the universe?"

I paused to choose my words. "He might exist, he might not. If he does, he has long since abandoned us to our own devices. I prefer to think that he is not there rather than that he does not care, but either will do."

"You disappoint me, Dr. Miller," Idaja shook his head "You must be—"

"I'm sorry to disappoint you, Mr. Idaja," I said, cutting him off.

"Such a cynical point of view," Idaja said. "Is that the right word, 'cynical'?"

"Well, it might be correct for some, but for myself I consider it a practical, reasonable perspective."

"Practical?"

"Yes. I see all gods at face value, merely icons and superstitions; it keeps the mind free from bias and other vague trappings that could be self-deceiving."

"So what do you believe in?"

"Myself."

"Most sad. If you would but study with great care many of the Eastern writings, specifically the text of Zoroaster, you would but see the inner workings of the universe and…"

I raised my hand to let him know I was not interested. Something about this fellow bothered me, and I hated that I couldn't put my finger on it. "Thank you for that suggestion, Mr. Idaja, but I already have, extensively."

"I see," Idaja said.

At that moment, the Raja sprang to life and immediately dominated the festivities. He stood up and clapped his hands, and the room jolted into motion. He bowed excessively, and everyone followed suit; they all bowed and scraped their way out of the room to excuse themselves. All of a sudden, they were in a hurry to leave.

"The Raja wishes to thank you a thousand times for your lovely hospitality and the most successful outcome of the quest," Idaja added at the door, bowing yet again. "May our paths cross again."

"Likewise, Mr. Idaja," I said, as I followed them to the front door.

Idaja waited to be the last one of the hoard to leave, then did an about-face on the front porch to say, "I cannot recover from the feeling, Dr. Miller, that I have met you somewhere before."

"Oh?"

"Yes." Idaja pierced me with his probing, spectacled eyes.

I returned the gaze, "And I, you."

"Strange."

"Perhaps we knew each other in another life?" I speculated.

"Yes, perhaps you are right," Mr. Idaja concurred. "We surely have met in another life. Yes, yes, another life." Mr. Idaja spun on his heel and left laughing.

"I'm sure I would have remembered such a pleasurable experience."

As he was walking away, giggling, Mr. Idaja waved his hand over his shoulder without turning and vanished into the night.

What a strange bird, I thought. People were an undesirable but necessary part of the business I was in. I would be the first to admit I didn't really like them.

My guests gone, I stood on the threshold of my own front door with my hand clutching the doorknob, looking out into the night. I shivered involuntarily as I contemplated the foreboding expanse in front of me—the outside world, where I never went. Quickly I closed the door. Breathing hard, I mopped my brow, which suddenly was moist with sweat.

The telephone rang.

I stopped short and waited for someone else in a nearby room to answer the extension. Surely Bea would hear it. It rang and rang. Finally, out of desperation, I went into my study and picked up the phone on my desk.

"Hello?" I heard nothing on the other end except heavy breathing. This unnerved me, although you could never tell it from my stoic front. "Hello, I say. Anyone there?" Nothing. Annoyed, I hung up.

I looked in the direction of the radio and said to the air, "I think the Cardinals had the day off. That's good. They can rest in the bullpen." I may have long ago given up my aspirations of playing for the Cardinals, but I knew their roster inside out. Simmons, Hague, Javier, Torre, Brock, Alou, Cardenal—a great starting lineup. I had every confidence in Carlton, Gibson, Reuss, and Torrez in the bullpen to deliver a sizzling season.

I walked over to the stereo and started it up by turning the volume knob with a click. With no game to listen to, I swung the needle arm over the edge of the well-worn record already on the turntable and lightly placed the needle on the first groove of my favorite Beatles album. I didn't play the Beatles when I had clients in the house—I have an image to maintain—but I find them relaxing. Moving to the other side of the desk, I absentmindedly fiddled with some Masai beadwork hanging from the elbow of the desk lamp. Humming along with the record, I mused over my most recent success. The new intercom system caught my eye—state of the art. I love finding an excuse to use it.

Pressing down one of the keys, I spoke into the box. "Bea, would you please come in here for a moment?" No answer. "Bea?"

Finally out of the box came a scratchy, "Yes?"

"Would you please come in here for a moment?"

"Sure thing."

I stood up and admired myself in a mirror on the side credenza. I licked the palm of my right hand and smashed down my cowlick, then adjusted my bow tie. What woman could resist? What woman, indeed. *Plenty*, I thought. I'd never really had a girlfriend in my entire life. I'd briefly dated a woman back at university, but lost her because of my other mistress, the school reference library, where I spent all my free time.

Satisfied with the picture of myself in the small round mirror, I removed the needle from the record player, turned the stereo off, and scooted back to my desk just in time for Bea's entrance.

"What's going on, Chief?" Bea inquired, as she pulled up a wooden chair to sit on the other side of the desk from me. She crossed those gorgeous legs.

I was smitten with Beatrix Peeters the first time I laid eyes on her. If love was a tree, she was the most beautiful, luscious, sweet peach hanging from the perfect limb on that tree. She was adorable. But I never told her how I felt. She was beautiful inside and out, and efficient to boot.

"Didn't you hear the phone?" I asked, politely.

"I must've been outside seeing off the caterer. And paying off the great chef, Depak Batt."

"Did they get away all right?"

"Smooth as buttercream, perfect timing."

"Fine, fine. Thank you for taking care of that. The great Mr. Batt can be a little eccentric if I understand his reputation correctly."

"Yeah, he's a little eccentric. Do you know he kisses the raw food before he cooks it?" Bea leaned forward.

"Kisses it? What for?"

"Good luck."

"Well, at least it's before and not after he cooks it. He does cook it afterward, doesn't he?"

"Yes, thank heavens for that."

I shivered at the thought of the alternative. "I was thinking, Bea, perhaps we should change the phone number here. Could you call first thing in the morning and do that for me, please? And see if we can keep the new number unlisted."

"Why do you want to change the number, Chief? Getting a few pointed calls, are you?" Beatrice smiled, knowingly.

"Yes, as a matter of fact, I am." I felt my brow furrow against my will.

"Ask me if I'm surprised."

"Do you know something I don't?"

"Probably. Your big interview made this evening's bulldog edition," Bea stated calmly as she produced the front section of the newspaper from under her steno pad and pencil. She handed the rag across the desk to me.

I was immediately disappointed. "This is the first section, page two. Why wasn't it front-page?"

"There's a little thing going on right now, east of us, called the Vietnam War. Ever hear of it?" Bea asked, with a slight smile. She liked to try out sarcasm on me.

"Well, yes, I have, but it's not as important as this," I said, as I folded the paper so I could read the article. "I wonder if many people have already read it?"

"Apparently, quite a few folks have, Chief."

"May I?" I asked and lifted my eyebrows as if I wanted the go-ahead from Beatrix to read out loud.

"Be my guest. Read on, Macduff!" she responded amicably.

"Oh, this is good! Samuel will be furious." I read out loud, *"In the growing controversy surrounding the theoretical existence of the Scroll of Nablus, two parties have emerged with opposing viewpoints. On the one hand, American expatriate Martin Samuel of the Cairo Institute, and on the other, our own world-renowned procurer of antiquated artifacts, Dr. Gustov Miller."* I savored and editorialized, "There you go, Bea, world-renowned."

Beatrix grinned as I continued with relish, *"In an exclusive interview granted this reporter at the home office of Dr. Miller, where apparently he remains cloistered, his opinions were expressed in no uncertain terms. 'He's way off base!' said Miller, referring to Dr. Samuel's attempt to find the much sought-after scroll. 'He couldn't find water in a lake!' Upon being asked if he had indeed been successful in confirming the existence and whereabouts of the storied Scroll of Nablus, Dr. Miller stated, 'I am saying nothing of the kind—yet. What I am saying is this: I know for a fact that Mr. Samuel will not, I repeat will not, find the Nablus Scroll where he is presently digging.' When asked point-blank if he had the scroll in his possession, Gustov Miller replied diplomatically, 'I am reluctant to answer you in a direct fashion, but I will be issuing a definitive statement regarding the results of my research within a week.'"*

I laughed out loud. "Oh, this will make Samuel livid."

As I went on reading and chortling to myself, Beatrix squinted up her face and asked, "Level with me, Chief, do you actually know where the Scroll is?"

"Well, I'm almost certain," I replied.

I started to ask Bea if she could keep a secret, but stopped myself short, knowing full well the answer. I looked at her, trying not to stare. She was breathtaking.

Getting up and moving to a bookcase on the eastern wall, I pulled on the facade to reveal a hidden compartment from which I removed a rolled-up map with handwritten notes all over the face of the weathered document. Rearranging the sundry items, both ancient and modern, on the vast worktable in the middle of the room and pulling the string on the overhead light to illumine the space, I proceeded to unfurl the map with glee.

"Come here, Bea," I said. "If it exists at all, and I believe it does, my best research indicates that it is located somewhere in this area, a good sixty miles south of Samuel's site." I tapped the index finger of my right hand on the spot several times in sync to my words as the notion settled in.

"How reliable is the research?" Bea asked.

"I'm sending James out there the day after tomorrow," I said as I lifted my head. "With a little luck, we should know something definitive within a week."

"Chief, do you really think this is the smartest thing to do?" Bea inquired.

"What?"

"Spouting off like this." Beatrix held up the newspaper article for emphasis.

"Why not?"

Bea said, "This is bad press."

Smiling, I answered, "Any press is good press."

"Doesn't this Samuel have a rather shady reputation?"

"Oh, that," I responded. "Well, yes, they call him the Damascus Butcher. He'll destroy a site, anything to get what he wants. Nothing or nobody stands in his way."

"Don't you think this could be a little dangerous?"

I allowed one eyebrow to rise slightly. Was Bea worried about me?

"Don't let the bow tie fool you, Beatrix. I can assure you that I am not rattled by Samuel or any of his cronies. I can take care of myself."

But Bea wasn't satisfied. "Chief, you don't need to take unnecessary chances like this."

"Like what?"

"Talking it up, defiantly like this, in the newspaper, making enemies."

"Thank you for your concern, Beatrix, but there is nothing to worry about." I dismissed the subject, airily waving my hand above my head. "And please, Beatrix, no need to mother me." A mother was the last thing I wanted Bea to be to me.

"Just because I'm concerned about you doesn't mean I am mothering you."

"Well, I appreciate your anxiety about this, but it's useless. Everything is under control." I put my hands, palms down, firmly on the table. "I can take care of myself."

"Famous last words," Bea mumbled.

I decided to pretend I hadn't heard her. "Did you get a chance to look at the household receipts?"

"Yes, everything balances out. In fact, we are a little under budget this month."

"Magnificent! I leave it all in your capable hands."

A pause.

I asked, "Any mail?"

"Bills, bills, bills, and this letter from a grateful Mrs. Lee for recovering her great-grandfather's pocket watch that he had received from President Lincoln."

She handed me the letter.

"That's sweet, but is there a check in there?"

"No, just admiration and appreciation."

"Oh. What about those expense vouchers?"

"That's my next project. I can tell you this much, this amulet job is going to be more than we originally thought," Bea stated.

"Why?" I prided myself on my exact budget projections.

"Well, I talked to Jim on the phone early this morning. He gave me a quick thumbnail of the expenditures; he ran into some costly, unexpected problems that had to be dealt with," Bea said.

"How costly?"

Bea thought before she spoke, "In the neighborhood of 'ouch.'"

"Ouch?"

"Yeah, somewhere between 'twinge' and 'agony.'"

"Ouch." I mumbled, before I went on. "He does get the job done, Bea, you will admit."

"Even so…"

"Very well, I will have a talk with him. When will he be back?"

"Tonight, any time now." Was that a hint of eagerness in her voice?

At that disclosure, the telephone on the desk rang again. Bea looked at me. I looked at Bea. Beatrix picked up the phone. "Lost and Found International, Dr. Miller's assistant speaking. How may I be of service?" She smiled, broadly. Pause. "Yes, he is." Pause. Bea's expression turned to suspicion. "May I tell him who's calling?" Pause. "Wait just a minute, please, I'll see if he is available." She cupped the mouthpiece in her right hand as she leaned over the desk and whispered to me, "It's a female voice. She wouldn't tell me who she is." I started to speak when Beatrix cut me short. "I'll take a message!"

I spouted, "No, I'll take it." Perhaps I could make Bea jealous by talking to a woman. I tried to grab the receiver from her, but she resisted by holding on.

"Maybe I should take a message," Bea said.

"I'll take the call," I insisted.

"I don't know."

"Beatrix, may I have the phone, please?" I gave her a big Cheshire Cat grin.

She yielded as I cleared my throat and took the phone. Placing my right hand over the mouthpiece before I spoke into the receiver, I added, "And stop worrying, Beatrix. Relax."

Putting the phone to my ear, I said in my best masculine voice, "This is Dr. Miller." Pause. "Oh, you read that, did you?" I was in my element. I languished back in my chair with my feet on the desk. Pause. "Well, it was nothing, really." Pause. "Thank you. You're very kind." Pause. "You have me at a disadvantage. You know my name, but I don't know yours. To whom do I have the pleasure of speaking?" Pause. "Pardon?" Pause. "Who? Hello? Hello?" I tapped the disconnect button on the saddle of the phone several times with my left index finger before I hung up the receiver. "She hung up. Most irritating!"

"I'll have the number changed first thing in the morning," Beatrix affirmed.

"Thank you." Collecting myself, I looked at Bea and said, "You really are a whiz, Bea; you're making yourself irreplaceable around here. I appreciate the extra time you've been putting in. I don't know what I'd do if you were to…" I trailed off before I brought up what I knew would be a sensitive subject, but I had been looking for an opening. "You know, Beatrix, you are so good at what you do around here, I might never let you go out into the field."

Bea sighed, "Now, Chief, when you hired me, you said—"

"I know. I know what I said. Everybody wants to travel the world, experience the adventure of exotic places. The outside world isn't all it's cracked up to be, Beatrix. And the truth of the matter is that this household would, once again, fall into a state of disarray without you at its helm. I need you here."

Bea leaned forward and took in a breath to launch her protest.

Before she could speak, I cut her off.

"No, I mean it, Bea. You don't realize how important it is to have these day-to-day responsibilities taken off my shoulders. It seems like I have doubled my investigative research time since I engaged you as my Girl Friday. Do you mind that term?"

"Not as long as it doesn't stop there," Bea replied. I knew what was coming. "When I applied, you represented the job as sort of an investigator trainee position that would eventually lead to some travel time."

"I haven't forgotten, Bea. You won't let me. So you want to travel, out there somewhere," I said, waving my hand ambiguously.

"Yes."

"Why?"

"After all, my major in college was anthro," Bea said.

"That's right."

"I used to dream of other cultures, languages, helping people, going to all those places I saw in the travel logs—so exciting."

"Why didn't you finish that degree?"

"I don't know. Maybe I will some day. Or perhaps God has other plans for me. I'm not sure."

"Didn't you also take some drama classes?"

"Yeah. At one time I wanted to be an actress."

"What would you take if you went back to school?"

"I don't know. Maybe I'd like to do some advocate work for people in need."

"What people?"

"Well, maybe overseas. Or tie-in with some sort of missionary organization or something."

I stood up quickly to make my point as I vehemently paced back and forth. She knew how I felt about this subject, yet she persisted in bringing it up. "I forbid it! It is absolutely a waste of your time and talent!"

I was actually yelling at Beatrix! I got hold of myself and stated more calmly, "If you don't mind my being candid with you—"

"No, speak your mind." Apparently I hadn't scared her off after all.

"You're a very commendable person, Bea. I don't want to see you waste your time and energies with such nonsense." I paused and then said, "I like you, Beatrix. You're smart, conscientious, and you must not limit yourself by any narrow religious view. You should be broadminded and open to new ideas and people— not confined by the beliefs of the past. You have such great potential!"

"Thank you, Chief. Coming from you that's quite a compliment."

"This preoccupation with religion you have expressed now and in the past is stifling you. You must cut yourself free from it." I hesitated. Was I letting my feelings for Beatrix carry me too far? I added, "For your own well-being, of course."

"I appreciate your advice, Chief, but I can't quite relieve myself of the weight of what he might want from me."

"Who?"

"Well, God."

"Oh, Beatrix, we have had this conversation before." I didn't want to be aggravated with Bea. Did she have to be so stubborn about religion? "That is perfect adolescent nonsense. What on earth could an imaginary God have to do with your choices? What on earth do you think he wants, anyhow?"

"I don't know," Bea replied. "I have thought at times that maybe I should be with a missionary organization or something."

"Beatrix! That's hazardous talk." I pointed my finger at her. "You are much too bright and have too great a potential to do that!"

"What do you have against missionaries?" Bea asked.

She sounded suspicious to me. Had she done her own investigation into my past?

"I have had passing experiences with missionaries and none of them good," I said. "Besides, that is not the issue—you are. You need to be warned, Bea, if you don't mind my saying so..." I trailed off. What was I going to say?

"Go on."

I righted myself, "To speak quite frankly, I think you are an underachiever, deluded by your antiquated beliefs."

After a silence Beatrix finally said, "I see, well, don't varnish it like that. Come on out and say what you mean."

"I am sorry if I have offended you, Beatrix;" I grabbed the lapels of my tweed suit, hoping for an impressive pose, "but I must be honest."

"No, no, I appreciate your concern."

"Thank you." I looked at Bea. Could she really not know how I felt about her?

Bea continued, "I appreciate the opportunity you have given me to prove myself here at LFI."

"Your efforts here are invaluable." I was stating the obvious.

"But I do find it difficult to ignore the voice of Providence, Chief."

"What a waste."

Silence.

I leaned back with a sigh. "But somehow, I expected no less resolution from you."

Beatrix was ready to launch now. "Chief, I know you would prefer not to touch on this subject matter, but all of us, including you, must eventually come to terms with Jesus." I knew this was a courageous move for Bea, but I raised my hand in protest—to no avail. When Bea made up her mind, nothing could stop her. Bea went forth assertively, "God created you, and Jesus loves you, Chief, whether you believe it or not."

This line of conversation might be considered by some to be an error of enthusiasm.

She had said the trigger words. I derailed her with a responsive strike. "Don't tell me about the love of Jesus, Beatrix! I know all about the 'love' of Jesus!"

"What do you know?"

"I know from personal experience that it is a pipe dream and that there is no such thing as the 'love' of Jesus!"

"What personal experience?" Beatrix eyed me directly. She wasn't backing down.

Abruptly, I turned my back on my assistant and clapped both hands together several times to cut her off. "Beatrix, please don't preach to me again and don't change the subject. I know what I'm talking about. Jesus as a 'Christ' is a myth. Jesus as 'love' does not exist! And as for you, young lady, it is my opinion—and I hope you respect it—that you need to see the world through fresh eyes, not through the eyes of some nebulous, nonexistent 'savior' but through your own eyes!"

Beatrix Peeters got up and walked around to face me. She looked genuinely concerned for me. "Chief, please listen to me." She pointed to the newspaper that remained on the desk. "You have taught me a great deal, and I acknowledge that, but right now you could be in terrible danger and I am worried about you." A beat. "I pray for you."

I couldn't help responding to her genuine concern and reached out to lift her hands. She responded—without thinking, I'm sure—by offering them. "Let me ease your burden there, Beatrix. It appears we're at a stalemate. I don't want to argue with you. I only want to help. I want you to get the most out of life you possibly can."

"Funny, Chief, that's what I want for you. I want you to realize that the most important thing in this life is to know God through his Son Jesus and to grab hold of his peace," Beatrix said.

Suddenly, she seemed to realize we were holding hands, and she removed hers. "I pray for you and your condition," she said softly.

"What condition?" I wanted to know. I was not aware I had a condition.

"Your hopelessness."

"What? I am anything but hopeless, and who says I do not have any peace? I have great hope in me and what I do and in a life of self-fulfilled purpose—a purpose that I create!"

"What about after this life?"

I broke off. "Here we go again, heaven and hell. Childish ideals. Outmoded concepts."

"Outmoded?"

"Yes, the lifelong power of the human mind is extraordinary, isn't it?"

"What do you mean?"

"To fabricate its own meaning. You have your beliefs that I don't begrudge you, and I have mine. It's fascinating, the need some people have to create a god of their liking in order to give themselves objective meaning and purpose."

"What if there actually is objective meaning and purpose?"

"There is none, I assure you. Religion is all convention and ceremonial mythology merely passed down by generation to generation through the human consciousness."

"What about faith, forgiveness, and moral order?"

"Forgiveness is a useless concept!" Bea was a bit taken aback by the vehemence of my statement. I collected myself. "These might be fine concepts for you but not always practical and never universal."

"Universal?"

"Beatrix, there are quite a few million Muslims, Hindus, and Buddhists that have a vastly different approach to religion than you do."

"I don't want to have anything to do with religion."

"What?"

"I don't want anything to do with religion; I want everything to do with relationship."

"Oh, please, Bea, it's so trite. I've heard this so many times before. How can anyone have a personal relationship with a God that doesn't even exist?"

"Through Jesus, his only Son—and he does exist."

"It's absurd and it's dangerous! If you please, Beatrix, not right now. I have some work to do…to prepare…and time is precious to me. It could be another late night and I think I'm getting a headache…" I trailed off, pretending to be engaged in some paperwork on my desk.

"I am concerned about you, Chief," Bea said.

No comment.

"Chief, you've been working pretty hard lately. How about a little walk? Maybe some fresh air and exercise might do you some good, clear your mind."

"You know perfectly well I never step foot outside this house." How could she suggest such a thing?

"Yes, I know. But I don't know why. Why, Chief?"

"In the first place, I do not have to justify my behavior to you or anyone. And secondly, I do not feel disposed to be so engaged. I have a lot of work to do this evening. Everything I need is in this house. My books, supplies, equipment. Besides, there is nothing on the outside but chaos and confusion, disorder and death. What is to be gained by venturing out? And I suggest that you be wary of the influences that are out there."

"What are you afraid of, Chief?"

"Nothing. Not anything. Why do you ask?"

"I don't know." An interlude. "Would it really be so bad to take a little walk outside, together…maybe to church on Sunday?"

This was a stubborn woman. How could she vex me and move me at the same time? Carefully, I said, "It is kind of you to care, but I have no need for church and its useless rituals."

"Okay, for the sake of argument, let's say you don't have to attend church."

"Fine."

"But, Chief, have you really looked for God?"

"God? You naively know nothing about God. I refuse to acknowledge the God of your faith. There is no sovereign God, and it's foolish to believe so."

I was painfully aware I was hurting her. I had practically called her stupid to her face.

Bea looked at me, and moisture rose up in her eyes. I had to say something, but I didn't know what.

"Beatrix…you know…"

Off in the distance, a doorbell rang. I had ordered the Big Ben sound specially from a company in Great Britain. We ignored it.

"We're at opposite ends of the spectrum, obviously," I said with exasperation as I moved away from Bea. "It is no use even discussing this with you."

"I respectfully disagree."

"You're as hardheaded as I am, Beatrix!" I said, spewing more than I meant to at the object of my affection.

The background of the house was again awakened to the Big Ben ringing of the doorbell.

❖

CHAPTER 8

The Mysterious Parcel

After Bea's exit to answer the doorbell, Dr. Gustov Miller had a moment to stand in silent contemplation, torn between regret about what he'd said and pleasure that he had not compromised his words. Recovering himself, he rolled up the map on his desk and returned it to its hiding place, then sat down absentmindedly in the wooden desk chair, and slowly started to spin around on its pivot.

He thought about a time when he was a little boy, before Africa, when his mother had taken him to the Woolworth five-and-dime to have a little lunch at the counter. He squirmed and spun around on the padded stool until his mom said, "Stop fidgeting, Gussie, and eat your grilled cheese. We need to go to the sundries department for some darning thread."

Gustov Miller stopped spinning as brief tears of sorrow bitterly squeezed from his eyes. He quickly caught himself and dabbed his eyes with a handkerchief just in time to witness James Morrison burst through the study door.

Jim Morrison was a confident young man, lean and rugged. He was six feet two inches tall with a healthy tan and a winsome smile. His white teeth contrasted nicely with his rich skin tone and medium-long black hair. His face was irregular in detail, and all of the various features thereon would presumably seem to add up to a confused collection of woeful countenance. But such was not the case. He was inexplicably handsome. His nose was bent, his jaw line was crooked, he had one blue eye and one brown, but none of those aspects dampened his boyish good looks and his masculine allure. Jim was casually dressed in blue jeans over hiking boots and a collared blue work shirt with the sleeves rolled up.

"Greetings, from the land of oil wells and sand dunes!" Jim said, flinging his arms out to his sides, "Boy, am I ever glad to be back in the good ole U.S. of A.!"

"James!" Dr. Miller shouted in return. Dr. Miller liked Jim Morrison. Not only was Jim a necessary part of the team, his "outside" man, as it were, but in some hidden ways Dr. Miller lived vicariously through Jim.

Jim asked, with his thumb raised over his shoulder, "What's wrong with Little Miss Sunshine?"

"Who?"

"Bea. She was a tad harsh at the door."

"Oh, nothing. She'll get over it." Without a space, Dr. Miller said, "Welcome back! Sit down, tell me all about it. How was the research I gave you?"

"Out of sight! Right on the money. I couldn't have done without it." Jim sat down and said, "I love going out, and I love coming back!"

"Such is life, James," Dr. Miller sighed in return as he noticed a book-sized package in Jim's right hand and a small tube-like parcel in the other. "What do you have there?"

"I don't have a clue, Chief. Special delivery, and this came by regular mail." Jim looked around and leaned over his side of Dr. Miller's desk. He whispered, "A very strange occurrence, isn't it, Chief, coming here at this time of night?"

"Not really, James."

"No?" Jim said suspiciously, "You don't think so?"

Dr. Miller returned the lean-in and whispered in response, "That's why they call it special delivery."

"Oh." Jim nodded knowingly as he sat down opposite Dr. Miller and plopped the plain, brown-wrapped package and the tube parcel on the desk.

"You were gone over six weeks," Dr. Miller said. "Any trouble? Did you find everything all right?"

"Is that all, six weeks? Seems like a year. Yeah, the research was great. The amulet was around the old guy's neck, right where you thought it would be, Chief."

"Excellent." Dr. Miller grinned in self-satisfaction.

"I did have a little trouble with the locals, though," Jim admitted. "You know, that's the trouble with people nowadays, especially Egyptian outfitters. Not an honest one among them."

"Really?"

"Nothing I couldn't handle, Chief. All in a day's work."

"Well, you are to be congratulated, James. Well done."

"Am I?"

"Yes, you are. You accomplished your mission with skill and expedience. The Raja was quite pleased. His whole entourage was here for supper this evening. The amulet arrived ahead of you by messenger, just in time."

"Good." Jim nodded, pleased. "How did it go with Old Turban Head?"

"Please, James, a little respect. The man is royal secretary to a Raja."

"Sorry, Chief."

"We passed a very pleasant evening." Dr. Miller spent a moment in abstract thought. "I continue to be puzzled by the significance that people place on such relics. On the one hand, I deeply appreciate the worth of unique items of ancient import, but on the other I fail to see the present religious value that drives such devotion and fervor. I suppose that the Amulet of Zoroaster is only significant inasmuch as the Raja and his company place so high a value on it. Their belief in it is the important thing."

Dr. Miller turned to inspect the package and the parcel, recently arrived on his desk at the hand of James Morrison. The plain brown wrapping of the book-sized package was secured by common jute twine. The address and return address were plainly printed in ink, and the postage was adequately and neatly affixed to the upper right-hand corner of the nine- by seven-inch parcel. In contrast, the small tube container was wrapped and addressed to Dr. Gustov Miller with no return address.

While Dr. Miller was thus engaged, Jim looked around to espy his quarry and quickly assess his chances for success.

"James," Dr. Miller said, with an intake of breath, "let me broach this subject and have it over with. I promised Beatrix I would talk with you about this."

"Shoot." Jim said, refocusing.

"From what you must have told her on the phone, the expenditures on this most recent endeavor seem to have been beyond what we thought they would be."

Jim squirmed. "Chief, it wasn't that much. I did have a little trouble with Hassan and the exchange rate. The Egyptian pound doesn't go as far as it used to. Besides, it costs more to bribe the locals than we thought."

"Very well, enough said, as long as you accomplish your mission! How about a cognac?" Dr. Miller seemed glad to change the course of the discussion.

"Twist my arm," Jim said, welcoming the subject change.

Dr. Miller hummed a suggestion of a Beatles tune as he lavishly poured a couple of drinks from a decanter on the sideboard. He handed Jim a glass, then raised his own. "To successful investigations."

"Successful investigations!" Jim echoed. Jim took a swig and said, "Bea can really be tough about things sometimes, can't she?"

"Well, she can, but that's good, I suppose."

"You think?"

"Oh, yes. I don't know what I'd do without her."

Jim thought the same thing but did not say it.

Dr. Miller added, "And you, of course."

"Thanks." Jim felt a bit like an afterthought.

Dr. Miller seemed to feel obliged to explain. "When Mrs. Sycamore quit suddenly, for reasons I could never ascertain, I found myself desperate for an assistant. Beatrix was the first one to apply and I hired her on the spot."

"Huh."

"She had an impressive educational background—anthropology and history classes, languages, accounting, even some drama classes. Actually quite an eclectic array of interests. Even though she had not finished her degree, that was the one thing that sold me on Beatrix. She had a great deal of curiosity about many things. I like that in a person. It wasn't until later that I discovered her religious prejudice."

"Is she still going on about that religious stuff?"

"Oh, yes, you know her. Stuck in her ways."

"Yeah, stuck in her ways."

"It's a shame how she simply will not let go of those old-fashioned concepts."

"Yeah."

"Can you imagine, James, that she still believes in a benevolent God and the veracity of a personal relationship with him? I just don't get it. She's not stupid."

Jim said, "Unbelievable."

"Yes, it is." Dr. Miller picked up speed. "She is in some ways a beautiful creature, but she will not let go of that crutch. I have tried to educate her, but she is resistant. She has such potential, but she insists on clinging to the stuff of the past."

A hush. Jim looked casually at Dr. Miller and asked, "Do you think she's beautiful?"

"Oh, I suppose, outwardly, but that soul of hers needs awakening." Dr. Miller looked nonchalantly sideways at Jim.

"Yeah, awakening."

"Yet perhaps it is her soulful passion that adds to her outward beauty even though her beliefs are misguided."

"Yeah, soulful passion."

"Why do you suppose people hang onto those outmoded ideas?"

"Oh, I don't know. Upbringing…security…fear…an old standby, maybe. Lot of reasons, I guess." Jim looked at Dr. Miller for approval.

"Yes, James, you're right, and it's too bad, considering the vast resources available to all of us through our own mental and physical prowess."

"Well, I guess some people feel they need a higher power or something to keep them going." Jim's stomach knotted up as he remembered the enigmatic ravens that provided food for him in his hour of need. He then added, "I went to church as a kid—my foster parents forced me—but religion never really did anything for me."

"Oh, well, yes, that was the party line adhered to by that generation and several before. It is a pity how the traditional western Christian concept of only one way to acquire a higher spiritual plane is so tunnel-visioned, wouldn't you say?"

"Absolutely."

"You have been out there, James. You know the world is filled with notions and legends about the creation of the universe. Many cultures have their own versions of the flood story and creation events and other myths. There might just well be, in all peoples, an acculturated need for the explanation of origins and some sort of need for divine presence. Or perhaps a kind of cosmic conscience dictates the necessity for such a prop to perpetuate these ideas."

"Yeah, I agree." Jim wasn't sure where Dr. Miller was going or why he felt inclined to go there right now.

Gently twisting the glass in his hand, Dr. Miller continued, "It strikes me as being a way to disavow responsibility for one's own actions and the consequences they cause, don't you think?"

"That's it." Agreeing seemed like a good tactic to Jim. And he did agree—for the most part.

"After all, man as he has evolved and matured continues to be a magnificent being and worthy of our contemplation—a contemplation that has its roots in primordial origins and finds its outlet in an individual need to seek significance and satisfaction where, in reality, there is none."

"Right on." Jim was starting to wonder about a refill on his drink.

"Indeed, if we have our heads screwed on right, fixed in an indifferent and bleak universe and it is up to us to find our own meaning and joy, wouldn't you say, James?"

"I concur, Chief."

"And poor Bea, with so much potential, is so stuck in her ways. It's a shame."

"A shame."

Jim thought about Beatrix and suspected Dr. Miller was thinking about her, too. But he wasn't going to let on. *Ah…Beatrix*. And he wasn't sure he wanted to know what Dr. Miller thought when it came to Bea's beauty.

Dr. Miller lifted his glass again, "To this life and what we make it, eh, James?"

"Amen to that, brother!"

"As the poet Beckett says: 'We are born astride a grave and a difficult birth, down in the hole, lingeringly, the gravedigger puts on his forceps. We have time to grow old. The air is filled with our cries…' And answer comes there none."

Dead air.

"That's a little depressing isn't it, Chief?"

"Nevertheless, our plight, right, James?"

"Right, Chief."

They hoisted their glasses, smiled big smiles and both agitatedly thought again about Bea and hoped for her essence.

While Dr. Miller moved his glass once more to his lips, he flinched and stepped back involuntarily as the phone once again rang sharply. He froze. Jim looked at Dr. Miller, wondering at the odd behavior, then picked up the receiver and said, "Lost and Found International, Jim speaking." There was a pause while Jim knitted his eyebrows. "Who's calling?" After a beat, Jim covered the receiver and said, "Long distance!" As Jim looked at his boss, Dr. Miller took another step backward and waved his hand, dismissing the call, pantomiming his unavailability.

"Oh, uh, he's not at his desk at the moment. Uh...may I...uh...take a message?" Jim hemmed and hawed. He listened again, then said, "I don't know. He didn't say." After another lingering silence, he said. "Okay, well, goodbye to you, too." He hung up the phone before he asked, "What was that all about?"

"The phone's been ringing off the hook," Dr. Miller admitted, as he wiped the palms of his hands discretely on his pant legs.

"Why?"

Dr. Miller retrieved the newspaper from his desk and handed it to Jim. "A recent interview hit this evening's paper." Jim immediately began to read. Dr. Miller put down his glass and went to the bookshelf hiding place to once again carefully remove the map and spread it out on the work table.

"This is where you'll be going next, here." Dr. Miller indicated on the map as Jim leaned over his shoulder to get a gander.

"Oh, yeah, Bea was telling me about that scroll," Jim voiced.

"You'll leave day after tomorrow," Dr. Miller affirmed.

"I get a day off?"

"No, tomorrow we'll go over the plan of attack. I'll give you your contacts and all the details you'll need."

"What time?"

"Late afternoon, four o'clock."

"Got'cha. Hey, Chief."

"Yes, James?"

"What's on this scroll, anyhow, this Scroll of Nablus?"

"To be honest with you, I'm not really sure. The research is sketchy. I know that it is old, about eighteen hundred years, and it is of extreme significance to the Saudi royal family, who are willing to pay an exorbitant amount of money for its recovery—something probably of ancestral prominence. I think I know where it is, but I look forward to learning of its contents."

"How will I know it when I see it?"

"You'll have to have an extremely discerning eye, James."

"Okay." Jim was not satisfied with Dr. Miller's answer, but he didn't want to show any weakness. "Hey, Chief," Jim stated, as he pointed to the newspaper article in his hand, "this Martin Samuel sounds familiar. Where do I know him from?"

"Remember the scandal at the Syrian digs, as well as other vulgar debaucheries?"

"Oh, yeah…," Jim responded vaguely, allowing a worried expression to escape his features.

"The Damascus Butcher?" Dr. Miller asked rhetorically, as if to remind Jim.

"Oh, yeah," Jim said, fully realizing. "Be careful, Chief, this might be rough."

"You, too, James," Dr. Miller said. "Watch your back." As if of one mind, they simultaneously picked up their drinks and dumbly tapped their glasses together to sip in silence. In increasing measure, as they worked together, they found themselves anticipating each other's moves.

"Smells funny in here." Jim said, wrinkling his nose.

Dr. Miller explained, "The upper-caste Indian royals had a rather unique fragrance about them." Dr. Miller returned to his desk and picked up the brown paper package tied with twine and started to give it the once-over.

While Dr. Miller was thus engaged with the parcel, Jim had an idea. He went to the window behind Dr. Miller and opened it slightly. "There," Jim said, as he started to tidy up the room a bit. Jim began to hum to himself distractedly as he eyed Dr. Miller and moved aimlessly around the room. Dr. Miller continued to focus on the package.

"Another drink?" Jim tested Dr. Miller's alertness.

Dr. Miller shook his head in the negative, as he inspected the parcel minutely.

Jim sauntered to the sideboard and poured himself a quick one while keeping an eye on Dr. Miller. Jim took a gulp and put down his glass. Slyly, he sidled to a large display case behind Dr. Miller, removed a small item, and noiselessly placed it in his pocket. Jim froze, staring at the back of Dr. Miller's head.

"There, that's better," Jim said, breathing deeply. Suddenly getting an idea, he yawned audibly and stretched his arms. "Well, I'm all in. I'll be going now. Got a busy day tomorrow."

Dr. Miller nodded as Jim worked his way to the door by tidying up as he went.

"See you tomorrow, Chief," Jim said. "This place needs a good cleaning up."

As Jim neared the door, his excitement increased. He barely caught and righted a floor lamp that he bumped into, wincing as he did. Sensing success, he reached for the doorknob and opened the door into the hallway.

Just before his escape could be completed, Jim was stopped by the voice of his boss.

"James," Dr. Miller said without looking up.

"Yeah, Chief?" Jim stopped.

"What are you doing?"

"Leaving."

"No, before that?"

"Straightening up a little?"

"Before that?"

"What?"

"What did you do behind my back?"

"When?" Jim laughed nervously.

"Just now."

"Got a drink?"

"How long have you worked with me?"

"A couple of years?"

"You know how I feel about drafts and the outside air. Please close the window."

"Oh, sure, sure. Sorry, Chief, my fault," Jim said, as he walked to the window and lowered the sash.

"Lock it, please."

Jim did so. "No sweat. Is that all?"

"Um, yes, and thank you for cleaning up, James."

"Don't mention it, Chief. Any time."

Dr. Miller waited until Jim made it all the way back to the door before he stopped him again. "James?"

"Yeah, Chief?"

"Please, before you go, would you replace the item you took from the display case?"

Jim smiled, putting on his best Mr. Innocent face, "What item would that be, Chief?"

"The one in your front right pocket," Dr. Miller voiced calmly as he raised his head and looked at Jim while leaning back in his chair.

"Oh, that," Jim admitted.

"Yes, the framed autographed baseball card from Lou Brock's first year with the Cardinals. No doubt it will someday be immensely valuable," Dr. Miller smiled unflappably. "The man can run like the wind. No one can touch him in the stolen base department."

Jim relented, looked at his shoes, and pulled the card out of his pocket to replace it where he had purloined it, among a collection of small but elite Cardinals items. He then said, laughing to himself, "Well, Chief, you caught me again. I thought I had it that time. So close! I was almost out the door. How'd you know I had it this time?" Jim pulled out from his pocket a small pad and pencil and pulled a chair up to the desk opposite Dr. Miller. Jim leaned eagerly forward to listen to the boss.

With a self-satisfied smile, Dr. Miller lit a cigar from the desktop humidor, and placing his hands on the back of his head, leaned back in his chair to recap.

"A combination of things," Dr. Miller stated, "all based on facts, not guesswork. First of all, I know you very well, and that gives me a distinct advantage. Secondly, the circumstances were too tempting—you had to try for it. Now I will show you the logic. Follow me." Dr. Miller easily slipped into his didactic mode as his gestures accompanied his words. He often thought he would have been an excellent teacher at a university, if it hadn't required him to leave his safe place and interact with large groups of students.

Dr. Miller rose from his chair to demonstrate. "You walk into the room, thus. You see me busy at work. You engage me with something that is seemingly irresistible, a special delivery package. What's inside? An intriguing tube parcel, wrapped with no return address. Strange. I love a mystery. You know that. I know you know that. At the sight of the delivery, I am captivated. You can see it on my face. A little conversation between us and the wheels start turning." Dr. Miller used his index finger at the side of his head in a circular motion to illustrate.

He continued, "Now's your chance. 'He's distracted,' you say to yourself. I notice out of the side of my vision a definite change in your posture and attitude. Your movements quicken. You take advantage of the fragrance in the house deposited by our guests and use that as an excuse to go behind me and open the window. I know you know how much I distrust the outside air; yet another distraction. You sense my mind a thousand miles away. You get another drink, survey the situation. You offer me a refill and make a comment on the quality of the air. You seize the moment, pick up the card, place it in your pocket, and feign a yawn to excuse your flight. You might have been better off to leave it at that but no, you continue to tidy up the room voluntarily as you make your way out, most uncharacteristically—and a bit clumsily, I might add. How am I doing?" Dr. Miller asked.

"Chief, that's pretty good. I'm that obvious, huh?" Jim scribbled several memoranda down in his notebook.

"No, not really, James. But to the trained mind, even those tiny subtleties, those nuances, are hard to ignore."

"That's amazing, Chief. How do you develop that kind of awareness?"

"The strictest discipline of the mind is required: concentration, observation, and focus. Of course, a well-rounded education is essential, James."

"But how do you get better at that sort of stuff? Are there any exercises to make you, like, more perceptive of that kind of thing?"

"Certainly. Stand right there and face that wall." Dr. Miller indicated to Jim to turn to the wall opposite from him with his back to the desk. Jim did so.

"Okay, now what?" Jim asked.

"Now, James, name every item on my desk and its current location," Dr. Miller said, as he pulled alongside his outside man, shoulder to shoulder, facing away from the desk.

"Right now?"

"Right now."

"Oh, uh, let's see…the phone's over here," Jim gestured, "and the…no, no, over on this side, isn't it? Yeah…a stack of papers over there…left hand side…pens in the middle…I guess…a blotter…the clock's in front…and a…," Jim strained, vaguely moving his hands and closing his eyes to envision the scene, "a table lamp…a…what-do-you-call-it…a…circle scribe."

"Compass," Dr. Miller said calmly, shaking his head.

"Yeah, that's it."

"Anything else?"

"Uh…no…yes, the tube…and a special delivery package!" Jim said, triumphantly.

"Good, what is the postmark?"

Jim was stymied. "I don't know."

"How much postage?"

"I don't know."

"Anything else?"

"No, that's it," Jim admitted, unconvincingly.

"All right, turn around," Dr. Miller said.

Jim did an about-face to regard the desk. Dr. Miller recited the following with his back to his desk and his eyes closed: "Let us see, you got the telephone correctly but the stack of papers was here when you were last in my office, not today." Dr. Miller moved his hands in front of him as if to place each object in the correct location as Jim observed. "The pens, the blotter, the clock, and yes, a compass. Most of the large permanent fixtures you remembered."

"I didn't do so bad, huh?"

"No, but look at the details you missed," Dr. Miller continued with his back to the desk and his eyes closed. "The small diary, paper clips in the clay Grecian vessel, magnifying glass, a rare book published in the 1830s on Tibetan cave runes, thumb tacks, erasers right here—so many little things that can tell you so much. A semiprecious onyx paperweight used to hold down notes on various Middle Eastern dig sites…stapler…lamp, all the necessary adjuncts to a well organized work space."

"Wow," Jim said. Dr. Miller never ceased to amaze him.

"This is just an example of the importance of observation and focus. The first rule of logical thought: observe and retain. The more often you do it, the easier it becomes. One can literally will the brain to control what one sees and draw faultless conclusions from that which one retains. Given enough data, that is," Dr. Miller said as he turned around to look at his protégé.

"Far out," Jim expressed, as he furiously wrote notes to himself. "I remembered the tube and the package!"

"Ah, yes, the parcels, well wrapped with brown paper," Dr. Miller said as he scooped up one of them and returned to sit down at his desk with the special delivery parcel squarely in front of him. "Let us look at this, for example. You brought it in here, yes, but where is it from?"

Jim knitted his forehead.

Dr. Miller said, "How much postage? Any return address? When was it postmarked?" No response. "So many clues left unheeded staring you in the face. Let's see, someone sent this special delivery to make sure it would arrive in a timely fashion. Now, when did this arrive and by whom?"

"Bea said about two hours ago, by special courier."

"And when did the tube arrive?"

"By regular mail today, I guess."

"Interesting. No return address on this one." Dr. Miller inspected the tube and then switched to the parcel and contemplated it closely. "Postmarked New York, yesterday morning, special delivery. This tells me, James, that in this case the sender wanted to retain his or her anonymity for some reason. He or she is a very precise person. Look at the handwriting and the care with which it is wrapped. Also it's worth noting that this person had to make sure I received this important package at this time. But why?" He turned his attention back to the tube. "Different handwriting, different senders. This tube is postmarked Chicago, three days ago."

Dr. Miller began to meticulously unwrap the book-sized parcel while continuing his commentary. "Neatly tied with twine. What can we glean from this item? An awful lot of paper…" Upon unwrapping the package, Gus stared at the contents. At first it was a blank stare, but it soon relented into a knowing one.

Removal of twine and paper had revealed a nine- by seven-inch framed black-and-white photograph of a young man standing beside a tree. Gus was frozen in disbelief. He remembered the tree, outside the old Busch Stadium the Cardinals used to play in.

"What is it, Chief, a picture or something?" Jim asked as he moved around to the other side of the desk to look over his boss's shoulder. "Just some dude standing there," Jim observed.

Dr. Miller looked at the framed photo and finally said, "This individual has a large mole on his left calf. The second and third toes on his right foot are webbed and he has a distinctive birthmark in the vague shape of Italy on his back."

"What?" Jim's jaw dropped open while he looked at the photograph more closely. He said incredulously, "Aw, come on, Chief, you're going to have to tell me how you figured that one out!"

Dr. Miller said distractedly, "I should know."

"Why? Who is it?"

"It's Andrew," Dr. Miller murmured, deep in thought, "my brother."

"Out of sight," Jim said, smiling. "I didn't even know you had a brother. He doesn't look like you."

"It's an old picture, but it's him."

"Where's he live now, New York?"

"That is the puzzler. I don't think so. I don't know for sure where he is, or even if he is. I have not heard from him in years. Ten or eleven, something like that," Dr. Miller thought out loud. "I had given him up for dead, or its equivalent, long ago."

"Why?"

"I'm not sure, call it a premonition."

"That's not very precise, Chief. Maybe he's not dead after all. Maybe he plans on popping up some time."

"No...well, perhaps. This is most perplexing. That might very well be like him. He is a...spontaneous...vibrant...person...and..." Dr. Miller tailed off.

"Well, maybe he didn't send it. Maybe a relative or a friend or someone."

"Yes, possibly, but I know of no such person in the New York area," Dr. Miller voiced. "And why no message? Strange."

"Beats me. Do you have any other family, Chief?"

"No, just one brother. Our parents passed away when I was young."

"I didn't know that. How?"

"In Africa."

"Africa! Really? What were they doing in Africa?"

No answer.

"Gun running?" Jim inquired eagerly.

"Nothing as exotic as that."

Jim waited for the coin to drop. Dr. Miller was lost in reverie.

Jim spoke again. "What?" No response. "Where were they in Africa?" Dr.

Miller appeared to be a million miles away, but Jim couldn't seem to quell his own curiosity.

Dr. Miller placed the framed photo facedown on the corner of his desk, and said, "Not now, please, James. Perhaps later. I would prefer not to reminisce at the moment. I have work to do. I will tell you all about my family some other time. If you will excuse me." Dr. Miller pointed to the door and then swung his chair around with his back to his outside man.

Jim took the not-so-subtle hint and got up to exit out the door. "Well, I guess I'll see you tomorrow at four." There was no comeback. "I'll just drop by in the afternoon to run through that new stuff." Dr. Miller still made no response, so Jim left.

Jim closed the study door behind him and went out the front door, where he paused. For some reason, standing outside on the sidewalk, he recalled the brief conversation earlier between himself and Beatrix where she referred to him offhandedly as the "plucky comical sidekick" of the organization. Jim didn't much like that moniker. He didn't say anything, but he thought about it plenty. Oh, he supposed he was Dr. Miller's sidekick in a way, but that's not how he wanted Beatrix to look at him. Then again, the whole interchange had been odd—as if she was glad to see him but wouldn't allow herself to admit it. He was glad to see her, gladder every time he came home from abroad that she was still there.

Inside, Dr. Miller sat for a while, then spun around to realize that Jim was gone and he was alone. After a moment, he lifted the photograph of his brother off the corner of his desk and set it upright to face him. Then he went to the bookcase and pulled down a book, a large black leather-bound King James Version Bible. He looked at the image of Andy in the picture before opening the book to the second page and reading the inscription: *"Presented to Gustov Miller on his twelfth birthday, with love from Mom, Dad, and Andrew. May God richly bless you."* Dr. Miller didn't know at his deepest essence whether he adored or despised that inscription.

Dr. Miller said aloud as he held forth the Bible, "Yes, Andy, I am interested in this, and justifiably so. But only as it is important to my field of endeavor, the historical significance of the early Christian Church, as I am interested, equally, in the history of all religions and cultures."

Dr. Miller unwittingly continued his soliloquy. "Can you imagine, Andy, the drama? Saint Paul the Apostle, in ancient Greece, very compelling. I have often thought what a magnificent story it would be for an opera or play to see Saint Paul walking up toward Mars Hill with the great minds of glorious Greece sitting about." As Dr. Miller spoke, he moved theatrically around the room with sweeping gestures. "I have even placed myself among them, the great thinkers of a great age. The Epicureans over here, the Stoics over there, the little separate dramatic scenes that must have occurred. These men scoffing at Saint Paul, while these men are attentive."

Dr. Miller went to the elaborate length of adopting a character with voice and stature. "This ignorant Hebrew, what could he know of higher philosophy? The ones over here with the wheels turning, hearing of this new religion based on the life, the death, and the resurrection of Jesus Christ for the very first time; the debates of the minds! Magnificent potential for compelling dramatic conflict.

"Paul surveys the effigies of all the Greek gods and his eyes rest upon the one marked 'to the unknown god,' just in case they missed one. He points to that one and says, 'I know who this one is.'" Dr. Miller demonstrated as if he had an audience. "Let me proclaim him to you! Are all eyes on me?"

Dr. Miller mused, *Imagine the moment. Magnificent, absolutely magnificent!*

He put down the Bible and picked up the picture, sat in his chair, and ran his hand along the glass that protected the photo as if to verify its solidity. "You should write it up, Andy. You and I and Mom and Dad should write it up."

The telephone went off again, but Dr. Gustov Miller neglected it. It rang eleven and a half times and then went silent. The man sat in his chair, motionless, for an extended time.

❖

CHAPTER 9

The Confidant

When Beatrix Peeters had stormed out of Dr. Miller's office, she had answered the clanging Big Ben front door. It had been Jim arriving at LFI. Their eyes had met, and she'd felt the familiar flutter in her stomach that she had come to expect when she saw Jim Morrison. But she had allowed her attitude from the conversation with Dr. Miller to spill over into this encounter. She had smartly welcomed back Jim by saying, "Well, if it isn't the plucky comical sidekick of Dr. Gustov Miller, returned home from the wars."

Jim had said nothing. Bea had smiled, more nervous than she looked, and flitted off to catch the last bus home.

As she sat on the bus, she realized she was a little mad at herself for what she'd said. It seemed to hurt Jim's ego. She really did not want to do that. If she could have kicked herself, she would have.

When she got home, she climbed into her pj's and thoughtfully consumed a bowl of cold cereal. There was a knock at the door.

"Who is it?"

"Angie," replied the voice from the other side of the door.

"Come on in."

Bea unlatched the door, and the two young women sat down on the sofa.

Angie said, "Is it too late?"

Bea said, "No, I was just mulling over the night's events."

"How do you think the supper went?"

"It was perfect, Angie. Everything went off like clockwork. The chef, Depak Batt, was great but a little weird."

"It comes with the territory, but that's good. Did Jim get back?"

Bea sighed. "Yes, he came by the house just as I was leaving. I had been discussing with the Chief, or maybe I should say arguing with him about, you know, God's leading and his love for us and how I had always wanted to be a missionary. I could tell he didn't want to talk about it, but he had to make sure he told me how wrong I was. Then the doorbell rang and the Chief told me to answer it. He really took charge of the whole conversation and I was actually kind of relieved by the interruption—especially because it was Jim." *If only I had said something nice to him,* she thought.

Pause.

Bea said, "Angie, I don't know why I am so incapable of making a convincing case for God's love for us and the reality of Jesus. Anyway, I answered the door and it was Jim. I was so glad to see him but I shot out some biting remark and whisked off. I guess I wasn't really ready to see him, and now I'm even more bewildered. Who knows what they think of me?"

"Who?"

"Jim and the Chief."

"After the dinner you pulled off, I'm sure Dr. Miller is more persuaded than ever how competent you are."

"I know. I'm pretty confident of my abilities on the job. The Chief calls me his Girl Friday, but for some reason I'm not always that confident in God. I haven't been able to influence either of them when it comes to Jesus. And I pray for them all the time."

Bea permitted her head to plop down on the armrest of the sofa, not quite sure if she wanted to cry or pray or both.

Finally, Bea lifted her head and regarded Angie. Throughout their history together, Bea always felt that Angie had a much deeper faith than anything she could muster.

Bea said, "Angie, I know this is personal, and you don't have to say anything, but I think I'm in love with Jim. I don't know if that's why I pray for him or if I am truly concerned about what God wants. I dream about spending the rest of my life with Jim, yet I don't have that same…I don't know, passion, about the Lord. I sort of let on that I do and when I share with the Chief, I believe what I say, but most of the time I think I'm questioning my own faith."

"Do you think Jim knows how you feel?" Angie asked.

Bea shrugged. "I feel like I should hide it, but he's a smart guy." She exhaled heavily. "It's so complicated. Tonight I got the idea that the Chief might have feelings for me."

"Why do you think that?"

"Just something about the way he looked at me. I can't make sense of it."

Angie asked, "Bea, do you believe that God wants the best for you?"

"I guess so, but sometimes he seems so distant."

"What do you think would happen if you were to marry Jim and he didn't have the same faith as you?"

"I don't want to think about that. I just want to believe that God will open Jim's eyes, and that he would believe in Christ." A pause. "Sometimes I think I want Jim more than God. God must be so disappointed in me. How can God love me when I feel this way?"

Angie said, "Bea, our hearts are not hidden from God. He is patient with us even when we question him. I know this is not easy. There are no simple answers, but love…I don't know if God will change Jim's heart, but I am certain that he will walk you through this."

Bea knew that Angie spoke from an intimate confidence in the Lord. Why didn't she have that for herself?

Angie continued, "We both have a busy day tomorrow; we can talk more tomorrow evening when it's all over. I just wanted to stop by to find out how the dinner went."

"Thanks, Angie."

Bea's friend left. After brewing a cup of tea, Bea sat down to read some passages in the Psalms and then pulled out her journal.

Prayer Journal: I hope I have not invested too much, spiritually and emotionally, in the unknown future. These thoughts I write down help me to sort out my feelings.

Lord, my heart doesn't believe what my mind knows about you. I admit to being a little angry about not seeing any change in the Chief and especially Jim. I want to believe and have confidence in the fact that you can change hearts. But it's hard.

I do believe, however, this is true. It's up to you to work your wonder in the hearts of Jim and the Chief.

I know, God, you have me here for a reason, and I pray as never before that your perfect purpose will be realized. I might not yet know exactly how you will work all the pieces, but I know it is your will that all men come to a loving knowledge of you, and I pray that this will be the end result in the hearts and minds of the Chief and Jim. Thank you for Jim…and the hope I have in you, Lord.

Bea turned off the lights, went into her bedroom, and fell into a restive sleep.

❖

CHAPTER 10

Madame X

The following day at precisely noon, Beatrix Peeters arrived at the office–home of Dr. Gustov Miller, Lost and Found International.

She walked to the place from the bus stop a block and a half away. She waved to Officer Milo Toole, who cruised slowly past the Miller mansion in his squad car on his ever-efficient late-morning rounds. Always the good neighbor cop, he heartily waved back.

Beatrix had a key. Dr. Miller was not up yet, which was not unheard of. Insomnia occasionally rendered Dr. Miller a petrified body that would stay in bed late into the day.

Bea picked up the newspaper, went through some mail, made coffee, and looked through the upcoming day's events. The crew that had come in to set up the ambiance of India would be there soon to dismantle everything. As she scanned the list of things to do, she was preoccupied and anxious. That morning she had made a brief entry in her diary:

Dear Diary: It's an apprehensive and at the same time enjoyable experience to think about the future. I regret being so caustic to Jim on the porch yesterday. Should I apologize? I forgot what he smells like—he has the fragrance of a man; I like it. I've got to play it calm and collected, though. I hope Jim shows up earlier than four so we can talk. Also, I should not have said what I said to the Chief. But he makes me so upset. I do pray for him. I pray for both of them. I'm not a debater. I'm much better at bringing up a good effective point twenty-four hours later—when it's too late. I think I should have challenged him more. Or should I have kept my mouth shut? Sometimes I just don't know what to do. I have to continue to believe that God is in charge and that he knows what's best.

Prayer Journal: My prayer is the same this morning as it was last night. I also pray for coolheaded resolution. Thank you, Jesus.

At 4:08 in the afternoon, with all vestiges of India gone from the house, the doorbell rang. Bea went to get it. It was Jim. They looked at each other and smiled. Beatrix walked back to Dr. Miller's office as Jim followed. She still had not seen her boss that day. She took up a position behind the desk in the boss's chair as Jim sat opposite her on the other side of the desk.

"So, what's up today, Sugar? How 'bout some java?" Jim inquired.

"I believe you are capable of getting your own coffee," Bea shot back.

"Maybe later."

They stared at each other in silence for a moment. Bea almost stopped breathing.

Jim finally interrupted the stare-down. "So, except for the briefing regarding the next case, was there anything on the schedule for today?" He leaned toward her with a big smile.

"I guess not. Why?" she asked warily. She stiffened and crossed her arms.

"I'm just asking. Sheesh!" Jim said. "Hey, why don't we take the evening off and go to a movie or something, just you and me?"

"Well, did you hear that," Bea said coyly, "the fun-loving comical sidekick thinks he deserves an evening off."

"No rest for the wicked?" Jim hinted.

Beatrix redirected the conversation. "How was your little junket, Jim? Was it exciting?" She leaned forward, genuinely interested. "A lot of intrigue?"

"Naw, nothing to it," he said, snapping his fingers, "just following a few leads and throwing around a little cash." Jim thought better. "Although I don't want it to sound too easy. You see, this guy the Chief told me to see, Hassan, was a tough nut to crack, but I had to go through him to get the amulet. I had no choice. That's where the extra expense came in. He took me for a ride, though, and I'd be telling a lie if I said that things went much smoother than I thought they would."

"I prayed for you, Jim."

She could see he was uncomfortable. *What was he thinking of?* He seemed humbled somehow. Bea thought that perhaps Jim was opening up; her pulse quickened.

Jim looked at the floor and mumbled, "Thanks, but, you know…"

"What?"

"Nothing."

The moment was gone. Bea said, "Well, it sounds exciting! Can I go on the next trip after you find the scroll?"

Jim said, "It's okay by me. Ask the Chief."

"He'd say no."

"The, uh, truth is, Beatrix, the Chief doesn't trust your self-control. A beautiful woman like you, traveling alone with a man's man like me…you just might get carried away and go crazy or something," Jim added with a boyish grin.

"Oh, brother. I think I could control myself. You're the least of my problems. You're harmless," Bea said, waving her hand dismissively, trying not to blush.

"Thanks. There goes one more male ego, shot down."

Bea said, "I admit I was worried when I didn't hear from you for awhile."

"You were? Thanks. Why?"

"Well…it's not just you. I'm concerned about the Chief, too. This next case, this Nablus Scrolls venture, could be dangerous. I don't like it."

"No more than any other case."

"What about this Martin Samuel guy, the Damascus Butcher? Did you read the article in the paper yesterday?" Bea asked. Jim nodded in the affirmative. "The Chief belittled him something awful."

"He wasn't very kind."

"That's an understatement. This Samuel guy is pretty rough, isn't he?"

"I've never met the gentleman, but I hear he's no cream puff."

"And the Chief goes spouting off to the press like that. It's not smart."

"Don't worry your pretty little head, darlin'. We can take care of ourselves."

After a pause and a raised eyebrow, Beatrix said, "Oh, spare me the machismo, Jim. Just be extra careful, okay?"

"Sure."

"And keep a watch on the Chief, too, would you?"

"Okeydokey, Smoky. It's nice to know you care," Jim said, scooting his chair closer toward her and, while reaching his hands across the desk, he inadvertently knocked over the picture of the Chief's brother.

Bea righted the framed photograph and looked at it. "What's this?"

"What?" Jim said looking into her eyes.

"This picture?" Bea asked, excitedly.

"That's the Chief's brother," Jim answered.

Beatrix quickly collected herself before she said, offhandedly, "Oh? It is?"

"Yes, it is," Jim responded, suspiciously, "You recognize him?"

"Why would I recognize the Chief's brother?" Bea answered.

"Why don't I believe you wouldn't?" Jim probed.

"It's just that the likeness is striking. I thought it was an old picture of the Chief, that's all."

"He doesn't look that much like the Chief."

"You don't think so?"

"No, I don't."

"I...I...he does to me." Beatrix paused before she continued, "When did the Chief get this?"

"Last night, special delivery." Jim said, "Yeah, the Chief was surprised too. He hasn't seen him for years."

"Did you know he had a brother?" Bea asked carefully.

"Nope." Jim regarded Bea skeptically, and Bea felt the heat of distrust.

She diverted the trail of conversation. She asked, "What do you think of brothers, anyway?"

"Brothers?"

"Yea, you know, brothers or sisters, or you know, families in general?"

"I'm all for them."

"You like families?"

"Yeah, I like them, from a distance."

"From a distance?"

"Yeah, you know, I never really had one, myself. So, I—"

"But someday maybe you'd like to have one—a family?"

"Well, maybe. I don't know."

"What?"

"I guess I think it would be all right, but the thought of settling down makes me feel a little uncomfortable...you know..."

"No, I don't."

"Well, kind of—"

"Yes?"

"Closed in, claustrophobic."

"Oh," Bea replied. She immediately wished she'd caught the disappointment in her voice before Jim heard it.

Another awkward instant followed as Jim cleared his throat.

Bea spurted, "When are you leaving?"

"Pardon?"

"When are you leaving on your next assignment?"

"Oh, I don't know, tomorrow, day after. You gonna miss me?"

"I'll try, but I doubt it." The heat rose in her cheeks and she hoped it was colorless.

"Ouch, that hurt." Trying a new tack, Jim asked, "Say, when I get back, why don't you and I go out and paint the town red?" That cliché just came out and it was too late for Jim to retract it.

"I don't go out with painters," Bea said coyly.

"I'll change my profession," Jim said.

"To what?"

"Anything you like, doll."

"Just for little ole me?"

"Just for little ole you."

"Would you really do that?"

"Just name it."

"How about a lion tamer?"

"A what?"

"A lion tamer, you know, taming lions."

"You want me to become a lion tamer?"

"What if I did?"

"You mean in the same cage with all those man-eating lions?"

93

"Yes, would you consider a career in lion taming if I asked you to?"

"I don't think it would be too good in there."

"What about me?" Bea said, leaning into him and touching his hand and luring him with her glimmering, fluttering, scintillating, gorgeous eyelashes.

"I don't think you'd like it in there, either."

"I was thinking of you."

"I like it when you do."

A pause before she said, "Well, at least there is some valuable conclusion I can take away from this conversation."

"What's that?"

"It's true."

"What's true?"

"Never have a witty repartee with a person who has the IQ of a hand puppet."

"Don't be so hard on yourself."

"Are you done?"

"Is there any hope for me?"

"We'll see. Maybe."

The two of them froze for a second, gazing into the other's peepers. Newton's theory about two dense objects in space being drawn together by a constant predictable gravitational force was proving true. Their lips were on a tense trajectory that made it seem like a collision was imminent.

Suddenly, the doorbell sounded. The instant was broken.

Beatrix, jarred into the moment, stood up quickly and asked, "What time is it?"

"Four forty-five," Jim whispered his reply, still leaning in, eyes half closed.

"Oh, four forty-five?" Bea bounced on tiptoes of both feet.

"Yeah, four forty-five."

Jim pulled back and observed Bea closely. "You look a little jumpy."

"Jumpy? I don't feel jumpy," Bea insisted. "Do I look jumpy?"

"Yes, you do."

Beatrix immediately sat down and smiled a big smile. "There, is that better? Do I still look jumpy?" The doorbell rang again.

"No, now you look stiff. Are you all right?"

Just then, Dr. Miller, all spit and polish, came through the door. He presented himself to the room and regarded his employees. He announced hurriedly, "I'll get it!" He turned on one heel and exited through the same door before it had a chance to fully close. Beatrix and James observed the abrupt entrance and exit before they turned their faces back to each other.

"How long was he there?" Jim wondered aloud.

Beatrix smiled and leaned forward, placing her chin on her curled right hand and batting her eyelashes again in the general direction of James Morrison.

Jim took in some air, preparing to speak, when the office door burst opened again to reveal an entirely new person. A woman entered—stunningly beautiful, elegantly dressed, about thirty years old, and nearly as tall as Jim. She moved like a slim dancer in a sage green silk dress, her long blonde hair cascading around her shoulders. She carried elegant gloves and a designer handbag. Quickly she surveyed the room, turned on the desk lamp, and sidled up to each window to draw down the shades without looking out. After she inspected the room, she sat down, adjusting her chair to face the other two. Bea and Jim looked at her with open mouths.

After a pause in which the room settled, Jim spoke. "Hi."

"Hello." She responded with a thick eastern-European accent.

"Who are you?" Jim wanted to know.

"Fine, thank you. How are you?"

"No, no, not how are you, but who are you?" Jim said slowly, emphasizing the words 'how' and 'who' in the sentence.

The stranger leaned forward, piercing Jim's gaze with her own. She parted her lips slightly before speaking. "Someone in trouble. Who are you?"

"Jim. My name is Jim," he muttered, trailing off. She was gorgeous, he was jelly.

Beatrix cleared her throat not once but twice.

Somewhere in the recesses of Jim's brain, he picked up the hint and gestured vaguely, "Oh, and this is…"

"Beatrix." Bea rolled her eyes and said plainly, "Beatrix Peeters. Hi."

"Hi," the woman said, still holding Jim with her gaze.

"To whom do I have the pleasure of speaking?" Jim said in return.

There was no answer.

"If someday I were to need to know your name for whatever reason," Jim said a little too loudly and slowly, "what name would I use?"

The exotic female leaned forward and partially closed her eyes with a whisper, "My name is unimportant. You are not Dr. Gustov Miller."

"That is true," Jim replied.

Beatrix quickly inserted, "Uh, let me go and find him. He couldn't have gone far. He never goes far."

Just then, Dr. Miller entered reluctantly through the hallway door. "Have you been introduced?" he asked.

"No, not completely," Jim said.

"Not yet," Bea said.

"Neither have I," Dr. Miller said. "May I? I am Dr. Gustov Miller and these are my able assistants, Miss Beatrix Peeters and Mr. James Morrison." After an unresponsive pause, he proceeded, "And, uh, Miss, uh…what was your name, again?"

"I have not told it to you yet," she said, confusedly.

"Ah, well, very good. Please sit," the Chief said, distractedly.

"I am already doing so."

Dr. Miller shook his head, apologetically, "Ah, yes, of course you are, Miss—?" Still no answer. "Then I will call you *Madame X*, after the unknown quantity."

"Rita," she shot back quickly.

"Well, good then, Rita," Dr. Miller responded, regaining the home field advantage. "Tell me, if you please, Rita, why do you clutch your handbag so tightly in your grip?" Dr. Miller slid behind his desk. Quickly glancing to Bea and Jim, Dr. Miller lifted one eyebrow and teased, "Intriguing, isn't it?"

Rita glowered at the man behind the desk. "You are Dr. Gustov Miller?"

"Yes, I assure you I am. I do a bit more around here than just answer the door."

"You must forgive me," the woman said. "When I first left Berlin ten years ago, I had no idea where I would find myself this day. I am not trusting of people, but my God has looked after me in times of great danger. I left behind my family and I cannot afford to reveal to anyone my true identity; I fear for my family still in East Germany. You understand?"

"Yes, of course."

"That is why I will tell you nothing of my correct name. So I am Rita."

"Very well, Rita, go on please."

Immediately, Rita stood up and nervously walked around the room, spieling her story. "I have been a citizen of the world, without a country for these few years, looking over my shoulder and not knowing what my future would be. My family, being there now, did attempt to be with the Communists. They hated themselves for it, but they had to survive. While many other Jews were oppressed, they successfully hid their identities during the Cold War and are ashamed of their actions, as I am of them. Today the Communists would discredit my family and abuse them if they knew. This is why I am careful. The Communists have ears everywhere."

Rita abruptly changed her line of thought. "A few months ago, while in Istanbul, I was looking through several shops in the open market. I was in an interesting store, filled with antiquities, when I met a curious, colorful piece of framed artwork of a veiled Persian woman. The frame was unusual, very old, so I purchased it. I paid the man what he wanted for it. When I was removing the painted portrait, I noticed on the backside a handwritten document that appeared to be some sort of map. I was strangely attracted to it. The man who sold it to me was a nomadic Arab. He said his cousin had found it in a cave just west of the Dead Sea and had given it to him to make some money."

"I could not read the map or decipher the location to which it referred." Rita paused then continued, "I think it might be of some interest to you…"

"How did you discern that?" Dr. Miller inquired.

"I am a Jew, Dr. Miller. Secretly, my parents would not let me forget my tradition in language as well as culture and religion."

"Oh, then this map, as you call it, might be of Hebrew origin?"

"Yes, and quite old, I would say."

"Why do you think it is of great import?"

"I am familiar, of course, with the Dead Sea Scrolls discovered many years ago, and my mind immediately went to the idea of a great archeological find."

"Naturally. Why did you come here?"

"I desire you to look at it and tell me what you think."

"Why me?"

"You are, are you not, Dr. Gustov Miller, the world-renowned investigator of religious artifacts and archeology?"

Dr. Miller nodded and smiled before Rita continued.

"Dr. Miller, your reputation for accuracy and dedication are well known," she said. "I have been following your accounts in the newspapers. The article in yesterday's edition is quite interesting. You seek the Scroll of Nablus. I was hoping you would be intrigued with my find and help me find out what it means."

"You have this map here with you?"

"No, of course not with me."

"Really?"

"Really."

Dr. Miller looked at her squarely. "Is that all?"

"But yes, of course, if I am allowed to go, I can retrieve the document."

Dr. Miller was silent.

Rita placed her hand on her upper chest. "Is there anything else?"

"I believe there is. Thank you, but you haven't been entirely honest with me, have you, Madame X, or Rita, or whatever your name is."

"I have not?"

"Would you like something to drink?" Dr. Miller asked, taking a sudden turn in conversation.

"No!" She stood up and then sat down. "Wait. Yes, water."

"James?" Jim got the hint and fetched a glass of water from the carafe on the sideboard. Bea did not move as she watched Jim hand the glass to Rita. She couldn't help but notice that he'd been transfixed by this strange woman since the moment she came through the door

Rita said, "Thank you."

"Thank you." Jim smiled and returned to his chair.

Dr. Miller said, "Something in your demeanor is furtive. The way you clutch your handbag, the manner in which you burst into my office, this mysterious map, your body language. No, you have other reasons for showing up here and now with this document."

Rita took a big gulp of water then muttered, "But I told you I do not have the map here. What do you mean, other reasons?"

"Reasons that I will soon discover, Rita." Dr. Miller sat immovable. "You are in danger and you need money." Dr. Miller's penetrating eyes froze her.

Bea and Jim sat motionless. Finally Jim gulped air as if he was about to break the silence. Dr. Miller promptly raised his hand, which stopped Jim from uttering a word. The soundlessness continued to the ticking of the stately grandfather clock.

Rita caved in first. "You are right, Dr. Miller. I am transparent to you. I am firmly convinced that this document will lead its owner to the Scroll of Nablus. I believe it is worth much."

Dr. Miller's restraint continued as he refused to speak and continued his annoying stare in the direction of the mysterious Rita.

"Ever since I first acquired this map," Rita spoke again, involuntarily nodding her head toward her purse, "I have had the feeling of being followed, as if someone is after me. It is hard to explain. Have you ever had that feeling, as if every move you make is being observed?"

"Yes," Dr. Miller said without thinking.

"It is extremely unpleasant, bringing back memories of my youth, my homeland."

"Have you actually seen anyone tailing you?" Dr. Miller wanted to know.

"Yes, I admit, but I could not make out his face—only a shadow, a form in a doorway or an automobile or a train. But I tell you this: he is evil and desires no good to me." Rita's frozen comportment ended as a harsh, desperate expression flashed across her face. "Can you help me, Dr. Miller?" Rita stood up and leaned over the desk, imploringly, toward Dr. Miller.

"Of course. Please sit down." His voice was soothing as he asked, "A refill?"

"Thank you." She dropped limply into the chair as Jim popped up to collect her glass and attend to her every request.

"A pillow?" Jim asked.

"No, I am fine," she responded.

Off to the side, Bea cleared her throat.

"You're in safe hands now. Did he follow you here?" Dr. Miller posed.

"I do not know. I tried to lose him. Or them."

"Do you suspect more than one?"

"I do not know what to suspect."

Dr. Miller paused slightly before asking, "May I look at the item, please?"

"I told you I do not have it here."

"Yes, you do. Please let me see it." Dr. Miller held out his hand.

Rita hesitated. She stood up and checked the watch that wrapped around her left wrist. Finally she spoke. "Yes, of course." She stood and turned her back to the desk to dig through her purse. "Here it is." Twirling on her heels, she produced a piece of folded, aged parchment that she held out with her right arm, over the desk in the direction of Dr. Miller. As he reached across the desk for it, Rita immediately retracted her hand and with little effort, tore the material in half and handed one piece to him.

"What on earth did you do that for?"

Bea and Jim knew Dr. Miller well enough to know how annoyed he was with this woman's behavior.

"It is my insurance."

"Why do you need insurance?"

"Look at it! Is it authentic or not?" Her face flared, wild-eyed.

"What is your game?" Dr. Miller mumbled more to himself, as he grabbed hold of the extended half.

"Look at it!" she reiterated.

"See here, it is extremely difficult to make a snap assessment of any such article."

"Is it of interest to you or not? Please, we have not much time."

Dr. Miller carried the torn material over to his work table, turned on the overhead work light, and retrieved his magnifying glass. First he examined the side with the portrait and muttered to himself, "Late sixteenth century, no doubt Persian, beautiful." Turning over the parchment, he continued to voice his thoughts, "Well, here are the crossroads, yes, here is the mountain pass…yes, yes and then…let me see the other half."

"No, not yet."

Dr. Miller sighed. "I can't be certain until I see your half. Where did you get this?"

"I told you."

"Give me that."

"On my terms."

"Which are?"

"Half of the treasure."

"What treasure?"

"Whatever there is."

"I don't seek treasure, I seek history."

"I seek both."

"What if there is nothing there but clay pots and ancient writings? Only scrolls of archeological interest?"

"Half!"

"Half the find—that's outrageous!"

"Half! Nothing less. I will not haggle!"

"No deal! I don't need this. I can find the Scroll of Nablus without it."

"Perhaps so, but this map is specific. It will save valuable time. It could cut days, even weeks, off the time needed to find the scroll—valuable time, precious time." She paused and leaned in to Dr. Miller with a vicious look. "Those wind-swept hills and valleys are dotted with caves, nooks, and eroded holes too numerous to count. How will you know where to start digging?"

Dr. Miller shot back, "If this map is so valuable, why don't you go and find the treasure yourself? Why do you come to me?"

"I would, of course, but I do not see how this map fits into the bigger area. There are hundreds of crossroads in that countryside. I need your expertise to fit it into the greater sector." Relaxing back in her chair she added, "As I see it, I need you and you need me."

"Are you suggesting a partnership?"

"It seems to be the only logical conclusion."

"I disagree. I don't need anyone. Here." With that, Dr. Miller tossed the half of the torn map that he had been holding. "Happy hunting!"

The woman stood up, collecting the other half. "You are making a grave mistake, Dr. Miller."

"Am I?"

"You need me."

"I don't think so. I'm willing to be patient. A few days won't matter."

"I wonder if your competitor feels that same way?"

"Who?"

"Martin Samuel." She paused to test the impact. "He would pay handsomely for this map."

"I think not," Dr. Miller said.

At the same time, Jim stood and yelped, "You wouldn't!"

Rita said evenly, "Why not? I have no loyalties."

Dr. Miller said, "Yes, but you see, Samuel does not know where this map fits into the big picture either."

Rita said, "That is what you say."

Silence.

Rita said, "I want that scroll, Dr. Miller!"

"You are not alone, apparently."

"What can I do to change your mind, Dr. Miller?"

"Nothing."

There was a thoughtful hesitation on her part as she scanned the room. "Perhaps you already possess the scroll, eh?"

"I'm afraid I do not."

"Where is it, Dr. Miller?" Rita snorted.

"Not here."

"You leave me no choice."

"What sort of a veiled threat is that?" Dr. Miller scowled.

The woman indicated the impulse to leave. "I am a woman of great determination, Dr. Miller."

"Oh, and what are you determined to do?"

"Soon, you will know." As she postured defiantly, the doorbell cracked the tension, giving everyone in the room a twitch and a release at the same time.

Dr. Miller popped forth, "Who could that be?"

"Is there another way out?" Rita said desperately.

"Yes, that way leads to the back door." Automatically, Dr. Miller pointed to a little-used door down the hall.

With a sudden spring-loaded dynamism, Rita bolted to the door. "I am sure we will speak again, Dr. Miller.

With that, she vanished through the door without even a click of it closing behind her. The only evidence that she had been there was a lingering foreign fragrance.

The doorbell rang and rang again. It was irritating.

❖

CHAPTER 11

The Intruder

The doorbell rang again. The ringer was impatient.

Dr. Miller took charge. "James, will you please see who that is at the door and tell them to come back later, or make an appointment, or leave a card or something? Just get rid of them. Beatrix, would you please check to see if our visitor truly departed?" Dr. Miller allowed his gestures to accompany his instructions as his two assistants split in the appropriate directions to vacate the room, leaving him alone.

Dr. Miller did not have time to digest the mysterious encounter because immediately the phone rang. He snatched up the receiver after the obligatory two rings and spoke a little harshly, "Lost and Found International, Dr. Miller speaking." Pause. "This is he. To whom am I speaking?" Pause. "What?" Pause. "No, I don't." Pause. "Look here, who is this?" Pause. "Of course, I'm sure I don't have it. If anyone would know it would be me, wouldn't it?" Pause. "I wish I did. It would save a lot of grief. Now, who is this? Hello? Hello?" Dr. Miller put the receiver down distractedly and stood there with his mouth open.

Beatrix burst back into the room. "She's gone!"

"What? Who?"

Bea looked quizzical, "You know, Rita, Madame X, she's gone."

"Oh."

"Who do you think she was?"

"I'm not sure."

"Was she on the up and up?"

"I didn't believe her story for an instant."

"Why not?"

"She sounded scripted, trite, like the words were not her own but borrowed from an old Humphrey Bogart movie. And the accent was Austrian, not German."

"Well then, who was she?"

"Don't know. Not enough information."

"Was her map real?"

"It was a real map all right, but to what I'm not sure."

"Did it fit into your location?"

"I don't know. It seemed to at first glance. I'd have to sit down and study it at length."

Bea regarded Dr. Miller. "Are you all right, Chief?"

Dr. Miller mumbled something. He was not himself. The sleepless night and his depressed state were wearing him down.

Bea said, "I don't like this."

"Now, Beatrix, relax. Nothing to get upset about." Dr. Miller collected himself. "We're under control. Hand me my magnifying glass, please. Let's take a look." He retrieved a large map from his work area and unfurled it again on the big work table, pushing things aside to make room for the oversized chart. He continued, "Now, if her map were to fit in here…"

Before he could concentrate, scuffling emanated from the hallway where Jim had gone to take care of the ringing doorbell. Bea and Dr. Miller cocked their heads to hear the roughhousing and expletives. Jim's voice rose above the ruckus.

"You can see him—but not now! He's busy and doesn't want to be disturbed."

The scuffling continued. A new voice emerged.

"Miller, pip-squeak, that's who I want. You can't stop me. Now move it!"

The scuffling was coming closer to the office, punctuated by thuds and bumps on the walls.

Dr. Miller scurried to put the map away and prepared to meet the oncoming melee.

The door burst open as Jim and a huge man dressed in a three-piece, dark-gray pin-striped suit came sprawling through with an unceremonious flurry that resembled a no-holds-barred, free-for-all wrestling match, pitting Andre the Giant against little Tricky Ricky Starr. Both of them ended up on the floor.

Once inside the room and collecting his person, the impeccably dressed big man gently separated himself from Jim. He looked around calmly, picked himself up, dusted himself off, and reclaimed his thick glasses and fedora in an embarrassed manner. His eyes darted about the environment. He was a barrel-chested fellow— six foot seven, if an inch—with piercing sky-blue eyes, white-blonde hair, and bad teeth. His pale skin and square jaw seemed to indicate the physical specimen of a rugged lumberjack with the pale demeanor of a bookworm. His alto voice amid the scuffling also belied his physique. Twirling his hat in his hands and looking at his shoes, he cleared his throat but did not speak.

Jim stood up as well and, closing the door behind him, said sarcastically, "No, no, please, come on in! You're always welcome here! Don't bother to schedule an appointment. Just make yourself at home!"

"What is the meaning of this?" Dr. Miller demanded.

The man glared at Dr. Miller and said, "Yous tell me," indicating Jim with his thumb. "This is the welcoming committee?" The big man's squeaky voice coupled with his size seemed to be at odds, a living contradiction of clichés.

"I demand to know who you are," Dr. Miller said.

"Oh, I'm terribly sorry. How rude of me. Here's my card," he said, deftly flipping a business card out of a silver cardholder he seemed to magically produce from somewhere. "Whom do I have the pleasure of addressing?"

"I am Dr. Gustov Miller, and these are my assistants, Mr. James Morrison, whom I believe you have had the pleasure of meeting, and Miss Beatrix Peeters, whom you have not. And you," Dr. Miller continued reproachfully regarding the business card, "Mr. Bruno Walters, you owe us an apology and explanation for bursting in here without an appointment and in this manner!"

"I do?" Bruno inquired, genuinely unaware.

"Yes, you do."

"Oh, well, yeah, I remain awfully sorry, Dr. Miller, for busting in here like that and messing the place up and all." There was a pause while everyone looked at each other. Bruno pondered Jim for a moment and then proceeded, "Oh, yeah, and, well, sorry, Sport. I hope that crack about your mother wasn't taken in the spirit in which it was not intended. Bygones be bygones, eh, Sport?"

As Bruno extended his hand and adopted a sappy grin, Jim cautiously relented and, extending his, said, "Okay, well, as long as you're truly sorry. From the depths of your heart, I mean."

"Yep, from the depths of my heart," Bruno responded, rolling his eyes.

The brute then turned his attention to the beautiful Beatrix Peeters. "And, you, Cupcake, can you find it in your capacious heart to forgive Bruno for any and all inadvertent indiscretions?" As Bruno advanced on Bea and easily extended his hand, she guardedly gave him hers. He politely removed his hat and delicately kissed her hand with his pinky finger raised to indicate a refinement which was laughingly out of place.

Bea quickly removed her hand and looked at it as if it was contaminated, saying, "For that, or something else you did?"

Bruno glanced at Jim and tossed his head in Bea's direction before he said, "I like her. She's got spunk." A big smile crawled across his face.

Dr. Miller asked, "What do you want?"

"I guess the amenities are over, uh?"

"What do you want, Mr. Walters?"

"Well, as you can see by my card…," Bruno began, then halted and motioned as if to invite himself to sit in the chair on the opposite side of the desk from Dr. Miller. "May I?"

"If you must," Dr. Miller relented.

"Thanks. Everyone, now, come on, sit down, let's put a cap on it here, huh, relax?" He fell into the chair while Dr. Miller and Bea also slowly sat. James remained standing and eyed Bruno suspiciously.

"As you can see by my card…," Bruno started again. He stopped and gestured to Dr. Miller for his card back again. Dr. Miller handed the card back to its issuer, and Bruno carefully read it, moving his own lips silently, and referred to it as he handed it back to Dr. Miller. "I am the managing director for the American Museum of Natural History."

Dr. Miller raised his eyebrows. "*The* American Museum of Natural History?"

Bruno smiled and nodded.

"Is Harry Shapiro still the curator?"

Bruno paused. "No, never heard of Harry Shapiro."

"You have never heard of *the* distinguished Harry L. Shapiro of *the* American Museum of Natural History?"

"Nope. This is the American Museum of Natural History, Sarasota, Florida."

"Oh," Dr. Miller said, looking a little closer at the card.

"Is there another one?"

"Yes, in New York."

"Never been there."

"I have."

"Ever been to Sarasota, Florida?" Bruno asked, warily.

"No, I have never had the pleasure," Dr. Miller replied.

Bruno seemed relieved, "Too bad. We're a small museum but someday we hope to be the biggest in all of Seminole County."

"Good luck."

"Thanks. And to that end, we have instituted a new acquisition program that has proved to be fruitful...heretofore." Bruno cleared his throat, smiled and went on. "Which brings me to my current assignment."

"Which is?"

Bruno shifted in his chair, saying, "Your reputation is impressive, Dr. Miller, to say the least, as well as your ability to acquire articles of extreme interest. It has recently come to our attention that you have possibly obtained, most recently, a particular item that, if authenticated, would be of great interest to myself and my associates."

"How recently?"

"Very recently."

"What sort of article is this?"

"Don't you know?"

"I acquire so many artifacts, Mr. Walters."

"This one is a piece of parchment about so big." Bruno moved his hands in front of him vaguely. "I...er...we...would be...are willing to pay handsomely for it...the article in question."

Dr. Miller paused to squint his eyes and tilt his head about twelve degrees to the left. "Do you have any prior claim to this item? Possibly as its rightful owner?"

"Who's to say who the rightful owner is?" Bruno went on, "But this is a business proposition, Dr. Miller. You're a businessman, are you not?"

"Ah, well, in that, uh, that case I should very much like to find such an article. It would certainly be worth my while, I imagine?"

Bruno tapped his forehead and thought for a moment. He readjusted himself in his chair, his eyes flashing around the room. He deliberately shrugged his shoulders forward and back a couple of times, seemingly to loosen up. He also allowed his head to roll slowly, twice one way and once the other, making his ears touch the tops of his shoulders. Bruno was agitated, and he showed it.

Jim speculated that if this were some sort of physical exertion that accompanied Bruno whenever he "thought," he would love to get this guy into a no-limit poker game.

Bruno finally spoke forth, "You don't have it?"

"No," Dr. Miller returned, "I don't have it, whatever it is."

Bruno stared at Dr. Miller.

"However, if I see such a parchment," Dr. Miller resumed, as he imitated Bruno by vaguely moving his hands to indicate the size of the thing, "I will give you a call. Tell me, what is inscribed on this parchment? How would I recognize it?"

"This is a little embarrassing," Bruno hemmed, hawed, and cleared his throat again. "But I am not so sure myself. I'm in acquisitions, not evaluations."

"How would you know it, if you saw it?"

"I would."

"How?"

"I got a good eye for that sort of thing."

After a beat, Dr. Miller asked, "And why is it of such value to you?"

"I want it."

"Well," Dr. Miller said as he leaned back in his chair, "I wish I could help you but, unfortunately, I have not run across such an artifact."

Bruno released some air through his nose before he pried, "Are you sure?" He raised himself out of his chair and buzzed his peepers around the office a third time, not waiting for the answer.

"Oh, I'm sure."

"Very sure?"

"Yes."

"Do you mind if I look around?" Bruno walked to the work table in the center of the room.

"Yes, I do!" Dr. Miller stood up. Jim stopped leaning against the wall.

"I mean at your books and stuff?" Bruno added.

"Well, it is rather late."

"I'm okay. I had a nap today. Hey, what's this?" Bruno had hoisted a piece of terra cotta stoneware.

"That is an extremely valuable Byzantine vase. Please be careful."

Bruno tossed it up with one hand and caught it with the other before he put it down. He smiled a big smile and spoke. "Oh? Nice, cute." He took a step and then stopped short before he continued, "Don't you think I know a valuable Byzantine vase when I see one? Huh, don't you?"

Dr. Miller did not answer.

Walking to the wall of bookcases, Bruno whistled, "Say, you've got a lot of books here. You read 'em?"

Again Dr. Miller did not answer.

"And your equipment—very impressive."

"Mr. Walters," Dr. Miller uttered.

Bruno grabbed a pair of scissors from the work table and started to play with them threateningly. Jim took a step forward. Dr. Miller held out his hand to stop him.

"You know," said the managing director of acquisitions of the American Museum of Natural History, Sarasota, Florida, "I'm authorized by the board of directors to offer thousands of dollars, maybe six, maybe seven thousand bucks." Bruno whistled, waved his hand at a ninety-degree angle and wiggled his eyebrows to indicate the generosity of the proposal before he went on. "If the particular item in question is genuine, that is."

"Well, as I told you before, I don't have the article in question, and if I did, I'm not sure I would negotiate with you," Dr. Miller asserted, as he leaned over the desk.

Bruno approached the desk and leaned into Dr. Miller. They were almost nose to nose.

"Why not?" Bruno wanted to know.

"Because I don't like your attitude."

"Yeah? Well, I don't like your tie!" As Bruno said the word "tie," he deftly cut Dr. Miller's off as it was hanging plumb over the top of the desk blotter. It fell to the desktop with a rustle.

As it happens, that day Dr. Miller had decided to forego the usual bow tie and wear a conventional necktie given to him by yet another grateful client. Dr. Miller gasped, stood upright, and blurted, "That was totally uncalled for!"

Bruno, imitating Dr. Miller, grew to his full height and shifted from second to third. "That was totally uncalled for!"

"Do not mock me!"

"Do not mock me!"

"Stop it this instant!"

"Stop it this instant!"

Dr. Miller turned red and silent.

"What's the matter, Doctor, does the widdle diddle cat got your tongue? Huh?"

Jim again had the impulse to jump forward, and once again Dr. Miller wordlessly raised his hand to stop him. After all, Bea was looking on.

Bruno said, "Look here, bright boy, if you've got that parchment you'd better cough it up and pronto or you'll be paying the price, for sure." He brandished the scissors toward Dr. Miller.

"I refuse to be intimidated!"

"Where is it, little Mr. College Graduate?" Bruno yelled as he pounded his hand on the desk.

Jim tightened up the distance between himself and Bruno, but Dr. Miller stopped him once more as he fought to muster his own courage. "Now look here, you. It is perfectly obvious that you are not the managing director of the American Museum of Natural History, either in Sarasota, Florida, or any other city for that matter. By the way, Sarasota is in Sarasota County, not Seminole County. This conclusion is obviated by your total ignorance of antiquated objects, or of historic or religious artifacts of any kind. You would not know the difference between a Byzantine vase and a bucket of dishwater!"

"Would, too!" Bruno inserted into Dr. Miller's monologue.

"And furthermore, you're rude—and boorish."

Bruno glared at Dr. Miller.

Dr. Miller continued, "Now, you either state your real name and your business here, or I shall be forced to ask you to leave immediately!"

Bruno smirked an unmistakable smirk. He dropped the scissors on the floor with a clang, stepped back a couple of steps and shoved his hand into the front right pocket of his coat. An unseen pistol took shape in the pocket. He spoke as he tossed his head to the left, "All right, everybody up against the wall!"

No one moved.

"Move it!" Bruno yelled.

No one moved.

Bruno straightened himself up and strode around the desk toward Dr. Miller, keeping half an eye on Jim. When the thug got to arm's length of Dr. Miller, he reached his open hand out and slapped Dr. Miller across his right cheek. Beatrix stifled a squeal by putting her hand over her mouth. Jim jumped forward but was held at bay by a pocket-filled gesture in his direction.

"Tough guy, huh?" Jim spewed.

"Tougher than you think, sport," Bruno shot back.

The brute turned back to Dr. Miller. Dr. Miller had melted to the floor in stunned intimidation. Dr. Miller, sitting there on the hardwood, tried to say something, but in fear and terror nothing came out, just, "I... I..."

Bruno laughed. "I tried to be a sweet guy, but no, you wouldn't take the money, would you?" He started to tear apart the office—emptying drawers, turning over tables, sweeping books to the floor—in a rage accompanied by growls and grunts, like a hungry dog rifling a dumpster behind a restaurant.

At one point during this melee, Jim started to lunge at the thug.

Beatrix screamed, involuntarily, "Jim!"

Bruno whirled on Jim and stopped him cold.

"Try it, pip-squeak!" Bruno threatened.

"Hey, that's not a gun in there," Jim sputtered and pointed to the thug's pocket.

"Well, then, come on, little Mr. Hero, try it and see for yourself, smart guy!"

"Jim, don't! Be careful!" Bea blurted.

"Yeah, Jim, don't. Be careful!" Bruno derided.

Bruno turned his attention back to Dr. Miller. "Come on, Miller, where is it?"

Bruno spotted something on the floor that Dr. Miller had, only yesterday, ignored. In his earlier frenzy, Bruno had overlooked the item, as well. It was the tube that had come regular post.

"Aha," Bruno breathed triumphantly, "what's this? Thought you could hide it from me, huh? I'm too smart for you by half, Miller!" Bruno picked up the tube and deftly unwrapped it. He one-handedly threw off the ragged paper jacket to reveal a cardboard, open-ended cylinder with a note on the inside. He gave it a quick read, "'To a good friend, enjoy!' What does that mean?" He threw them all down in disgust—the note, the cardboard tube and the wrapping paper. "That's nothing. Come on, Miller, where is it?"

Since the slap in the face, Dr. Miller had retreated to the wall behind his desk and was curled up on the floor, cowering in shock. "I...I...," was all that came out of his mouth.

Jim tried to rally the troops, "Come on, Chief, let's rush him. He can't get both of us."

"Jim!" Bea reiterated fearfully.

"You'd better keep a cap on it, bright boy, if you want to see another sunrise." Bruno continued to ransack the office, violently tossing things aside but finding nothing.

"You can't locate anything in this place. It's a mess!" Bruno said, observing the shambles he caused. "I'll give you one last chance, Miller. Where's the parchment?"

Dr. Miller started to whimper, "I...I don't know."

"Where is it?" Bruno made a broad menacing move.

"Please, please, don't hit me again." Dr. Miller was shivering with a force that caused Bruno to step backwards and consider.

"Careful, there, Miller, you're gonna have a heart attack." Bruno crinkled his face in disbelief.

Dr. Miller mumbled, "Please, please leave."

Beatrix added, defiantly, "Yeah, you big bully, get out of here."

Jim topped Bea, "Get out or I'll knock your head off!"

Unimpressed, Bruno looked around the room yet again before snickering to himself and relenting. "Okay, okay, but I'm not through with yous," he said, pointing his pocket at Jim. And then looking piercingly at Bea, he supplemented, "You either, Cupcake."

Bruno backed up to the door, worked the knob with his free hand, and slipped out noiselessly.

Jim and Bea turned to their boss. "You okay, Chief?" they both said.

Dr. Miller collected himself and swallowed hard as he nodded, "Yes, yes. I am fine. Please make sure Mr. Walters—or whoever he is—finds his way out."

"You all right?" Jim insisted.

"Yes, yes. Please go."

To his relief, they complied with his request to ensure Bruno Walters had indeed left the premises.

❖

CHAPTER 12

The Scroll of Nablus

Hardly believing what had just happened, I picked myself up slowly. After a long moment of breathing deeply, I began to move aimlessly around the office and started to straighten up. I replaced books and examined damaged goods. Somehow the shelf of Cardinal memorabilia had remained unscathed. The old Bible was on the floor. I was tempted to leave it, but visions of my parents wafted through my mind. I whiffed the pages with my right thumb and replaced it on the shelf.

After a few minutes of absentminded clean-up, the door burst open. I jumped, but I was greatly relieved to see James Morrison striding through the door.

"It's just me," Jim said. "He's gone for good, I hope."

"Good, good riddance." I picked up another book.

"What are you doing, Chief?" Jim inquired.

I pretended to clean up, "Uh…nothing, James."

"Why didn't you box that guy's ears off, Chief?"

How could I explain to Jim behavior that I could not explain to myself? "Well, I thought discretion the better part of valor, you know."

"You all right?"

"Yes, yes, just a little shaken, that's all. He hit me."

"I know."

I touched my pained cheek and looked weakly at my fingers. "Is it bleeding?"

"No, you'll be okay." Jim hesitated and then reached out sympathetically to me

115

and placed a friendly hand upon my shoulder. "You'll be okay."

I looked upon Jim the way a struggling neophyte looks up to the grizzled veteran right after being struck out with the bases loaded on three pitches. The shame, the ignominy, to be the final out in the bottom of the ninth, causing your team to lose the game and the series to the archrivals.

I sighed. "Look at my office."

Jim started to help me pick up clutter. "Do you think he was after the same scroll or parchment everyone else is after?" he asked.

We continued to halfheartedly pick up the mess with the same enthusiasm that people pick up their belongings after a great tornado tears through their fragile trailer park: with dread and reluctance.

"The scroll," I said in answer to Jim's question. "Yes, undoubtedly he was. Can you see my magnifying glass anywhere, James? And the map?"

Things started to happen.

The phone rang. I jumped involuntarily, about a foot and a half, at the noise. After I landed, I stood there transfixed, motionless. The phone rang again, but I ignored it. It kept ringing.

Finally Jim could stand it no more and picked up the handset. "Lost and Found International, James Morrison speaking." Pause. "He's right here. Hold on." Jim put his hand over the mouthpiece. "Chief, it's for you."

"No, no, say I'm not here."

"Too late."

"I'm unavailable," I said, crossing my arms and taking a step backward.

Jim removed his hand and spoke into the phone, "Just a second...." He replaced his hand before he spoke to me. "Come on, Chief, I already told him that you are here."

"I am unavailable," I repeated.

"It's all right, Chief. Here." Jim held the receiver out to me. He wasn't going to take no for an answer. Why did he think it was so important for me to take a phone call right then?

I edged toward the phone. Distractedly, I picked up a piece of paper strewn on the table during hurricane Bruno and pressed it over the mouthpiece. I suppose I'd seen something like this in a movie. I lowered my voice as I spoke. "Hello?" Pause.

"Yes, this is he." Pause. "Who are you?" Pause. "Unless you tell me who you are, I am slamming down this phone!" Pause. "Stop hounding me!"

I realized the absurdity of the piece of paper over the handset and removed the paper, while I allowed my eyes and brain to work in unison to register the nature of the paper I was holding and its meaning. In an instant—which seemed an eon—I grasped the fact that the paper in my hand was ancient and faded. As the gravity of the realization mounted, I slowly put down the handset, not on the cradle of the phone but rather on the work table. The voice on the other end of the line continued to babble like an automated voice.

Allowing the full impact of the discovery to hit home, I looked at the piece of paper. It was ancient to be sure. Automatically, I began to hold it delicately like a rare, valuable object. It was a parchment, an old parchment. I looked at it again and blinked. It was still a parchment, an old parchment. I laid it out on the floor of my office, casting debris aside, and smoothed it out carefully. My voice finally came to me as I muttered, "My magnifying glass, James, where is it? Quickly!"

Jim scattered what he had tidied to find the magnifying glass in question.

"I think this is it! I think it—" My voice raised in excitement.

James finally found the glass and handed it hastily to me.

I spent some time closely examining the piece of paper. "This is it!" I said, at last, triumphantly.

"What?" Jim shot back.

"I tell you, I've found it!" I bounded to my feet and started to jump up and down in place like a schoolboy at recess. "The scroll, James, the Scroll of Nablus!" Jim started to jump up and down as well, mimicking my unfettered joy.

"This is it, I tell you!" I repeated. We jumped up and down in unison, raising our voices to a girlish pitch, an absurd pair of explorers finding the treasure at last.

"Wait a minute," I said, reining in exhilaration. "Wait a minute. Where did this come from? How did I get this? I don't believe it."

"I don't know, Chief," Jim volunteered. "Is it real?"

Carefully, I bent down and turned over the document to discover another layer of paper on the backside of the parchment. I deliberately separated the one layer from the other.

"I don't believe it. It was the wrapping paper for the tube that came through the mail yesterday. The tube, with the note." I scrambled for the note and read it. " 'To a good friend, enjoy!' The parchment—the paper it was wrapped in."

"What?" Jim exclaimed. "The wrapping paper?"

"My acid kit! Where's my acid kit?"

"Where is it?" Jim launched into searching mode.

"I don't know!"

We were like kids on Christmas morning tearing through the presents.

"Where was it?" Jim inquired.

"On the table." I pointed.

"I can't find it."

"It's got to be here somewhere."

I pulled aside some books to exclaim, "Aha, here it is, and fortunately, it looks undamaged. Now we will get something substantial to work with, some facts instead of conjecture." I was regaining my equilibrium.

"What are you doing?" Jim asked.

"This will tell us the approximate age of the document," I answered. With the gleeful abandon of a Dr. Jekyll, I swept off the table and carefully placed the parchment on its surface. I then precisely mixed a solution of the different vials and deftly loaded an eyedropper.

"How long will it take?" Jim asked me.

"Ten, fifteen minutes tops," I assured him.

"Can't you speed it up?" Jim inquired.

"No, this will be just fine. Relax, James, I think we are onto something big here. Everything is under control."

I was about to swing my arm over the document and apply the solution to the corner of it when the electricity went out, as if on cue. The timing was perfect.

The room went black, dark as dark could be. In the blackness, I skittishly dropped the eyedropper accidentally on the table, as I let out an involuntary yelp.

A shriek and a muffled scream came from another part of the house. Then silence and then a door slam, which sounded like the front door.

We stood absolutely still in the pitch darkness, listening to the silence.

❖

CHAPTER 13

The Ransom Note

After inclining our ears for more sounds from the blackness and for what seemed like the longest time hearing nothing more come out of the dark, we started to stir.

My own voice sounded thin as I broke the silence. "James...James...are you here? What happened? The lights?"

"I don't know," was the response. "Are you all right, Chief?"

"It's so dark!" The tremor betrayed my agitation. "Why did the lights go out?" No answer.

"James, speak to me," I demanded.

Jim found his voice. "Maybe Bea forgot to pay the electric bill?"

"Would you find out, please?" I stammered, cracking at the seams.

"Sure, Chief, relax. Bea! Bea?" He began to grope toward the kitchen, perhaps thinking Bea might be there.

"I've got some matches here somewhere," I said, rustling toward my desk.

"Bea!" Jim called again. His knee hit a chair.

"James, be careful," I said. I let out a mild expletive. "The match box is empty."

"Bea!" Jim called once more.

"The fuse box, James," I suggested, collecting my wits. "Out on the back porch, to the right of the door. There are matches on top of the electrical panel."

"Okeydokey, Chief," Jim said. He groped his way to where he thought the door might be. "Ow!"

I heard the office door open and footsteps fade away. My eyes gradually became adjusted to the slight ambient light. Fumbling for the window shade, I tugged it. With the shade up, just enough moonlight drifted through the window to couple with the sparse light emanating from the hallway door.

I panicked. "No, wait, James. Don't leave me. James?"

"I'll be right back." The voice drifted in from down the hallway.

I forced myself to think. "There's a flashlight here somewhere. Beatrix!" I shouted out. Why hadn't she come running by now? "James!" I yanked open three drawers before I found the flashlight. "Eureka! Please work, oh God, please work." I turned on the flashlight, and it threw a beam of radiance exactly where I wanted. I looked around, daring to let out my breath.

Just then the lights came on with a jolt.

"That's it, James, you've done it! Good work!" I yelled out into the ozone. "Blessed light," I muttered to myself.

"Bea! Bea!" Jim's voice moved from room to room. Bea did not respond.

I surveyed the damage as Jim scurried about the place.

"Where's Bea?" Jim wanted to know, bursting into the room once again.

I stood motionless. "I don't know. She's not in the front room? Or the kitchen?"

"She was out here in the hallway a few minutes ago," Jim said as he stalked outside the office once again. "Bea!" His voice had acquired an anxious tone.

I was drawn back to the work table, where I discovered an acid spill oozing from the eyedropper onto the surface of the wood. "What a mess," I said to the air as I fluttered around looking for a rag to clean it up.

Jim returned with increased urgency. "I can't find her anywhere."

As I blotted up the acid, I responded over my shoulder, "That's strange. Surely she would have said something before leaving."

"What's that?" Jim asked.

"The acid spilled," I replied.

"Oh, that's just great. Now we'll be able to tell how old the table is?" Jim retorted. "I'm going to find Bea."

"Don't go," I blurted, "stay here. Why don't you wait a few minutes and give her a call. She might have been tired and gone home." Desperately, I did not want Jim to leave me alone.

Jim looked at me with a quizzical expression, "I don't think so. I think I should try and—"

Interrupting Jim in mid-sentence was the piercing crash of glass shattering and then a dull thud as a baseball screamed through the window and, by chance, hit me between the shoulder blades, causing me to crumple to the floor in pain.

Jim reacted without thinking. Following his instincts, he scooped up the baseball and ran to the window to see if anyone was out there. He saw a man running hard to the south. Somewhere car brakes screeched to a halt.

Jim turned back to me as I was lying on the floor moaning and gasping for air. Jim gave me the once-over, "You just got the wind knocked out of you, that's all. No blood, you'll be all right." He hoisted my limp torso to an upright position. Slowly I revived.

As I got my breath back, I whispered, "What hit me?"

Jim opened his hand and revealed the baseball wrapped in paper and bound with rough jute. He found the scissors and cut the twine to get at the paper. The baseball rolled loose as Jim fumbled with the paper. Jim read it at first to himself and let out an uncontrollable wail.

"What is it?" I managed. The fingers of one hand closed over the baseball rolling slowly toward me.

"There's a note."

"What does it say?"

"No, I can't believe it! It's too—"

"Let me see."

Jim was off like a shot. He ran out the office door shouting over his shoulder, "Bea! Beatrix!" he shouted again and again into the empty house. "Bea's been kidnapped!"

I sat there on the floor in stunned disbelief, blankly staring into space, holding the baseball. It was old—I estimated more than twenty years—but in remarkable condition. It was at the same moment vaguely familiar and an utterly ridiculous intrusion. I slipped it into my jacket pocket as I looked toward the broken window.

Jim raced back into the room. "It can't be true," Jim said. "She's not here. What are we going to do?"

"Let me see." I held out my hand to Jim.

"Bea's been kidnapped," Jim repeated.

"Let me see the note!" I insisted.

Jim would not let go of the note. "She's not here, Chief. What are we going to do?"

"I don't know."

"What do you mean, you don't know?"

"I don't know. James, the note! Read me the note!"

Trembling, Jim opened the paper and read again, "If you want to see Miss Peeters alive again, come to Central Park, New York, at midnight on the seventeenth. Be at home plate, diamond number one. Bring the goods, or else blood will flow, and fingers will be cut off one by one. No cops!"

"Let me see it," I repeated.

Jim finally handed the note to me. I retrieved my magnifying glass and pored over the ransom note with concentrated effort. My examination was thorough, albeit distracted.

"The seventeenth, that's two days from now," Jim estimated.

"I'm calling the police!" I started toward the telephone, which was still off the hook with the receiver lying on the work table.

"No, keep them out of it for now." Jim grabbed the phone and cradled it.

I gasped. "Has the phone been off the hook all this time?"

"Looks that way, Chief."

"I don't even know who it was," I muttered, appalled at what I had done.

"Why does that matter now, Chief? Focus! Bea!"

"James," I explained patiently, "whoever was on the other end of that telephone was privy to all the events which have just transpired."

"Oh."

"We don't know who we're dealing with, and now a third party knows everything."

"Oh."

"Don't you think it would be prudent to call the police now?"

Jim shook his head. "No, I do not."

"Why not?"

"The note says no police."

"Oh, of course," I said, then balked. "But they all say that!"

"What?"

"All ransom notes say, 'Don't call the police!'"

"They do?"

"Yes, they do. Don't you watch any detective movies?"

"Not really."

"I do. We have got to call the police."

"No, Chief, I said no. I don't want to put Bea in any more danger. Besides, we knowingly are in possession of an ancient artifact, one that probably would end us up in jail. You know that it's illegal to transport this across international borders. Remember the trouble we had in London when they found that wooden Persian vase in my luggage? They would never believe our story. Let's look at the note again."

"Oh, well, there's really not much here," I stated, lifting my head from the subject correspondence. I proceeded to stare blankly, my eyes out of focus, into the room.

"What's it mean, Chief?"

I did not give an answer, but continued to look out into space. The magnifying glass dangled in one hand and the note in the other.

"What are 'the goods'? Huh, Chief?"

No answer.

"Huh?" Jim reiterated.

I still said nothing.

"Bring the goods?" James persisted. "Is it this Bruno Walters guy? Or Rita? Or Martin Samuel?"

There was still no answer, only preoccupied thoughts running through the synapses of my brain.

"Come on, Chief, we got to get moving!"

Jim was nervously fidgeting up and down while we sat in frozen tableau—one unable to stop moving and the other unable to move. Jim looked down and I looked down.

Jim repeated himself. "Chief, let's go, come on!"

Finally, I spoke, "I can't." My voice carried no guile, only a nearly imperceptible shame. Had all my years of careful planning come to this atrocious moment?

I knew Jim could not fathom the turmoil swirling deep inside me. I'm not sure I understood, myself, what prompted this reaction of total withdrawal. I didn't even know my own heart.

"What do you mean, you can't?" Jim pressed.

"I can't." I sat transfixed in my office chair.

"What's wrong?" Jim waited for an answer that was not forthcoming. He whirled my chair around and faced me eyeball to eyeball. "Why not?"

"I can't go outside."

"Look, Chief, I know you don't go outside and all. You like to work from your little office here and do all the research stuff you do, which is very good and helpful. I honestly don't know what I'd do as the field guy if you didn't give me the lowdown and all. I mean, it's terrific. But honestly, Chief, what do you mean you 'can't' go outside? What does that mean? Talk to me."

"I can't. That's all."

"Tell me why."

"I can't."

Jim slapped his own face and rubbed the length of it in frustration before he determined his next move. "Look, Chief, I guess that's really your business, not mine. After all, you sign my paychecks, and all I do is run around the world taking all the risks. But right now Bea's in trouble, and we're the only people who can help her. Are we on the same wavelength here?"

"Beatrix…," I said blankly.

"Yes, Beatrix. She needs us."

"I should never have accepted her application. It is entirely my fault, exposing her to all this danger."

"Yeah, Chief, danger. She needs us. Let's go," Jim said, starting toward the door.

"I can't go out there," I repeated. Couldn't Jim see that I was serious? I finally returned Jim's focus as I waved my hand in the general direction of the outside atmosphere.

Jim gave thought to his next tack. "She needs you, and I need you. You're the brains, I'm the muscle."

"We make a pretty good team, don't we, James?"

"Yes, a very good team."

The phone jangled, jolting our nerves.

I froze, and Jim leaped to pick up the receiver.

"Hello." Jim listened. "No, this is Jim Morrison. Who are you?" Pause. "He's right here." Jim held the phone out toward me. I scooted my chair back and crossed my arms while shaking my head in defiance. This was not the time for a phone call. Jim reluctantly drew in a breath and with a bit of disgust resumed the conversation with the phone. "You have to deal with me." Pause. "Who are you? Where are you?" Pause. "Why should we?" Pause. "I know what you want, and you know what I want. Don't play dumb with me. I got your note and I'll be there with the goods." Pause. "Well, you ought to know. You're the one who wrote it! Yeah, Central Park, midnight on the seventeenth." Pause. "Yeah, two days. Baseball diamond number one." Jim slammed down the telephone.

"Who was it, James?"

"I don't know who it was."

"What did he want?"

"It sounded like a 'she,' but it was hard to tell."

"Well, then, what did he or she want?"

"The meeting—"

"I know that, but what? Was there a ransom demand?"

"She or he wants to negotiate—for the parchment."

"Why did you tell her or him to meet us in Central Park?"

"Well, it was his or her idea, not mine! It's on his or her note!" Jim shook the crumpled piece of paper in my direction.

"How do you know it was him or her on the phone?"

"What?"

"Do you know who wrote the note?"

The light bulb went on. "Oh. Maybe it was somebody else?"

"Maybe. "

"Oh." The other nickel dropped. "Maybe it was somebody other than the note writer, whoever he or she might be."

"Maybe."

"This is confusing." Jim distractedly put the crumpled ransom note into his pocket.

All of a sudden, the doorbell rang. I shook with distress, stood up, and shamelessly fell on my knees, twirled my chair, putting it between myself and the entrance to the office. "In God's name, who is that now?"

"Should I get it?" Jim asked.

"Wait," I answered.

The doorbell rang again and again in rapid succession.

"What should I do, Chief?"

I continued to cower.

"I'm going to get it," Jim decided, though he did not move. "Okay, I'm really going to answer the door." Jim stormed out through the office door and stomped toward the entrance way.

I yelled after him, "Careful, James."

"I'll be right back," Jim shot back over his shoulder.

When Jim was almost to the door, a loud frantic rap of knuckles on the wooden portal suggested the person didn't really trust the bell.

At the door, without the presence of his nervous boss, Jim's cagey instincts kicked in. He turned on the porch light and the entrance hall light. Opening the front door, he let it slowly swing open at its own pace, while he quickly ducked into a dark recessed alcove just to the right of the door. He would have the advantage of surprise. He needed it.

Silence.

❖

CHAPTER 14

The Investigation

Jim could not see who was at the entrance, but just in case, he dummied up and waited for whoever rang the doorbell to make the first move.

Still nothing.

Jim heard heavy breathing, as if the person outside had just been running. Then Jim heard some slight foot shuffling, then the clearing of a throat.

"Hello? Anybody here? Is everything all right? Hello?" came the voice.

Jim recognized the voice, but still said nothing.

"It is Officer, uh, Detective Toole. Anyone at home?"

Jim stepped out from the shadows and asked, "Milo?"

"Mr. Morrison? Hi, Mr. Morrison. Yes, it's me, Detective Toole. Is everything all right?"

"Uh, yeah, sure," James scrunched up his face in disbelief. "Did you say *Detective* Toole?"

"Yes, well, rookie Detective Toole."

"Rookie detective?"

"Yes, sir, Mr. Morrison." Milo caught his breath. "I passed the detective test two months ago on my fourth try, and today is my first day on the force in my new position. You see, the first part of the test is pretty cut-and-dry, it's all about detective stuff and all. You know, sniffing out clues, interrogation, following up on leads, that kind of detective rigmarole and all. The second part is a little more involved."

"Milo—" Jim started to interrupt the fellow.

"There's all this junk you got to know about the law," Milo continued, "and suspects' rights, and how to collar the perpetrator, and admissible evidence, and court procedures, and things like that. I had a hard time getting past that part of the test, if you know what I mean. Boring things that you'll hardly ever use, at least I don't think so. But that's the hard part of the test. That's why it took me four times to pass it. I had to do a lot of studying."

"That's great, uh…Milo…er, Detective Toole. What can I do for you? It's a little late, and I'm right in the middle of something here."

"Oh, yeah, sure. Is Dr. Miller here?"

"Yeah, but—"

"Could I talk to him?"

"It's a little late."

Milo shouted out into the house, "Dr. Miller?"

At the onset of a muffled vocalization from the other room, Milo moved swiftly in the direction of the home office of Dr. Gustov Miller. Milo went through the open office door and saw no one. He then halted, turned to Jim, and asked, "Where's Dr. Miller?"

"Chief?" Jim inquired into the room.

"Yes?" was Dr. Miller's reply from behind the chair where he was cringing.

Jim sauntered a little closer to the desk area and said delicately, "Uh, Chief, Detective Toole, uh…is here to pay you a visit."

Dr. Miller peeked his head out from behind his chair-shield.

"Hello, Dr. Miller," said Milo.

Dr. Miller said matter-of-factly, "Oh, hello, Detective Toole. Congratulations, Milo. You finally passed the test, eh?"

"Thank you, Dr. Miller. Thank you. There's a ninety-day probation period, and then I get a grade-level pay raise."

"What a relief to know you are on the force as a detective now."

"Well, you know…" Milo shrugged his shoulders, grinned a little and looked humbly at the ground.

"So…"

"So, what are you doing back there behind the chair? Are you all right?"

"Oh, yes, I dropped my scissors." Dr. Miller groped on the floor. "Ah, here they are. Well, good then, good." Dr. Miller picked himself up from in back of the chair and replaced the scissors on top of the wildly messy desktop, then resumed his chair as if all were normal. He made no attempt to clean up. "Fine. Well, Milo, what brings you here at this time of night?"

"Oh, yeah, thanks for reminding me. How could I allow myself to get so easily distracted? Why am I here? I saw the guy—are you all right, Dr. Miller?"

"Yes, I'm fine. What guy?"

"The fellow that threw that rock or whatever it was through your window."

While Milo pulled a small notepad and pencil out of his light-brown trench coat, Dr. Miller and Jim connected with a silent, frantic look.

"Doggone it, I busted the lead. Do you have a pencil sharpener?"

"Uh…" Dr. Miller looked feebly around and then grabbed a pencil that was conveniently at his fingertips. "Here, use this."

"Thanks, I owe you."

"Keep it."

"Double thanks."

"So, who was that guy who threw that rock—or whatever it was."

"That must have been terrifying," Milo observed.

"Well, yes, it was a difficult moment." Dr. Miller straightened what was left of the tie Bruno Walters had cut off.

"Well, not to worry, Dr. Miller, the law is here now."

"Thank God for that," Jim inserted.

"Well, where should I begin? I was driving home after a long day of paperwork at the station house." He paused, licked the pencil lead and made a few notes as he muttered to himself something unintelligible to the others. "This helps me think," he assured them, pointing his pencil to the pad, and then narrowing his eyes, he pointed to his head.

"I was driving home, coming up Sixth Street, when I made my usual right turn onto Highland here." He pointed toward the north. "Well, it was a pretty clear evening out and I could see pretty well." He made some more notes. "So I noticed in your yard, around to the side here, a skulking figure. At that instant, I witnessed him throw something through that window there and shoot off as soon as he spotted me. Well, I pulled over, put the hand brake on and shut off the engine. I hopped out of the car and took off after him, back out here and over your back fence and on through to Roosevelt." Milo allowed his gestures to accompany his recounting of the incident.

"Amazing, Milo, wasn't there any trepidation on your part?" Dr. Miller asked.

Milo reacted with eyes half closed and a mild laugh. "No, no, Dr. Miller. I'm a detective now. I don't know the meaning of the word!"

"I'm sure."

Milo halted to make some more notes and then the pencil lead snapped. "Darn it, do you have another pencil?"

Dr. Miller hurriedly scrambled through the side drawer of the desk to find a replacement. He once again gave an eager glance to his assistant, who registered a fleeting panicked expression.

"Thanks, Dr. Miller, I owe you triple."

"No problem," Dr. Miller said through his clenched teeth.

"Where was I? Oh, on Roosevelt. So, he cut left and went down to Fifth where he turned right on…what's the name of that little alleyway there? Anyway, that's where I lost him, darn it. You know where it is, right by the old Kincade place there on the corner. Anyway I doubled back here as fast as I could to see what was up."

Milo shrewdly took the initiative and started his way to the window, stalking it like a cheetah sneaking up on a helpless baby hyena. He measured it up and down with his keen eyes.

Dr. Miller stood up and took a step toward Milo. "So, you say it was a 'he'? Are you sure?"

"Of course." Milo stopped short. "Well, it was pretty dark. I guess I'm not absolutely sure." He turned flatly to Dr. Miller, relaxed his shoulders, squinted his eyes again and asserted, "Be it a man or a woman, he could run like the devil!" Milo resumed his investigation of the window area and the office in general.

Jim looked at Dr. Miller and exaggeratedly mouthed in silence the words, "What are we going to do?"

Dr. Miller pantomimed back mutely, "I'm thinking."

Finally Jim piped up. "Well, Milo, uh, Detective Toole, that is one exciting story, certainly something to tell your grandchildren about. But thank God it's all over and nobody got hurt."

Milo raised his hand squarely to Jim. "This is nothing…I once had to single-handedly corner a bull that had escaped from the Fenson barnyard. I almost got gored. Now that, my friend, is something to tell your grandkids." Milo thought a while. "But before I can do that, I first got to have children, and before that I got to get married, and before that I got to find someone to marry, and before that I got to be on the lookout for that certain someone—"

"And now is the time to start that search," Jim jumped in, picking up on the future chain of events.

Milo pushed aside that last remark and quickly shifted his concentration and repositioned his pencil to make further notes. "Hold on. Let me do it by the book. Time…place…victims… Now, where were you when this incident occurred?"

Dr. Miller said nothing, so Jim answered, "Right here in this room."

Milo spread his hands and underscored the size of the room before he asked, "Where, exactly?"

Jim gestured. "I was over here, and the Chief was over there."

Milo quizzed in order to confirm, "Here, or over there?"

"Here, here," Jim emphasized, "precisely here! Look, Milo, it's over and done with—"

"Let me just make a note of this. Victim A—that's you, Mr. Morrison—was here, and Victim B, that's the good Dr. Miller, was precisely there."

"Yes."

"Okay, all witnesses get into your positions, exactly where you were when the aforementioned object came flying through the aforementioned window."

"Is this necessary, Milo?" Dr. Miller said weakly.

"As the ranking officer in charge of the investigation, I am obliged to demand your full and unhampered cooperation." Milo gazed at both A and B until they moved reluctantly into their positions. He continued, "Thank you. Now exactly what time was it when this object came flying through the aforementioned window?"

Jim volunteered, "I don't know. I didn't look at the clock." Dr. Miller just shrugged his shoulders when Milo espied at him.

"Oh, well, we'll say about ten-fiftyish, give or take a couple of minutes." Milo pondered for a while and then carefully erased the entry and rewrote it to his own satisfaction. "There," he uttered. "They like accuracy in a court of law and at the station house. All righty then, what was the object in question thrown through your window?"

"A baseball," Jim said. "Is this really necessary, Milo?"

"Oh, it's necessary, all right." Milo deliberately scrawled yet another note and then suddenly had an idea. "Wait, I almost forgot, I've got to describe the perpetrator to the best of my ability while it's still fresh in my brain." Milo agonized and wrote down a lengthy paragraph or two while Jim and Dr. Miller anxiously permitted precious time to slip away. Milo read it over a couple of times and then smiled with self-satisfaction. "Okeydokey. Now where were we?"

"A baseball," Jim supplied.

"Ah, yes."

Dr. Miller was losing what little patience he had with Milo's process. "Look, Milo, it is very late, and my head is splitting. Let's just say that it was a baseball and call it a night, huh? I'm sure it was just some kids who got a little overly excited."

"Well, all right, I guess. I'm just trying to be thorough, you know." Milo erased some things on his note pad and added some others. "May I see that ball in question?"

With a sigh, Dr. Miller reached into his pocket and handed the ball to Milo.

"Thank you," Milo said. "Umm. Reminds me of my lucky ball, the one I caught in left field at the first Cardinals game I ever went to."

"Congratulations," Dr. Miller said.

"I go to as many games as I can, you know," Milo said. "Maybe you and I could go together some time. I know you're a fan."

Jim jumped in. "Is there something else you need, Milo?"

Milo let the weight of the ball make his wrist sag. "Was this all that came through the window, a baseball and nothing more?" Just then, Milo dropped the ball on the floor like it was a red hot coal. It rolled to a stop against the side of the desk. "Doggone it! Where's my brain, tonight?" Milo reached into his coat to pull out a pair of gloves. He carefully put them on and bent down to pick up the ball.

"Oh, it's probably too late now anyhow. Our fingerprints are all over it by now; dumb, dumb, dumb."

"Don't be so hard on yourself, Milo," Dr. Miller mitigated.

Milo thought for a second and then sniffed a little further down the trail asking, "Do either of you have any idea who would have done such a thing as this?" Milo shuttered his eyes, shook his head and tossed the ball up and down unwittingly in his gloved hand.

Jim started in, "If you ask my opinion—"

Milo dismissed Jim with a wave, as he looked directly at Dr. Miller. "Do you have any suspicions as to the motive of the crime?"

"He doesn't know," Jim snapped.

"Yeah, but—"

Dr. Miller inserted, "Look, Milo, if you ask me, it was a group of neighborhood kids who did it on a dare or something, just a prank, nothing more. Just a ball gone wild. You know how kids are these days. All things considered, it was a relatively harmless incident and I would be partial to dropping the whole matter. But we certainly appreciate your vigilance in this episode, Milo."

"Well, if you think so," Milo was not convinced.

"Yes, he thinks so," Jim squeezed in, sounding as convincing as possible.

"Still, I'm going to have to include this in my report, Dr. Miller."

"I have no doubt," Dr. Miller agreed. "Now, if there is nothing more, Milo," Dr. Miller referred to his wrist watch. "Oh, look at the time."

"If you really think so."

"I do. It's late."

"Well, if you say everything is okay, Dr. Miller?"

"Everything is fine, Milo, and thank you." Dr. Miller stamped on a facial expression of nonchalance.

"Okay, I'll be leaving now, I guess." Milo surveyed the room again as he put the ball on the table and replaced his gloves and notepad into his pockets. He subsequently put the pencil behind his right ear before he summed up, "This place is a mess, Dr. Miller. How can you work in here?"

"Uh, I know where everything is." Dr. Miller stood up and nonchalantly recaptured the baseball, returning it to his pocket.

"Oh well, to each his own, I always say."

"Good night, Milo. James, would you please see Detective Toole to the door?"

"Sure, with pleasure." Jim crossed and opened the office door to the hallway. "Good night, Dr. Miller."

"Thank you again." Dr. Miller stood up.

"All right." Milo reluctantly followed Jim out to the front door and laconically exited the house with a slightly flummoxed demeanor.

Jim smiled and casually closed the front door behind Milo Toole. He then dashed back into Dr. Miller's office.

❖

CHAPTER 15

Facing the Outside

Jim prattled forth, "Hey, Chief, we got to get going. What's the deal, here, anyway?"

Like a somnambulist, I walked over to the bookcase and pulled down the King James Bible from the shelf and shuffled silently back to regain my desk chair. I didn't really look at the Bible, just rifled the pages unwittingly like a little child would stroke his comfy blanket.

"What are you doing, Chief?"

I did not answer, could not answer.

"We don't have time for that now. We've got to get going."

Jim let out a deep breath and then purposefully walked over and deliberately waved his right hand in front of my face, trying to test my awareness, I suppose. I must have appeared to be in another galaxy.

"Come on, Chief, what do you think? I mean who do you think that Rita chick is, anyway? Do you think she's involved in this kidnapping? Or this Bruno guy? Huh, Chief, what do you think?"

"I don't know," I finally said.

"Well, who do you think this Bruno guy is anyway, and why is he after the parchment so heavy?"

"I'm not sure."

"They both must want that parchment pretty bad, huh? I mean to kidnap someone." Jim paused again and looked at me expectantly. "Don't you think, Chief, this Madame X broad or maybe even that Martin Samuel guy has something to do with this? Chief? Are you with me?"

I had no answers, and I wished Jim would cease his incessant pestering. "I don't know, James. I'm confused. I don't know what to think."

Jim rocked back and forth in his chair while I continued to mindlessly thumb the pages of the Bible.

"I need you to engage here, Chief."

I couldn't take much more of this. "Everything is happening so fast," I blurted. "There's got to be an answer. Sail along so nicely for so long and then all of a sudden, in one night, total anarchy. Why? It's disturbing. Why me, why now?"

Jim's jaw hung open. "Why you? Why Bea?"

"Yes, yes, of course, why Bea? Why Bea? Why any of this. I hate this!"

"So do I. Come on, Chief, let's find out when the next train leaves going east."

"Train? East? Why?"

"Well, we gotta get to New York, don't we? Central Park, New York, New York?"

I dropped my head to gaze into the pages I was turning. "I have got to find the answers somewhere."

Jim crossed over to me and violently ripped the King James Bible from my hands and threw it across the room, where it smashed on the far wall. Stunned, I watched it slide down the wall and fall open on the floor. "Not now, Chief," Jim said. He was actually yelling at me. "Now is not the time to be intellectually inquisitive! Now is the time for action!" He grabbed my coat sleeve. "We've got to save Bea!"

"Save Bea."

"Yes, now!"

"You go, Jim, I can't."

"Come on, Chief, you're the brains of the outfit. I need you."

"No, I can't."

"Bea needs you!" Jim grabbed me by the collar and jostled me. "Don't you understand, she needs you now!"

"I can't...Don't hurt me!" Against my will, I started to whimper.

Jim released me. "Okay," Jim yelled in my face, "all right, you win, I'm going without you. Goodbye!" Jim whirled around and left the room with a determination that only he could muster.

In the safety of my solitude, I relinquished my whimper into a full-blown cry of desperation and despair. I blindly thought about asking God for help, then, "No, no, I will not serve a God like that! I am in charge, not God!" I seemed to be convulsing from the inside out.

Jim came storming back into the room. "Chief, please! Bea's in trouble!"

Reining in my emotions, I remained behind the fortress of my desk. "Jim, why are you torturing me? You save her. You can do it."

"I need you, Chief, I always need you. Come on!" Jim reached down and out of frustration he did the unthinkable—he slapped me across the top of my head, the way you see people do it in a slapstick movie or the Three Stooges.

I yelped.

"Come on, you baboon! Move!"

"I can't, Jim. God, oh God, don't hit me. Maybe you can save her."

"What is your problem? Maybe God can and maybe he can't. Maybe God wants us to do the saving, or maybe God doesn't care. Did you ever think of that?"

"God doesn't care…" I gasped for breath. "I can't go out there…I can't."

"Why not?"

"I'm afraid."

"Of what?"

"Of the outside."

"What do you mean? The outside what?"

"Everything!" I screamed as my secret oozed its way through my being and out through my throat. All my defenses were gone. "Everything! People, noise, confusion, death, murderers—everything!" I pounded the desk with my fist so hard that Jim took a step backward. "I'm helpless! I'm powerless!" My outburst ruptured into crying again.

Jim had never seen me like this before. I'm sure he didn't have a clue what to do. Finally he said, "You're going to have to put those feelings aside right now. This is a matter of life and death for Bea! Come on, now, Chief, I know you care about her!"

I sputtered through my tears and my trembling, "I do!" If only Jim had any idea how I really felt about Bea.

We ogled each other for a full twenty seconds with opened mouths. An unvoiced exchange sprinted between us.

"I'll be with you, Chief!" Jim said more calmly as he took me by the shoulders. Those same shoulders slumped under the strain of despair. Jim added, "God will be with you. There, is that better? God!"

"I don't believe in a God who cares—"

"I'm not sure I do, either, but right now I'm open to being convinced."

There was simply nothing left inside me. Jim stormed out again, and I still could not follow. In my numbness, I heard myself saying words I would not have believed I would say. I was praying! "God, I hate dealing with you. If you are actually up there and actually care, then please don't let anything happen to Beatrix."

I laughed out loud. I didn't believe in God, yet I was talking to him. I couldn't help but think of my parents as I fingered the baseball in my pocket. Andy. He would know what to say.

"Mom, Dad, where are you? If I go out, will you be there? Please God, if I go out there, please be with me." My fist clenched the baseball now. I stood up straight, resolved.

"James! Wait!" I began to lurch across the office. Was I too late?

The office door opened and Jim stuck his head in. "Right here, Chief."

I was startled. "Did you hear all that?"

"Yup!"

"I'm going with you."

"I heard. Let's go."

I couldn't believe I was simply—brazenly—going to walk out the front door of my house. "Wait, the parchment!"

"I'll get it." Jim shot back into the office and rummaged for the document. I watched, motionless, as Jim picked up the Bible he had flung to the floor. What made him do that, I don't know. Perhaps he was thinking about Bea.

Bea. We had to find her. Jim clutched the Bible as if it were Bea herself.

Jim returned to the hall and handed me the scroll. "Why don't you keep it?" I suggested.

"Why me?"

"I trust you, James."

Jim finally handed the Bible and magnifying glass to me. He folded the parchment carefully and tucked it into his back pocket.

About a million disturbing thoughts raced through my mind. What a wretched ordeal I had gotten myself into. I looked disgustedly at the book in my hand. What was this Bible to me but the crowning symbol of the faithless abandonment of a dead God? Yet I had just spoken to this God. Desperate measures, to be sure. Did I hate myself at that moment, or did I hate God?

"What's the Bible for?" I asked Jim.

"I don't know. I just picked it up without thinking." Obviously Jim lied, probably thinking once again about Bea.

"I don't think we need it." I put the magnifying glass into my pocket and dropped the Bible to the floor. I thought perhaps Jim was going to object, but he didn't. If he was honest, he would have to admit that the book meant nothing more to him than rules he didn't believe in.

We stood alone in the hall, wary of the step we were about to take.

❖

CHAPTER 16

The Timeline

I rushed out of the front door of my own house like a frantic termite, and then at being exposed to the open air, I stopped dead on the porch and re-entered the interior hallway. I detoured up the stairs, with Jim close behind.

"Wait, Chief. Where are we going?"

"By my calculations, considering the distance to New York, we have approximately nine hundred and eighty-some-odd miles, as the crow flies, to cover in about forty-eight hours. Make that forty-seven. We lose an hour to the time change." I did the math in my head. "That makes for a journey of a little more than twenty miles per hour. Is that manageable, James, or is that a challenge?"

"Piece of cake," Jim asserted.

"Good. I suggest we put our watches on Eastern time right now. It's now a little after one o'clock A.M. on the sixteenth."

"Let's get to New York quick to see the lay of the land."

"Wait," I said.

"Wait for what?"

"We need a B."

Jim halted. "Yeah! We need to get Bea."

"No, no, we need a plan B."

"Huh?"

"We need a backup plan. If plan A is going to New York and doing our own negotiations, wouldn't we be wise to call ahead and have some allies on the scene? I've got some acquaintances in New York. I can call them and ask for assistance."

"Who are these people? Can you trust them?"

"I think so."

"I don't know. We can do this, Chief. I don't trust anyone."

"Let me get my personal address book with phone numbers."

"You can't call them now, Chief. It's the middle of the night. Let's get moving."

"We'll do rapid packing and then we're off to the train station to catch the next train east."

"Good, yeah, right!"

"Do you want to stop by your place to get some things?"

"No, no, Chief, I'm going with what I have on." After a thought, Jim ventured, "Hey, Chief, maybe we should take a plane. That would get us there quicker."

I hesitated, "Oh, no, James, I don't fly."

"How do you travel, Chief?"

"Uh, I don't."

Jim smiled, "You don't take anything, do you, Chief? Plane, train, boat, car, nothing."

"That's right."

"So what difference does it make, plane, train, whatever?"

I swallowed hard. He had a point.

"Do you even have a driver's license?"

I looked at my employee sheepishly. "No." While I owned a 1968 Mustang, it was strictly for staff use.

"Let me handle the travel arrangements," Jim said.

"Well…"

"Come on, Chief."

"I'm afraid to fly."

"Have you ever done it?"

"No."

"Then how do you know?"

"Just the thought."

"Let's face it, Chief, you're afraid of everything."

"I guess you're right. I am."

"Let me handle the details. I'll drive," Jim asserted. He then added, "We'll need some cash."

"Oh, of course, I'll be right back." I went down alone to my study, looked around out of well-formed habit and pulled aside a painting that hung on the eastern wall to reveal a safe. I worked the combination and pulled out a big wad of currency. I then closed the wall safe. Turning to my desk, I pulled open the left bottom drawer and extracted an item. If I was going out into the world, I might as well wear my Cardinals cap.

I dashed back upstairs to where Jim was waiting.

"Will this be enough?" I asked, showing Jim the loot.

"Oh, yeah, plenty."

A few minutes later, we shoved off in my car.

The weather had turned bad, an early morning drizzle with a steady wind. A storm was rapidly moving in.

❖

CHAPTER 17

Countdown: 47 Hours (1:00 A.M.)

Jim made his way through the weather to the airport. Dr. Miller cowered in the passenger's seat, clutching his deployed umbrella, all the way to their destination.

"Chief, I think you can put away your umbrella now. There's very little chance of it raining inside the car."

"This is fine, just like this, thank you."

"It looks a little silly."

"Oh, I suppose it does," Dr. Miller said, keeping it open all the same.

Jim pulled up to the main departure area. They could see cruising by that the ticketing gates were unmanned.

"We'll have to wait," Jim said. "I'll park where we can see when they open."

Jim pulled the car around to a parking area and pointed it at the terminal. He turned off the motor and curled up behind the wheel, his eyes closed. Dr. Miller, still holding his umbrella, sat silently. He prayed that silent prayer again and somehow made it through the next few minutes. Dr. Miller dreaded the worst and tried not to hyperventilate, his mind ablaze with past and future scenarios.

Constant rain pattered against the roof of the car. To Dr. Miller it was somehow comforting. He listened to the slow breathing of his traveling companion as Jim fell into a shallow sleep.

Against his expectations, Dr. Miller drifted off as well. He dreamed he was being held captive all alone for some unknown reason in a grass-hut prison cell on a tropical island. The cell was bamboo lined and quite sturdy against the bluster of a droning rain. Under the thatched and locked door, an unknown force delivered two meals a day without a word or a reason. This pattern repeated itself day in and day out for an indefinite period of time. Dr. Miller did not know, nor did he ask, why he was incarcerated. He just knew that he was, and he just lived with it. In this dream, his only occupation was to walk the length and breadth of the dirt-floor cell and think silently to himself about useless items. This bothered him. Why did he waste his time with so futile an occupation? The noise of an engine stirred him as he realized it didn't belong in the dream.

COUNTDOWN: 43 HOURS (5:00 A.M.). The noise happened at about five in the morning. A man pulled up in a covered Jeep with an engine that sounded like it was about to fall out. Pulling in next to Dr. Miller and Jim, he looked at them suspiciously. Dr. Miller nudged James, who rubbed his eyes and glanced toward the terminal. It looked open, but the storm had worsened while they dozed.

"Looks like we need that umbrella now," Jim said.

Huddled underneath it, they dashed toward the terminal. A man in a gray uniform looked them up and down. "Luggage?" he asked.

Jim shook his head. "No thanks. When's the next flight to New York?"

"Are you nuts?" the man said. "There's a couple of flights, one American and the other Pan Am. That one's scheduled to take off at 11:15 and it's routed through Atlanta and then on to New York, but that ain't gonna happen, my friend, if this weather keeps up."

"What do you think are the odds it will take off?" Jim wanted to know.

"Slim to none!" was the curt reply. "This storm is supposed to be a whopper. We could be socked in all morning!"

"Great," Jim moaned.

The man said, "Besides that, I heard the pilots talking about a sick-out."

"A sick-out?"

"Yeah, they don't like their contract with Pan Am. A work stoppage? Can you believe it? Bunch of greedy so-and-so's."

Dr. Miller was relieved. "James, I think it would be wise to avail ourselves of ground transportation. How about taking the train east?"

"Okay, Chief, about-face." With that, they ran back to the car. Jim backed out of the parking space and headed back into the city and the train station.

The rain pounded the area like an angry cleaning maid beating the rugs.

They pulled into the train depot parking lot. Jim parked the car and went directly to the counter to inquire after the next train east. Dr. Miller followed reluctantly.

COUNTDOWN: 42 HOURS (6:00 A.M.). "No, you just missed the early one," said the narrow-eyed man behind the caged ticket booth. "It pulled out ten minutes ago. The next train leaves here a little after ten."

"When does it arrive in New York?"

"Don't know. That one goes to Chicago. You'd have to switch there to the New York train."

"Well, give us two tickets for Chicago," Jim said.

"Do they have a sleeper?" Dr. Miller whispered to Jim.

"Do you have a sleeper?" Jim relayed.

"All booked," the grumpy clerk responded.

"Okay, just the two regular seats, then."

Jim held his hand out to Dr. Miller, who was tagging along like a little brother on a field trip to the local zoo with his older sibling. He was outside, and out of his league.

Dr. Miller pulled some money out of his pocket and forwarded it on to Jim, who transferred it to the guy behind the counter.

Dr. Miller stood slouched over warily, nestled behind his leg man, all the time looking around in wide-eyed wonder at sights he had not seen in so many years. The umbrella remained deployed over his head.

A handful of people waited in the station. "Wow, look at all the people and the commotion here, James."

"Yeah, it's quite a hotbed of activity," Jim said sarcastically. "Chief, do you have to have that umbrella out over your head in the middle of the train station?"

"It makes me feel more comfortable, contained."

"Well, it's embarrassing, Chief. People are staring."

"Sorry." Dr. Miller reluctantly contracted his umbrella.

147

"Come on, let's sit over here and wait."

The two sat on a bench inside. On the back of the bench was a brass plaque that stated, *No sleeping on bench.*

Jim regarded the sign and spoke to it. "I can't sleep anyway."

Dr. Miller then had a thought. "James, why don't we just drive to New York?"

"Well, I'd have to do all the driving because you don't drive. And it might be slow going with all this weather. It's a long way to New York."

"Nine hundred and eighty miles to be more precise."

"And besides, it gets a little close in the car after a while. I need to get up and walk around every once and a while." Jim couldn't bring himself to use the word "claustrophobia" with the Chief.

Dr. Miller nodded his head, "We'll take the train." Dr. Miller then tentatively went over to the newsstand and tried to buy a newspaper. The stand was closed, but he discovered the front section from yesterday's paper lying on the counter. He brought it back to the bench and carefully placed it on top of his head, then leaned back on the bench as he gave into the weariness swallowing him up.

"Chief," Jim whispered, "I'm not sure which is worse, the umbrella or the newspaper."

"It blocks out the light," Dr. Miller said, coming up with what sounded like a good rationale for his odd behavior. Saying the umbrella made him feel comfortable had sounded feeble even to him. He needed a new excuse for the newspaper. "Sorry if it embarrasses you, James, but I want to get a little shut-eye."

"Yeah, maybe I should try, too," Jim echoed.

They settled back and closed their eyes.

Dr. Miller had another dream. He was all alone and floating on a homemade raft in the middle of a nameless lake. Rain was falling all around him, but he was not getting wet. This inconsistency bothered him very much, and he tortured himself for not being able to resolve the fact that he was fully exposed to the rain, yet was perfectly dry at the same time. How could this be?

It seemed like no time had passed when Dr. Miller felt a kick at his outstretched feet. He startled awake and pulled the newspaper from his head to behold Detective Milo Toole standing over him.

❖

CHAPTER 18

Suspicious Passengers

OUNTDOWN: 40 HOURS (8:00 A.M.). "Well, if it isn't Dr. Miller and his trusty companion, Jim Morrison."

"Milo, what are you doing here?"

"Funny, I was just going to ask you the same question."

As Dr. Miller fumbled for words, Jim came to his rescue. "Just sitting here waiting for a train."

"You know, you can't sleep on these benches, you two. City penal code one ninety-two, subparagraph B clearly indicates, and I quote, 'Within the limits of the city, public benches are not to be used for loitering or sleeping.' And I have just been a witness to you violating that law, gentlemen."

Jim piped up, "We didn't know it was illegal."

"Ignorance is no excuse. I'm going to have to write you up." Milo pulled out his citation pad.

"Oh, Milo, do you have to?" Dr. Miller interjected.

"The law's the law, Dr. Miller."

Jim spoke up. "Hey, Milo, I thought you were off at six A.M."

"Officer Hubber called in sick. I'm working his shift."

"You're a one-man force."

"I sometimes like to think so." Milo pondered. "I see you're wearing your Cardinals hat, Dr. Miller. Looking sharp! I'm off at noon, just in time to go see the Cardinals play today if it doesn't rain."

"Ah, very well," Dr. Miller said. "I believe Steve Carlton is scheduled to pitch. He's having a record year."

"I go to all the day games," Milo said. He reached into his raincoat pocket and pulled out a ball. "Funny I should run into you again so soon. Now I can show off my lucky ball, the one I caught in left field at the first game I ever went to." He tossed the ball up in the air and caught it with the same hand. "You probably wonder how I go to all the day games. I work the night shift. I put in special to stay on that shift now that I made detective." He tossed the ball again.

Dr. Miller eyed the rising and falling ball as he discreetly put his hand in his own pocket to feel the ball there. If Milo walked around with one baseball, what would prevent him from having a second ball? One which he perhaps would throw through the window of an unsuspecting researcher?

"So, what train are you waiting for?" Milo asked.

"The ten-ten to Chicago," Jim answered.

"What is the nature of your visit to Chicago?"

"Well, if you must know, Mr. Curious," Jim said, "we are going to a…class reunion…in Chicago."

Milo kept tossing the ball, and it was getting on Dr. Miller's nerves. He shifted uncomfortably on the bench as he wondered what a detective was doing lurking around a train station. Surely detectives had better things to do than detect bench-sleepers in the train station.

"I hate those things. Before I went to mine, I speculated that all my friends would have high-paying jobs and be successful and all…you know, lawyers and doctors and stuff. And you know what?"

"What?" Jim asked with a sigh.

"This is the strange part," Milo said. "They were all just regular people with regular jobs and all. I was actually the most impressive out of all of them, being on the police force like I am, a real success story by their standards, you know?"

"That's great, Milo, good for you," Jim piped up.

"Yeah, and now I'm a detective."

"Yes, you are."

Milo thought. "What was I doing?"

Dr. Miller volunteered, "You were going to write us a ticket." Anything to deter Milo from telling his detective saga again.

Jim nudged Dr. Miller and rolled his eyes. He must be more tired than he thought to have walked into that trap.

"Uh, but you don't have to if you don't want to," Dr. Miller said.

"Well, okay, since it's your first offense, I think I am within my public mandate to let you off with a warning. But in the future, I do not want to see you fellows sleeping around on a public bench area ever again. Is that clear, gentlemen?"

"Clear as a bell, Rookie Detective Toole," Jim said with more brightness than the situation called for.

"Have a nice trip, Dr. Miller and associate." Milo walked away, tossing the ball.

Dr. Miller had a bad feeling.

COUNTDOWN: 39 HOURS (9:00 A.M.). The newsstand was now open. Dr. Miller got up to purchase a newspaper, and Jim, a devout Spiderman fan, went along to look at the comic book display.

"Wow, the new ish'. I haven't seen this one. Chief, can you loan me a buck?" Jim relished his comic books. Dr. Miller paid the young woman behind the counter.

Jim settled into his Spiderman adventure, and Dr. Miller devoted some time to the news.

The urgent object of their journey nagged their individual attention, in which both men desired to immerse themselves. They were on their way to save Beatrix Peeters. The distracting entertainment value of their separate reading materials surprisingly only made the time drag on even more. Instead of being a diversion from the current problem, it proved to be merely a chore of great effort. Each man found himself privately reading a sentence or paragraph only to realize he had not actually comprehended the material. They would glance up at different times to refer to the other, who seemed to be absorbed in the paper in front of him, only to refocus and then with new vigor, attempt to read the same section over again. They did this with mixed results. Each of them was not very successful at enjoying his time of reading. They were worried about Bea.

The pair of travelers perked up when they heard over the loudspeaker the announcement they'd been waiting for.

"The 10:10 to Chicago, now boarding on track four. All aboarrrd."

Finally they could move. There was something to do. It felt good to advance. Jim and Dr. Miller went into the club car and found their seats. The weather outside was still wet and windy with no evidence of let-up.

"I'm starvin' like Marvin. Let's get something to eat," Jim said.

The two men sat in the dining car perusing the menus that the waiter handed over. The train slowly pulled out of the station and headed north.

After a hearty breakfast of flapjacks and pork products, hash browns and orange juice, the men retired to the observation car to settle down and silently observe the passing countryside. There was little to observe through the rain-drizzled window. The heaviness of the meal also brought a languor to their dispositions and the weight of their purpose did not invigorate. Lost in their private—yet common—concerns about the beautiful Bea and her plight, they leaned their heads back to allow themselves to be overtaken by sleep.

COUNTDOWN: 36 HOURS (12:00 NOON). "Wake up!" whispered the far-away voice. "Wake up, Dr. Miller!"

The voice was of an exotic nature with a flavor of Eastern Europe and made both the men arouse from their slumber in that twilight between sleep and wakefulness. In Dr. Miller's left ear and in Jim's right, the familiar yet foreign intonations jarred them to consciousness.

"Follow me quickly!" the female voice urged in hushed tones.

The two men in unison started to move before they were aware of the source of the alarm. They fully shook off the gossamer mesh of sleep only to zero in on the mysterious Madame X, or Rita, who had jolted them to response. She was off down the aisle, frantic as a hummingbird. They moved rapidly behind.

"What is it?" Jim wanted to know.

"Follow me," she urged.

"Wait!" Dr. Miller tagged along.

The few other people in the observation car lifted their heads and followed with their eyes as the curious party scurried out. Rita hot-footed them to the adjoining car, where she led them to a sleeper compartment for which she had the key. Dr. Miller and Jim were now fully awake, having been plied with adrenaline.

Once behind a closed door, she suspiciously peeked out the window and lowered the shade. She flicked on the interior light and expelled a breath of relief.

"What is this all about?" Dr. Miller insisted.

Rita looked at the fellows with a dire expression. "You are in great danger."

"From what?" Jim wondered.

"From you?" Dr. Miller wondered.

"Not from me, Dr. Miller, but from him," Rita said.

"Who?"

"Do you realize you have been followed?"

"Who by?" Jim asked.

"By whom?" Dr. Miller corrected automatically.

"By whom?" Jim relented.

"How well do you know this man, this Mr. Idaja?"

"Who's that?" Jim interjected.

"The royal secretary to the Raja?" Dr. Miller quizzed back.

"Yes, him. I have seen him on this train."

Dr. Miller cogitated. Then he said audibly what was going through that mind of his. "What would Idaja be doing on this train?"

"I do not know what," she said.

"Was the Raja or the Rani or any of the retinue with him?" Dr. Miller asked.

"No," was her answer, "he was traveling alone."

"Curious."

"Old Turban Head," Jim quipped.

"Mr. Idaja is the royal secretary to the Raja," Dr. Miller reminded James once again.

"Sorry."

"That is not all," Rita added.

"What else?"

"This Walters man is also on the train."

"Bruno Walters? On this train?" This news made Dr. Miller sit up straight.

"Yes, and he may not be alone."

"How many are there with him?" Jim asked.

"I do not know for sure, but he is not on holiday, I think."

"Bruno Walters." Dr. Miller slid down the wall of the small compartment, his back against the door, until he folded himself up, sitting on the floor clutching his knees.

"Come on, Chief, let's take him on," Jim stated.

"No," Rita said, "it's too dangerous."

Dr. Miller eyed the mysterious Rita. "And what are you doing here, Rita, or Madame X, or whatever your name is?"

"I am here protecting my investment."

"Oh, that's right, you think we're in partnership, don't you?"

Rita said nothing.

"So you followed us," Jim reckoned.

"Yes."

After a moment Dr. Miller ventured, "Are they after me—or maybe you?"

"I am frightened," Rita confessed.

"I bet you are," Dr. Miller said cynically.

Rita looked at Dr. Miller scrunched up on the floor and observed, "Aren't you?"

Now it was Dr. Miller's turn to remain silent.

"Look," Jim said, "it's time for action."

"If they are after you," Rita said, "maybe you had better give the parchment to me for safekeeping."

Dr. Miller and Jim looked at each other.

"What makes you think I've got the thing?" Dr. Miller asked.

"Don't you?"

"Do I?"

"Your eyes betray you, Dr. Miller." Rita turned to Jim. "Or maybe your friend, here…"

This moment of heavy pause was shattered by the sounding of the train whistle, which caused Rita to sit up. Subsequently, the sensation of lessening momentum caused the figures to lean in unison toward the front of the train. The train was stopping.

"What's happening?" Dr. Miller asked. "We're stopping."

Jim went to the window to look out. "Looks like a scheduled stop."

Rita gushed, "Let's get off!"

"No one panic here," Jim said.

"Maybe she's right. Maybe we should get off the train," Dr. Miller said.

They heard a rap on a door down the hallway and then some ensuing commotion.

"What's going on?"

"Shhh, listen."

Dr. Miller got to his knees and placed his ear to the door. The others followed his lead and added their ears to the door. Silence was shattered by a loud knock on the door that caused them all to recoil. Rita recovered and stated coolly in a sing-songy lilt, "Who is it, please?"

"The conductor."

"Oh." The three inspected each other. Rita ventured, "One moment, please."

The trio anxiously adopted nonchalant poses, Rita pretending to brush her teeth, Dr. Miller grasping a curling iron, and Jim suddenly absorbed in the latest issue of *Vogue*.

Rita unlocked the door and asked lightly, "What is it?"

"You have to debark the train for about a half an hour," he said.

"Why?"

"Got to switch out this car for maintenance."

"Great," Jim said sarcastically under his breath as he realized his magazine was upside down. It was too late to correct it.

"Thank you." Rita shut the door.

"Well, I guess we'd better go," Dr. Miller said, and the other two concurred.

As the conductor moved on down the line, all three scurried to gather up Rita's things and wordlessly moved down the corridor, turned to the right and down the steps out onto the platform.

It felt good to Jim to be outside, even if it was in the rain. On the other hand, Dr. Miller felt draped in a blanket of consternation while outside.

Dr. Miller suddenly wondered, "Jim, where is my luggage?"

Jim said, "I don't know, Chief, probably back in the trunk of your car at the train station parking lot."

Dr. Miller breathed in and out.

❖

155

CHAPTER 19

Countdown: 35 Hours (1:00 P.M.)

The station building was boarded up with the word "condemned" painted on a hammered-up two-by-six over the door. The temporarily exiled passengers stood there, unsheltered, making the best of an uncomfortable situation.

Sullen Dr. Miller had his coat draped over his head as he stiffly looked ahead and wondered where he had left his umbrella. Rita adopted an I-don't-care attitude, pulled out a cigarette, and lit up. Jim threw back his head, closed his eyes, opened his mouth, and felt the raindrops fall into his throat. He loved the freshness of that.

Dr. Miller flinched and slapped at his right temple when the guy standing next to him allowed the edge of his umbrella to stray in that direction. Dr. Miller fearfully turned that way and noticed under the umbrella Mr. Idaja was standing next to him, humming. The umbrella looked strikingly familiar, but of course Dr. Miller could not prove it was his.

"Mr. Idaja?"

"Ah," Idaja turned to Dr. Miller, "if it is not my friend, Dr. Miller. How are you?"

"Well, I'm fine…a bit wet. How are you?"

"I'm fine as well." Idaja moved his umbrella, providing Dr. Miller some shelter. After an awkward moment, Dr. Miller asked, "What are you doing here?"

"The conductor requested of me to leave the train so they could exchange the sleeper car."

157

"I know that, but what are you doing on this train in the first place?"

"I am going ahead of the Raja and Rani to prepare for their stay in New York. What are you doing here?" Idaja inquired.

"Uh…" Dr. Miller looked blankly at Mr. Idaja and then turned to his left to see Rita and Jim looking curiously at him and his companion.

"You remember my colleague, Mr. Morrison?" Dr. Miller lifted his voice.

"Yes, of course, Mr. Morrison. Quite remarkable. I understand you had something to do with the recovery of the Amulet of Zoroaster."

"I was somewhat of a participant, yes." Jim glanced at his boss.

"Well, it is a small world, isn't it," Dr. Miller stated.

"Indeed it is, but I would not wish to carry it on my back." Idaja chuckled at his own witticism.

The others did not think it was as funny as he did.

"And your attractive friend here?" Idaja pointed to Rita.

Rita had already taken a step away from the investigators, huddling with her belongings. She was looking vaguely off in the opposite direction.

Jim picked up the hint. "I don't know who she is."

Dr. Miller supplemented, "Uh, yes, we've never had the pleasure."

At that, Rita turned to the gentlemen and said, "My name is Rita, and I am not traveling alone."

"Well, pleased to meet you, Rita," Dr. Miller said.

"Likewise," Jim appended.

"I am also most cordial to make your acquaintance, Miss Rita."

"Hello." She looked the other way.

Idaja riveted on Dr. Miller, "Did you say your reason for being here?"

"I didn't say, but actually we are on our way to a class reunion in Chicago."

Idaja said, "How nice, I'll be transferring trains in Chicago to go to New York."

Jim said, "Oh, well, have a wonderful time."

"You, as well."

They stood side by side without another word while the cars were switched out. Finally the conductor yelled, *"All aboarrrd!"*

As the soaked passengers grumblingly embarked, the conductor repeated to every patron, "Sorry folks, but it had to be done."

❖

CHAPTER 20
Left for Dead

OUNTDOWN: **34 HOURS** (2:00 P.M.). As the passengers slogged onboard, Dr. Miller and Jim left Rita behind to keep the distance that she had initiated. Idaja went into his sleeper, Rita into hers, alone, and the two men trudged back into the observation car, heavy with wet clothes.

As uncomfortable as they were, they gladly took a seat.

"I can't take this broken sleeping pattern," Dr. Miller complained. "It's wearing me down."

"You'll be fine."

"I'm cold."

"You'll be fine, Chief."

The two men sat there. Jim let his head fall onto the headrest. Dr. Miller followed suit.

They dreamed about Bea.

Jim dreamed that Bea was somehow a marble or pinball. She was injected into a large sort of whirling machine that bashed her around like a molecule inside a boiling firebox. He tried to jump into the machine to save her, but could never do it for fear or inability. He groaned in his sleep with anger and frustration.

Dr. Miller dreamed that Beatrix was walking along a high suspension bridge, way above a huge, empty baseball stadium surrounded by blackness. She fell through the guardrail of the bridge and tumbled down out of control. Dr. Miller leaped after her but never caught up with her. Frantic, he woke before either of them hit the stadium floor.

Dr. Miller bolted awake. His jarring movement caused Jim to do the same. After they both had a moment to regard each other and shake off the sleep, they shared a silent moment of concern for Beatrix Peeters.

"I gotta go to the head," Jim said.

No sooner had Jim left the car than Dr. Miller noticed a presence over his right shoulder. It was Bruno Walters pressing the back of his seat.

Bruno quickly moved into the seat next to Dr. Miller, which Jim had just vacated. Violating Dr. Miller's space, he leaned into the man intimidatingly.

"How you doing there, Miller?"

"Walters…"

"I want to have a little talk with you."

Dr. Miller looked around the car and noted that they were alone. A chill of fear surged through him.

"About what?"

"Not here. Let's go to someplace else," Bruno said.

"I'm very comfortable here, thank you."

"No, you're not."

Bruno grabbed Dr. Miller by the arm and dragged him quickly out the rear of the car and onto the loud, jostling platform between the cars. The window to the access door was open, and the misting rain was dampening the air. Bruno pushed a terrified Dr. Miller up against the door to the outside. Rain and wind pelted Dr. Miller in the face.

Bruno took his time to silently pull out a pack of Lucky Strikes. "Smoke?"

Dr. Miller just shrank against the door and shook his head.

Bruno pulled out a cigarette and a lighter and cupped his hand against the elements in order to allow the flickering flame to ignite the tobacco. He exhaled as he put back the lighter and the pack.

"So, Miller, where's your little pal now, huh?"

"Who?"

"You know, that little Jim guy?"

"I…"

"You what?"

"I…"

"Is that all you can say, Miller, 'I,' 'I'?"

Dr. Miller was silent.

Bruno removed his lit cigarette from his mouth and waved it in the direction of Dr. Miller threateningly.

"What do you want, Walters?" Dr. Miller managed to say.

"What do you think, bright boy? The parchment."

"Why?"

"Money, glory, praise, and money, in that order."

"I don't have it."

Bruno shook his head. "Okay, I asked nicely. I tried. It's my own fault for trying it the polite way. I deserve what I get."

With one agile move, Bruno flipped the cigarette out the open window in the door and, grabbing Dr. Miller by the jacket collar, unlatched the door with his elbow and hung Dr. Miller out the door. The landscape passed below at forty-five miles an hour. Dr. Miller was petrified, sure he was going to die.

Bruno was strong. He held Dr. Miller with one hand and searched the doctor's pockets with the other.

The passenger train started to slow as it often did when a freight train was given priority to pass on the other side.

"Where is it, Miller?"

"I don't know."

Bruno slapped Dr. Miller's face with a forehand and then back the other side with a backhand. He rifled through the doctor's clothing again.

"Bingo! What's this?" Bruno scooped out a big wad of paper money from Dr. Miller's pocket. Dr. Miller did not answer.

"Ah, just dough. That's the best you can do, Miller?" Bruno snarled.

"Don't…you—"

"Don't what?"

Dr. Miller accusingly said, "Philistine." That was the worst insult he could muster under the circumstances.

"What did you call me? Huh? What'd you call me? You are such an overrated guy, you think you know everything. You don't know me. What a jerk. I've never even been to that part of the country. Filisteen?" Bruno slapped Dr. Miller again. Dr. Miller gave no answer, but closed his eyes and clutched tightly to the one hand Bruno used to keep Dr. Miller from falling off the moving train.

"Where is it?" Bruno lifted Dr. Miller and started to shake him.

Dr. Miller said nothing but trembled inside and out.

"I'm gonna keep this cash on account of I have costs to cover. This has been a expensive little venture."

"No!"

"No, what?"

Dr. Miller didn't answer.

Bruno found Dr. Miller's wallet and address book. He quickly scanned them and cavalierly flipped them out the side of the train. "What's this?" he said, his hand in Dr. Miller's jacket pocket.

"What does it look like?" Dr. Miller fiercely wished Bruno would leave the baseball alone.

"A baseball? Why would you walk around with a thing like that in your pocket?" Bruno tossed the ball into the wind as Dr. Miller stifled a gasp.

"I'll bet your little buddy has it, huh?" After another thorough shakedown, Bruno disgustedly regarded Dr. Miller. "The great Dr. Miller, huh? You're a hopeless freak!" At that, he wrenched loose Dr. Miller's grip and flung Dr. Miller off of the train, away from the tracks below.

Bruno greedily stuffed the cash into his coat pocket. He jeered at the retreating Dr. Miller flailing in the bushes, but for a short period of time. For right then and there, the always enthusiastic Jim Morrison turned the corner of the door between cars just a bit too late to observe the malevolent Bruno savoring his recent expulsion of the aforementioned Dr. Miller.

Jim, after taking care of nature's call, had returned to the observation car to discover the absence of his boss. In fact, he noticed the car was empty. He sat for a while, thinking that Dr. Miller had gotten up to stretch his legs or something. But after a few moments his ambivalence turned to concern and subsequently his concern turned to apprehension.

Jim began to search the immediate area only to move in the direction of the adjacent car. When he opened the door, he found Bruno leaning out of the train, observing the passing scenery.

"Walters?"

Bruno turned to spot Jim and immediately stood to his full height.

"Oh, if it isn't the little sidekick, Jimmy."

"Morrison to you!"

"Morrison. We were just talking about you."

"Who?"

"Me and your boss. You're just the guy I wanted to see."

"What do you mean?"

"I just tossed your precious Dr. Miller out of the train. I hope he's all right."

Jim stiffened. "What have you done!" He jolted toward Walters and attempted to grab him up high.

Bruno countered with some upper body strength of his own. "Bring it on, Jimmy, bring it on."

In a terrible tussle, the men wrangled back and forth using fists as well as brute force. During the melee, they managed some exchange of dialogue.

"Where is it, bright boy?"

"What do you mean?"

"The parchment."

"Take it if you can, you beast."

The two men bashed back and forth in the small space between the rail cars with kicking and fisticuffs the likes of which has rarely been seen. At one time or another, both men almost fell out of the train through the flapping door as the locomotive resumed speed.

At first the spry Jim appeared to have the upper hand in the conflict, but soon the tide shifted to Bruno's iron-like strength. Jim, finally realizing the advantage of living to fight another day, luckily cold-cocked the brute with his off hand and skittered back into the railcar and down the aisle toward the rear of the train. Bruno lay temporarily stunned at having lost the battle but not the war.

Jim moved as fast as he could through the cars without arousing the attention of any fellow travelers. At the end of train, he discovered a ladder that allowed ascent to the top of the car. He took it. By now the train had resumed full speed, and the going was brutal. Jim walked along the top of the railcar into the rushing wind, sure that Bruno was following. He was right. Looking back behind, he espied the thug mounting the top of the car in unmitigated pursuit.

Jim ran and leaped the distance between the cars as he moved forward.

Bruno did the same.

As Jim struggled forward, he looked for some means of resolution to this doomed course of action. If he jumped to the ground, he'd be splattered like a ripe peach thrown against a brick wall. If he stood his ground, Bruno would pummel him. He was desperate as he kept staggering forward.

Bruno was constant in his stalking.

The click-clacking of the train suddenly changed in timbre as the engine sped over a trestle spanning a wide gully, which accommodated a river. Jim looked down. It was a big river. He didn't know what made the water look deep enough, but it did look deep enough. Maybe it was the abyssal green-brown color of the watercourse, or maybe it was the proximity of the ruffian who was close behind, or maybe it was just the time of day—but for whatever reason, Jim decided to jump.

So he did.

❖

CHAPTER 21

Destitute

COUNTDOWN: **32 HOURS** (**4:00** P.M.). I just sort of lay there, nestled in the top branches of a luxurious, leafy bush that didn't seem to strain under my weight. I checked out my various body parts to see if they were all intact or if any were missing or broken. Apparently I was okay. I stared for a while at the overcast sky, the unrelenting rain smacking my face and running into my mouth, nose, and ears. In a strange way, I felt content to just lie there in contorted repose.

I appreciated the fact that I was indeed in the outside world. This caused me to tighten up with no little consternation. That, in turn, alerted the plant and brought about my cascading a bit downward through the network of branches. I grabbed a solid-feeling limb instinctively. That allowed me to swing vertically and hold on with both hands for all I was worth. When I dared to open my eyes and look down, I realized I was merely six inches off the ground and safety.

It seemed reasonable to let go.

The ground was muddy and hard to traverse. I worked my way out of the web of twigs and bramble to find myself in a wooded area transected by the railroad tracks, on a slope that fell away from the built-up rails. I paused and decided to go back along the edge of the slope to look for the contents of my pockets—my wallet, my address book, and the baseball. I searched for a long time, scanning the landscape, kicking at rocks, scraping away the brush, and had almost decided it was pointless when I saw it.

It had rolled to a stop at the base of a tree, so nearly covered in grass that I was flabbergasted that I'd actually seen it—the baseball! It was considerably scuffed up, but there it was. I scrambled down the slope to retrieve it, feeling the grin spread across my face. This wasn't an ordinary baseball, I was sure of that. I didn't know what it had to do with Bea, but somehow I was convinced I was meant to have that ball. Finding it again after the way Bruno threw it off the train was confirmation. I wiped it against my pants leg and just held it, feeling its weight in my hand.

With the ball once again in my coat pocket, I ran an inventory of my assets: no money, no wallet, no James Morrison. Not a very promising ledger.

I sat down in the mud.

✤

Meanwhile Jim came surging to the surface of the river as it pulled him along its flow. He gulped a big breath of air. As he drifted away from the bridge, he looked back and saw no evidence of a train or anyone pursuing him. Ironically, it was kind of peaceful—but also cold. Jim swam easily toward the shoreline. He was a good swimmer. As a teenager, he had worked for a summer as a lifeguard at the local public plunge, and the experience was paying off when he needed it.

When he got to the shore, he lay there for a long while in numb remission, breathing heavily.

Bea.

The Chief.

After a while, Jim picked himself up and started to move.

✤

Countdown: 31 hours (5:00 p.m.). I got up and began to move away from the tracks, muddling through the undergrowth and dense foliage until I stumbled out of the wild woods and onto a dirt road. There was not a sign of human life. I did notice some wildlife hunkered down, enduring the weather, something I was not inclined to do.

On the other side of the dirt path was a cultivated cornfield. The stand of corn was impressive, about five to six feet high, but not nearly ready for harvest. Time and nature would take care of that.

I turned left and started to walk along the other side of the road. I didn't know what I should be looking for, but it seemed prudent to keep moving. After some distance, I heard a vehicle approaching from the rear. Turning to see what was coming, I saw a speck slowly making its way along the one-lane road toward me.

I panicked and ducked into the cover of corn stalks, not knowing who might be in the car. Gradually the vehicle approached, and slowly it passed by. I could see a round-faced, devoted farmer touring his fields alone in an old pickup truck on a day when he could do little else. The farmer did not see me but was focused rather on the current state of his crops, as farmers constantly are.

As the truck slowly pulled away, I came out of hiding and deliberately continued down the road in my own melancholy way. I thought about my depressing plight, Beatrix Peeters, and Jim Morrison, in that order.

✦

Jim continued through the wilderness. He thanked his zodiac sign, whatever it was, for the good fortune he enjoyed. *There was indeed someone out there somewhere, looking out for me, whether you believe in that sort of thing or not*, thought Jim, *just like the raven that took care of me in the desert*. Maybe someone was praying for him. Jim thought of Bea, not for the last time.

Jim walked at a ninety-degree angle through the brush by the bank of the river until he came to a winding, dirt path that followed the contour of the tributary.

Which way to go?

His concern for his boss drove him to follow the river upstream to the trestle from which he had leaped. He had to find the place where Dr. Miller might be lying broken and in urgent need by the side of the railroad tracks. *Poor Chief*, Jim pondered, *he's pretty helpless out here.*

✦

COUNTDOWN: 30 HOURS (6:00 P.M.). I was rent between this dreadful disaster of my own circumstance and that of my workmates and friends. I had not felt this notion for many a year, and it began to work on my soul. Even though I was more than a bit tired and hungry, I kept on moving. Down the dirt road I trudged until I came to a T where I had to make a choice. I turned left. After a passage of time, the road opened up to a cleared parcel and a small farmhouse in the distance.

The smoke coming from the chimney and the bucolic setting made for an inviting draw. As I got closer, I plainly saw a pastoral scene complete with barn, chicken coops, pig pens, and all the accoutrements of a working family farm. Because of the weather, the occupants were inside the house, cozy and dry. A warmth emanated from the place like a nostalgic postcard, even down to the old pickup truck parked out front.

I thought about my childhood setting and the family I'd once had. I'd lived in a picture like this once. But no more. My parents were long dead, and I didn't even know where my only brother lived.

I skulked up to a lean-to on the back side of the barn and took cover in the shelter of its roof in order to escape the constant drizzle and think about my next move.

I found a sweet comfort in being under a closed roof, even if it was not my home in St. Louis.

❖

Jim arrived at the overpass that spanned the river gorge. He walked up the slope of the ridge to the plateau of the tracks, then headed back south on the bridge over the watercourse, retracing the path of the train.

He looked down at the river below and counted himself crazy for having done such a foolhardy thing as throwing himself off the top of the moving train and into the water. How did he know it was deep enough? He shivered at the thought of what could have been.

Jim figured that if Dr. Miller had survived the fall off the train, he would be lying in agony not more than a mile or mile and a half away, somewhere along the eastern stretch beside the tracks in the wooded area that lay south of the trestle.

He proceeded to carefully walk that distance.

❖

COUNTDOWN: 29 HOURS (7:00 P.M.). I sat in the little shed behind the barn as the rain clattered against the corrugated metal roof. And as I sat there, the distinct aroma of roasted meat blended well with potatoes and carrots wafted through the air. What a grand meal that would make. My stomach started to respond to the aroma. I thought through the process of actually going up to the door of the nearby farmhouse and asking its occupants if I could join them in this evening repast. I had heard of the farmhouse hospitality concept, but I had a difficult time placing myself in the context of its use.

Obviously my reticence at being assertive in this area was due in part to the fact that I had not stepped foot outside my own house in over seven years. A little over seven years ago, I had been forced to go to court on behalf of one of my clients, and it had been an extremely unpleasant experience. I swore to myself I would never do it again under any circumstances. Until seventeen hours ago, I would have said my agoraphobia was overwhelming. But here I was, and still breathing.

Mapping out a plan of attack and the words I would say, I acquired some momentum. It took a while, but the hunger pangs brought me around, and I yanked myself up to my feet and stepped back out into the rain toward the farmhouse door. I placed my right foot on the first tread of the stairs that led to the landing in front of the farmhouse entrance, instinctively trying to minimize any squeaks and moans that would, of course, be present in an old front porch. Having successfully mounted the porch, I peeked into the front window, but saw nothing; a lined drape blocked the outside world. Stealthily I pulled open the screen door, which caused a little creak that in turn engendered an involuntary tick in my face. I listened intently at the door for any conversation or hubbub that might help me in this quest for some beef stew or potatoes or any derivative thereof.

Bracing myself, I lightly tapped on the door of someone else's home, something I had not done in so long that it made me nervous. Through my fear, I took a deep breath. I thought about praying, but what was the point? I could knock on a door under my own steam.

No response. I rapped with my knuckles even louder. The drone inside stopped, and I ascertained that someone was on the way to answer the door.

After a beat, the door swung open and I was eye-to-eye with a stout fellow with a sweet, clean-shaven face that looked remarkably like the farmer I had observed touring his corn patch in the aforementioned pickup truck.

The farmer narrowed his eyes at me.

I found my voice. "Excuse me, I'm terribly sorry, but you see, I had a rather unfortunate accident and I find myself in the need of some assistance."

"Accident?"

"Well, yes," I laughed, embarrassed. "You see, I accidentally fell out of a train that was passing through these parts and, uh, fortunately my fall was broken by a thick bush at the side of the tracks."

The farmer mulled over my explanation in silence. I realized then that it had sounded much better when it was rehearsed during my mental preparation. I smiled. I should have thought of a more believable lie.

"Accidentally fell out off a train?"

"Well, it's hardly the sort of thing one would do on purpose," I said, my nerves trembling. "I was between cars, you know, and I leaned on one of the access doors and it was not latched properly, obviously, and I fell...off...out."

"Hmm," the fellow thought. Making the mental leap, the farmer asked, "What kind of assistance do you need?"

"I don't really know my way around these parts and I need, perhaps, a place to stay, just for tonight—and maybe some food, if you have any to spare. I would be on my way tomorrow morning, first thing. I would gladly offer to repay your kindness with the coin of the realm but once again, unfortunately I find myself penurious."

"What?"

"Broke."

Once again, the look. The farmer spoke, "What did you say your name was?"

"Uh, Miller, Dr. Gustov Miller."

"Dr. Miller...hmm...any relation?"

"I beg your pardon?"

"Any relation to the Dr. Miller who lived in Birdsall? The vet?" The farmer pointed with his left thumb in the direction of what could only be Birdsall.

"No, I'm afraid not," I said.

The farmer slyly thought of an angle. "I've got a sickly cow. Maybe you could look at her for me?"

"I'm not a veterinary doctor."

"What kind of a doctor are you?"

"History, archeology, and world religions."

"Don't have any need for such a doctor."

"Well, I could pay you back later...when I get back home...later."

"Where's that?"

"St. Louis."

After a silence the farmer said, "Well, you seem like a decent enough fellow, a little careless maybe, but I don't want any of your money. Come on in, but leave your muddy shoes out on the porch here. The missus will have it no other way."

"Thank you."

I breathed a bottomless sigh. I removed my wet shoes and entered the cozy domicile.

I was directed to sit at the dining room table, where the woman of the house sat.

"This is Betty, and my name's Roy."

"Nice to make your acquaintance."

"Yours, too. Do you like pot roast?"

"Very much so."

"Potatoes?"

I had guessed right. "Yes, it's my favorite."

"Good, help yourself."

Betty had not yet cleared the dishes, so she introduced a new place setting on the table and pleasantly indicated there was plenty left for me. Apparently this couple had no children.

We passed a very pleasant meal together, with Roy and Betty sipping coffee and munching apple pie while I deposited some meat and potatoes, followed by the aforementioned apple pie and coffee. It turned out to be a very agreeable supper and conversation. I couldn't really have asked for a more amiable reintroduction to outside contact.

My thoughts naturally turned to my own past and the many Sunday afternoon meals with my mother and father and younger brother. Ah, the halcyon days of my youth, when I hadn't a care, before Africa. This could have been Werner and Edith Miller, hospitably taking in a stray and contentedly offering a simple fare.

❖

CHAPTER 22

Moving from the dining room table to the parlor, I didn't have to go far. I lifted myself up, walked six paces around a flowered, slip-covered sofa and plopped down.

Roy followed. Betty did the dishes. I raved about the meal and that, of course, made Betty minimize its sufficiency and apologize for its lack of adequacy. I politely offered to help clean up, but Betty refused.

As Roy and I sat there, the farmer went on an extended monologue about the agriculture business. It was difficult to concentrate on or participate in the discourse, due to the length of the day, the fullness of the stomach, and the distraction of concern. I was, of course, preoccupied with the quest that I was on and the people involved.

What was going to happen to Bea and Jim?

I was pulled back to the moment when the farmer asked, "What was it you do?"

"Sorry?"

"What was it that you said you do for a living?"

"Oh, I run a business that recovers missing articles."

"What kind of articles?"

"Anything, really, old or priceless, anything missing or lost. Anything of ancient import, or extremely valuable, or rare, religious items."

"Huh, sounds highfalutin' to me. Do people actually pay you to do that?"

"Yes, and quite handsomely."

"Where're you from?"

"St. Louis."

"I mean, originally, your roots."

"Fairfield, a small farming town." An image of an alfalfa field floated through my mind, and I could almost smell the annual church picnic.

"How'd you get mixed up with finding rare things?"

"It just sort of happened, I guess."

"Was your daddy a farmer?"

"No, a pastor."

"What denomination?"

"Baptist."

"Betty and me are Methodists."

"Oh."

"What church do you go to?"

"I don't go to church."

"Why not?"

"I, uh, sort of got out of the habit, I suppose." This man had just told me he was a Methodist after generously taking me in; I could hardly tell him that I hated God for killing my parents.

"Your folks still in the ministry?"

"No, they're both gone."

"Gone?"

"They're dead."

"Sorry to hear that."

"Me, too."

A pause for thought.

Roy said, "Well, they say the acorn falls not far from the tree."

"I beg your pardon?"

"Well, finding rare lost religious artifacts might just lead you back to your roots."

"I don't think so."

"My father was a farmer and his father before him. And if there's one thing I know, it's that a tiny seed, well planted at the right time, can most often, even in spite of neglect, naturally grow into the spittin' image of the parent."

I drew in some air, about to speak before Roy cut me off. Roy said, "Don't say anything right yet; think about it first."

I took the opportunity to appear to do so. During my deep reverie on the matter, I was overcome with drowsiness and being categorically affected by the dissatisfaction of an interrupted sleep pattern, I excused himself and asked my host for directions to the guest room. After thanking my host and hostess profusely for their kindness, I closed the door of the downstairs guest room, hung my wet clothes on a hook on the door, and fell into bed, exhausted.

I thought of Beatrix Peeters.

I thought of my parents.

I thought of Andy.

And at last I slept.

At 6:00 A.M., a dream startled me to wakefulness. I didn't remember it, just that it was unpleasant, and I could not go back to sleep. I slipped on my mostly dry clothes and hoped I could get away without another dissertation on the plight of the American farmer. I made my way quietly to the kitchen, where I palmed a couple of day-old biscuits, and hurried out of the house just as I heard stirring upstairs. I had to find Jim. More importantly, we had to find Bea, together, before the calendar turned another day.

I continued down the dirt road that had led me to the farmhouse. Upon coming to a crossroads, I wished Jim were there. How was I to know which way to go? The sun had come up to my right, so I had my bearings. I decided to travel north along the railroad tracks in the general direction of Chicago. I could only hope that Jim would wait for me there and somehow we could find each other and make it to New York before midnight.

The idea of a finding a pay phone crossed my mind. But I didn't have a dime. Besides, who would I call? The only two people who might hope to hear from me were lost to me at the moment.

I pressed on.

✤

CHAPTER 23

The Waitress

COUNTDOWN: **19** HOURS (7:00 A.M.). Jim slept in the forest.

Working his way along the tracks in the morning, Jim suddenly halted. He paused to look down and regard a misplaced wallet splayed open but looking familiar. He picked it up and saw immediately that it belonged to the Chief. It was empty of money, but the business cards were there. *Lost and Found International— Dr. Gustov Miller, President.*

Jim yelled out into the atmosphere, "Chief, hey, Chief!"

No answer.

However, this serendipitous discovery gave him new energy. He literally beat the bushes within proximity of his immediate location and found nothing.

Jim moved down the tracks, looking about him all the while with no results. Impulsively, he cut over in a perpendicular direction until he came to a dirt road some distance off but running parallel to the train tracks.

He pondered if it was good news or bad news that the wallet was found without its owner.

Jim looked down the dirt road, both ways. He didn't know which way to go, so he spit on his hand and slapped the heel with the other hand and allowed the direction of the spittle to determine his course. It splattered off his palm toward the right.

Scanning the horizon, Jim felt he needed to find some point of reference in order to fix his orientation. He felt in his back pocket. To his relief, the parchment was there, along with another valuable item he had not revealed to the Chief. He looked in his own wallet and it was dismally empty: a driver's license and some business cards: *Lost and Found International—James Morrison, Acquisitions.* It was still soaking wet.

Jim thought of the Bible lying on the hallway floor in the Chief's house and that made him think of Bea. *Beatrix, you all right? You know that I'm coming?*

A few minutes later, his internal request for an orientation point was answered. A wet Jim Morrison ambled into a small town.

He thought of finding a telephone, but who would he call? Bea? The Chief? It impressed him, the lack of funds he commanded. He imagined the visual effect his appearance would have on the locals. They would no doubt think him to be a transient bum in need of a handout. The type of folks in these parts, Jim thought, firmly believed in self-sufficiency.

There was, in the center of this tiny town, a confluence of two roads. On the four corners of this intersection stood a gas station, a post office, a John Deere equipment store, and a Lutheran church. Jim also noticed a small diner, named Ned's, right next to the John Deere tractor outlet. It was open for breakfast and lunch. He went in.

"Howdy," Jim said, trying to fit in.

Two customers hunched over the counter, awaiting the services of one chef and one waitress.

"Hello," replied the waitress, "I'm Cindy."

Jim could tell by the badge stitched on the waitress's clean, white uniform that she was not fibbing. Indeed, her name was Cindy.

"Where am I?" Jim inquired.

"Ned's."

Jim tried another tack. "How far away is Chicago?"

"It's about ninety-five miles, and no, I don't have bus fare."

"How do I get there?"

"If you're walking, which you are, you'd take Main Street here to the stop sign and then turn right, and keep on walking about…," Cindy dictated blandly, accompanying the oft-spoken directions with helpful hand gestures.

"Ninety-five miles," Jim completed her sentence for her.

"That's right."

"Thank you. Is there anything else open in town?"

"Nope."

"Thanks again," Jim said.

"And you'd better get a move on, darlin'. You're not getting any younger."

"Neither are you," Jim said politely, and left.

Jim stood outside Ned's and wondered whether he should try to go back and search some more for the Chief. What if he was lying half dead somewhere by the side of the train track? Should he press on ahead along the route they were going? Jim really had no idea where else to look for the Chief. The chase aboard the train, the adventure of floating downstream, the search for the Chief, the overnight stay in the bush, and then the subsequent stroll to this forsaken town left him sadly out of it. If only he had the help of a Dr. Miller directional map, it would be easy. Jim needed Dr. Miller to find Dr. Miller.

Sure enough, nothing else was open in town, so Jim sloshed down Main Street, and there was the stop sign Cindy had told him about. He turned right, and again Cindy was correct: a long, straight double-lane asphalt road headed north and south. Following instructions, Jim turned right and headed north.

❖

CHAPTER 24

Deadly Curves

C OUNTDOWN: 15 HOURS (9:00 A.M.). Reaching a point of desperation, Dr. Miller tried his hand at hitchhiking. He had heard it was possible to actually procure a ride if a person extended a thumb to a passing car in the direction he wanted to travel. Dr. Miller got up the nerve to try, to no avail. Because there seemed to be only a few older beaters traveling this country dirt road, the thought of bumming a free ride felt like a low-life way to get around. Normally he would have thought this behavior beneath him in any circumstances, but normally he could not have imagined finding himself in these circumstances. He tried a few different techniques to acquire a ride, but they all failed. After walking some distance, he remembered he had a couple of biscuits. He took one out of his pocket and started in on his breakfast.

As Dr. Miller trudged along, he experienced a sudden shiver; he hesitated, realizing he was outside. He started thinking, *How could I have forgotten that fact— being outside?* Waving his right hand horizontally above his head, he pondered the open sky and started to draw his coat over his head, but he resisted the urge. Upon realizing that he was not as anxious as he certainly should be, he thought, *Strange, indeed, that I should be so much more at ease under these conditions than I ever imagined. Yet it is a reality.* He began to analyze why this would be true. *Am I getting more at ease and confident, or am I just tired and dulled from the arduous journey? What is happening to me?*

He heard another car approaching from the rear. He thought about trying again to hitchhike, but shrugged off the notion as being useless.

The noise of the car wound down to an idle as it pulled alongside the despondent Dr. Miller. This caused Dr. Miller to turn his head to the left in order to see the car and its driver.

The driver had indeed stopped the '65 Ford Falcon and had reached across the front seat and opened the passenger side door in an inviting manner. Dr. Miller peered into the car to see its inhabitant.

He heard the sweetly stern tones of an Eastern European female. It was the exotic Rita.

She said, "Get in."

✤

Jim continued his walk north. This two-lane blacktop had some serious traffic, so Jim immediately started to hitchhike. He didn't get a ride. Maybe he didn't look pathetic enough. He looked at himself, and he thought himself to be very pathetic indeed. Maybe he was too pathetic.

He attempted every method to acquire a ride known to the world traveler.

He gave up and focused on some berry bushes alongside the road, but the berries were not yet ripe. Their presence served only to stimulate his hunger further.

All of a sudden, a car pulled up behind him. Jim stopped and turned to recognize the smiling man behind the wheel. It was Mr. Idaja. Jim stood there with his mouth open.

Idaja said, "Please to get in. I am driving."

✤

COUNTDOWN: 14 HOURS (10:00 A.M.). Rita asked directly, "Dr. Miller, do you have the parchment?"

Dr. Miller shifted uncomfortably in the right front seat. "I do not."

"Who does? Mr. Morrison?"

Dr. Miller's silence betrayed the truth.

She said, "Where is he?"

He said, "I don't know," which was the unfortunate truth.

Dr. Miller turned his head to the mysterious Madame X. "How did you happen along here and now?"

"I have told you, I will not allow my part of the parchment to leave me."

182

"Look, Rita, or whatever your name is, I have told you that we are not part-ners in this matter."

"I must protect my share of the treasure."

"You have no share." Dr. Miller felt like he was talking to an oil painting, as if he were trying to get through to Whistler's Mother.

Dr. Miller said, "How did you know I was here?"

No answer.

"Where did you get this car?"

No answer.

Dr. Miller looked out the front window of the Falcon. "Why are you going so fast?"

Rita said, "We must find Mr. Morrison."

The Ford Falcon was doing about fifty-five and gradually increasing in speed. By Dr. Miller's estimation, this was a bit too fast on this country road, and his dis-comfort level rose correspondingly with every increase in miles per hour.

Dr. Miller fastened his seatbelt. "Do you even have a driver's license?"

No answer right away. Finally Rita asked in return, "From this country?"

Dr. Miller said, "From any country!"

"I used to have one."

"Great."

The pace of the vehicle was now clearly exceeding what Dr. Miller believed to be a safe speed.

"Please slow down."

Rita did slow down, but not enough for Dr. Miller.

"Where are we going?"

Rita said, "We must find Mr. Morrison."

"You know where he is?" Dr. Miller asked hopefully.

Rita said, "We must find Mr. Morrison."

"But—"

Rita said, "Shush!"

Dr. Miller grew anxiously silent. His white knuckles betrayed his dread.

The car sped northward. Dr. Miller had his eyes on the road.

✦

Jim thought for about a second, then obediently climbed inside the black Buick Special.

"Mr. James Morrison, is it not? Dr. Miller's assistant?"

"Yeah, but—" Jim closed the door as the Buick pulled away.

Idaja said, "Have a little sustenance, if you please. You appear hungry."

Mr. Idaja with one hand manipulated the steering wheel as the car gained speed and with his free hand produced some sandwiches from a brown paper bag on the front seat.

Because of Jim's malnourished state, he merely acquiesced to Mr. Idaja's suggestion. He peeled back the tinfoil to reveal two pieces of bread with something in between. He took a bite without asking. He grimaced. "What is this?"

Idaja said, "It is a sandwich, as you Americans say, with soy-curd in the middle. Do you like it?"

Jim didn't really, but he said he did and ate it gladly. He had eaten worse.

Idaja said, "There is also some coffee in that thermos."

"Thanks."

The car went north.

Jim said, "What are you doing here, anyway, and how did you—or did you—know that I was walking on the side of this road?"

"I believe I told you, I am previewing sites of destination for the royal family. I do believe Chicago is north of here?"

"But you were on the train?"

"I took a little side trip to assess the countryside. The Rani is very interested in American culture and desires to see as much of it as she can. I just happened to spot you and recognize you. How did you happen to be off the train?"

"It's a long story." Jim didn't feel like reliving the incident.

Idaja asked, "Strange us meeting again like this, is it not?"

Jim said, "I guess." After all, stranger things had happened.

Idaja had been putting the pedal to the metal and was passing trucks with regularity.

Jim said, "You're going a little fast. Have you driven in America much?"

"No."

"Do you have a license?"

"No."

"Great."

"Where is Dr. Miller?"

Jim said, "I wish I knew."

Idaja said, "I, as well."

"Why?"

No answer. Idaja hummed.

They sped on in silence.

✤

COUNTDOWN: 13 HOURS (11:00 A.M.). They were making good time—a little too good.

Dr. Miller, keeping his eyes glued to the oncoming rush of roadway and landscape, had little desire to chat with the driver. Most of the conversation shared with the lovely Madame X proved to be circular in nature and less than fruitful. Dr. Miller decided to sit there, shut up, and hold on, hoping that they were moving toward Chicago.

Few other cars were on this country road, but that was about to change. Rita, at the helm of the vehicle, barely slowed enough to negotiate a hard right turn, causing Dr. Miller to shift radically to the left and press up against her.

When the car had settled on the perpendicular course, Dr. Miller collected himself and said, "Pardon me."

Rita said, "It is all right, Dr. Miller."

This new right angle announced an upcoming traffic signal that allowed for a high, wide, and handsome two-lane blacktop highway that coursed in a north-south direction.

Rita came to a screeching halt and then flipped on the left-hand directional.

As the car sat idling, waiting for the green, Dr. Miller asked, "Which way are we going?"

"North."

"Why?"

"We must find—"

"Mr. Morrison," Dr. Miller finished her sentence for her.

"Yes," she said.

185

At the turning of the light from red to green, she jolted left and lost no time in making it to highway speed. Dr.Miller was relieved in a way because the speed of the vehicle befitted the condition of the road.

Even then, the eager Eastern European passed other trucks and cars as if she were imitating Mr. Toad.

They went on, in excess of the speed limit. Dr. Miller saw the advantage to going this fast, however. He and Jim had been slowed down during the first part of their journey and now had only a little over twelve hours to make it to New York if they were going to rendezvous at Central Park at midnight. And first they had to find each other. He took some small comfort in Rita's determination to find Jim.

As they were approaching Chicago, Dr. Miller figured they had to average over sixty miles per hour of the remaining trip if they were going to make it on time at all. He wondered about Bea and what torture she might be suffering right now at the hands of her captors.

Dr. Miller picked up on the spirit of the chase. "Can't this thing go any faster?"

"Yes, I believe it can, sir."

Dr. Miller was sorry he said that as the car's speedometer needle started to advance on virgin territory.

❖

Jim, too, let his mind wander to the possibility of what might be happening right now to the lovely Beatrix Peeters. He shivered at the thoughts of his own imagination.

The calculations that Jim quickly went through indicated the need for speed. "Could you drive a little faster?"

Idaja said, "Yes."

The pace increased, as did Jim's heart rate. Weaving in and out to pass the slower traffic made for an exhilarating ride. Yet on they went.

Idaja's behavior behind the wheel belied his agility and speed. He tilted his turbaned head and calmly hummed a little tune and smiled as he adroitly moved around the slower cars. As violent as the outside was, all was placid on the inside of the car—except for Jim's body language that attempted to influence the movements of the vehicle by gyrating in its seat.

Idaja asked, "Are you all right, young man?"

"Yeah, fine," Jim said. "You're a pretty good driver for a foreigner."

"In Bombay you must drive this fast or you will be driven over from behind."

"I'll have to go to Bombay someday—if I live."

"If you live—that is a good one! You Americans are always with the humor." They streaked on.

The road added more traffic as they approached Chicago. Because Jim was looking ahead to thoroughly enjoy the near-misses that were unfolding by the minute, he did not notice the red lights blinking from a distance in the rearview mirror.

❖

CHAPTER 25

Countdown: 12 Hours (Noon)

D r. Miller was pleased and displeased at the same time with the rate of speed at which the car was moving. He appreciated the fact that they were moving along at a good pace to make the appointed time and destination, but displeased with the nauseous, carsick feeling in the pit of his stomach.

He glanced at Rita and noticed her looking in the side mirror. This preoccupation of hers caused Dr. Miller to turn and look as well.

He couldn't help but observe a black Buick Special gaining ground on them at an alarming pace. On it came.

The Buick passed the Falcon as if the Ford were in reverse.

Rita's head swiveled appropriately as it tracked the passing car.

"Mr. Morrison!" she said.

Dr. Miller said, "James?"

The Buick was past them in a blur.

"I must catch him," she said.

Before they could accelerate to pursuit speed, Rita was forced to pull over to the right to allow for the passing police car that appeared to be matching the speed of the Buick.

Then Rita picked up the pace. "I must find Mr. Morrison."

Oh, no, Dr. Miller thought, *we have just cut to the chase.*

❖

Idaja said, "Uh-oh."

This engendered a look from Jim.

Jim asked, "Uh-oh, what?"

Idaja said, "I believe I am being sought."

Jim turned. "The cops."

Idaja stepped on the gas. "I must avoid them."

Jim said, "You're going to have to pull over."

"I cannot, for you see, this will be a great embarrassment for the entire royal family, and I cannot allow such a thing to occur."

They passed several other cars. Being transfixed on the pursuit vehicle, Jim did not notice that they passed Dr. Miller and Rita.

On they went, keeping the police car at an equal distance behind.

The sign read: *Chicago 50.*

An off-ramp ahead pointed the way to a nice four-lane intersecting freeway heading east. Idaja swerved and took it. The police car followed.

On they went violently eastward at a speed of which Bert Munroe would not be ashamed.

After an extended chase in which the smooth Mr. Idaja realized that he was not shaking the police car, he tried a new tack.

Idaja said, "Hold onto yourself!"

Jim, of course, being the adventurer that he was, liked to think of himself as being able to calmly accept the wild maneuverings of such a hair-raising pursuit. But even Jim, if asked, would readily express his opinion that this zany bit of crazy corkscrew machinations on the part of Mr. Idaja was beyond the limits of good sense and prudent action.

Jim clutched the door handle and the seat cover. His body was rigid.

With one quickly calculated glance and movement, the daring Mr. Idaja swept the steering wheel to the right and slammed on the brakes just enough to fly across all four lanes of the highway, barely catching the off-ramp that led to a rural frontage road.

This maneuver almost caused an eighteen-wheeler in the right-hand lane to buckle in front of a horse trailer filled with prime show animals.

Once at the stop sign, Idaja did not bother to actually stop, but rather he turned right without slowing.

The red lights behind the Buick Special followed quickly with a safer lane change and highway exit but with equal élan.

More red lights, however, blinked in front of the Idaja Express. The royal secretary was rapidly approaching a railroad crossing. The red lights coupled with the clanging bells and the slowly lowering crossing guardrail did little to impede the pace of the Buick. In fact, against the very nature of the safe and sane driving dictum, Idaja did not hesitate to speed up.

Jim did a quick estimation of the respective speed rates of the automobile in which he found himself and the freight train that was making good time heading east.

They had about, he thought, a fifty-fifty chance of making it. *No, wait,* he thought, *make it seventy-five–twenty-five; yeah that's more like it.* The fact that he was in the right front passenger seat and that his side would receive the initial impact of the oncoming train did not escape the shrewd Jim Morrison.

Jim grabbed the dashboard and closed his eyes. Mr. Idaja did not.

With the gas pedal fully depressed and elbows and knees flailing, Mr. Idaja cunningly turned the steering wheel left and then a fast right, weaving his way through the railroad crossing and to the other side just as the freight train with a full head of locomotion whizzed through the intersection.

There was no margin for error. Even Jim was stunned with admiration and awe. Idaja was as calm as a Calcutta cabbie.

"Let me out of here!" Jim said. He just wanted to kiss mother earth.

Idaja said, "As you wish." He pulled over, off the road, and stopped abruptly.

Jim fell out of the car and kissed the dirt shoulder of the road.

Idaja reached over and closed the door.

"Forgive my rudeness," Idaja said, "I really must be on my way if I am to evade the local constabulary. Farewell, my friend." He sped off convincingly.

The train eventually passed. It seemed to take a long time because of the frantic pace that had preceded in time.

The cop car continued down the road in delayed pursuit, followed hotly by a Ford Falcon with a driver that looked remarkably like the exotic Rita. Jim scratched his head.

Because Jim was down on his knees getting reacquainted with terra firma and he was slightly below road grade, she did not notice him.

The three vehicles sped into the countryside with the Buick seeming to have what would appear to be a distinct lead. And after witnessing the driving abilities of the deft Mr. Idaja firsthand, Jim shook his head in doubt at the possibility of the Indian ever being caught.

Jim paused for some refreshing moments of self-collection. He stood up slowly and scrambled up to the road level.

✛

Countdown: 11 hours (1:00 P.M.). Rita followed the police car as best she could. She hurtled eastward, on into Indiana.

As the police car up ahead was gradually pulling away from the Falcon, Rita thrust the Ford onward for all it was worth.

Dr. Miller said, "You're not a bad driver."

Rita said, "Thank you."

"But you are going way too fast," Dr. Miller said, reaffirming his grip on the dashboard.

"I must find Mr. Morrison."

Yes, but I would like to be alive when we do, Dr. Miller thought.

"Would you care to drive?" Rita asked.

"No, I would not care to drive."

"Sit back and relax. I am in complete control."

The caravan went on eastward. Rita noticed up ahead that the blinking red lights of the squad car disappeared. She moved to the right lane and estimated an off-ramp that must be the one the Buick had taken.

She was correct. At a stop sign, she looked both right and left. Dr. Miller had the idea to jump out of the car while the jumping was good, but Rita did a California rolling stop and turned a sharp right. Up ahead on the perpendicular asphalt road was a train track that ran east-west, parallel to the main highway. A long freight train was barreling through, west to east. The crossing guard rails were down, complete with flashing red lights and the familiar clanging bells.

Waiting at the railroad crossing was the squad car. Apparently, the Black Buick had made the crossing prior to the advent of the train. This, no doubt, left the

192

frustrated police pursuit to idle anxiously at the crossing, waiting for the freight train to get out of the way in order to resume the chase.

Rita cautiously pulled up behind the police car and halted. She leaned over the steering wheel as if that would somehow expedite the train.

Dr. Miller saw his chance. He undid his seat belt and opened the passenger side door.

Rita said, "Where are you going?"

"To solid ground."

"I must find Mr. Morrison."

"Good luck." He slammed the door behind him. He would find Jim on his own.

Rita looked at Dr. Miller and then at the road ahead. She sat in the driver's seat peering at the squad car in front of her. She waved to Dr. Miller as if to dismiss him.

Dr. Miller moved away from the car and back down the embankment on the side of the road. He stood there among some bushes that covered the rural landscape.

After the long freight train had finally passed, the crossing rails lifted and the police car was once again off after the Buick with renewed vigor. Without a look back, the Falcon piloted by the mysterious Madame X also accelerated into the breach.

Dr. Miller stood there in silence, soaking in the aftermath of the car chase. He had made it. He had survived, so far. The sky was still overcast, but it was not raining. Where was he? He was somewhere in Indiana, perhaps, south of Gary, some seven hundred miles west of New York, New York. Maybe even the same number of miles from Beatrix, or so he imagined. He walked up the embankment to the road top. He looked both ways. There was not a car in sight. He slowly started to walk north, back toward the highway.

Behind him he heard a voice.

"Chief?"

Dr. Miller turned.

❖

CHAPTER 26

Escape in the Air

COUNTDOWN: 10 HOURS (2:00 P.M.). The two of them just stood there and looked at each other, stunned.

Dr. Miller said, "James?"

Jim said, "Chief?"

They fell together like long lost chums, chattering like careworn veterans at a VFW reunion. After they jumped up and down with joy, they started walking east along the frontage road beside the tracks, arm in arm.

"James, what happened to you. Where have you been?"

Jim explained the last twenty-three hours in detail.

"Oh, by the way, Chief, here's your wallet."

"Thanks." Dr. Miller asked, "Did you find my address book?"

"Nope."

Dr. Miller said, "So much for plan B." He slipped a hand into his jacket pocket and fingered the baseball.

Jim said, "Sorry. Chief, what happened to you? Where have you been?"

After describing his adventures, Dr. Miller asked, "Still have the parchment?"

Jim said, "Right here." He indicated his back pocket.

They strolled together for a moment in silence, savoring the fellow feeling. They stopped simultaneously and looked ahead with worried eyes at the frontage roadway before them.

They both said at once, "Bea!"

Dr. Miller looked at his watch. It had stopped working. Jim looked around, frantically. His eyes fell on something. Dr. Miller looked at Jim and then followed his gaze to its focal point. Dr. Miller saw a biplane, a crop duster. He looked back at Jim. Dr. Miller said, "No!"

Jim said, "Yes!" His legs started rapidly moving in the direction of the airplane.

Dr. Miller said again, "No!" but he followed Jim.

The airplane in question sat idly at the end of a long, dirt strip about a hundred feet away, running parallel to the road the men were on. The dirt strip insinuated a runway. Not too far from the two-seater biplane was a typical country house with a large, detached barn that appeared to serve as a hangar in bad weather. No one was around.

As Jim got closer to the plane, Dr. Miller's anxiety level rose.

Jim climbed up on the bottom wing and inspected the cockpit. Jim said, "Hot dog, the key is in here."

Dr. Miller said, "No! I refuse!"

Jim climbed aboard.

Dr. Miller said, "No!"

Jim said, "Electric starter." He tapped the gas gauge with his right index fingernail, "Twin tanks, lots of gas. Let's go!"

"Wait a minute, James. You know how much I hate to fly…"

"How do you know? You've never done it."

Dr. Miller countered, "You can't even fly the thing."

"Remember when you sent me to Algiers and Morocco to find those Moorish artifacts for that rich North African dude?"

"Yes."

"I had to fly a plane pretty much like this one from Casa Blanca to Marrakech. I was self-taught, sort of a learn-as-you-go thing."

Dr. Miller didn't like the sound of this.

Jim said, "Quick, get in." Jim started the thing up and the engine turned over the first time.

Dr. Miller said, "No, I—"

"Get in, Chief!"

Dr. Miller looked toward the house and saw a skinny, bald guy in his underwear flailing and running toward them with a twelve-gauge, double-barreled shotgun.

Meanwhile, Jim had worked the plane into takeoff position and had started to push forward on the throttle.

The owner of the plane released a warning shotgun blast into the air.

Jim was holding the lurching plane as it was poised for takeoff. Jim said, "Get in, Chief, *now!*"

Dr. Miller didn't know what to do. The angry, armed man was almost upon them when Dr. Miller was forced into a frantic move.

Dr. Miller said involuntarily, "God, help me!"

Not able to wait any longer, Jim released the brakes, and the plane lunged forward. At the same time, Dr. Miller scrambled onto the lower wing, clutching a strut, and then with one motion, hoisted himself aboard, flinging his body into the rear seat of the craft, head first. The shotgun-toting fellow dropped his weapon and grabbed onto the rear tail structure and held on for his life.

Jim strained at the controls of the plane, while Dr. Miller's wingtip-clad feet writhed in panic-stricken agitation straight up and out of the rear seat of the crop duster, and the bald man in his underwear was being dragged along behind.

Finally the skinny character let go and came to rest in a large puddle of mud. He shook his fist helplessly as the airplane gained speed and Jim guided the thing off the ground and into the air. It wasn't a pretty takeoff, but it was a takeoff. Jim guided the ascent of the plane and headed due east.

Jim yelled, "I didn't think I could do it."

No answer.

Jim said again, "I didn't think could do it, Chief."

No answer.

Jim turned around to see two legs sticking up vertically in the rear seat. Jim said, "Come on, Chief, stop fooling around. Bea needs us."

Slowly Dr. Miller adjusted himself to a sitting position. Once he was righted, he silently breathed a deep, cleansing breath and closed his eyes. He moved his lips almost like he was praying; he looked relieved.

Dr. Miller said, "I'm okay...now."

"Good," Jim said, as if he'd know all along that Dr. Miller would be fine.

Dr. Miller looked down at the passing landscape. Maybe he wasn't so good after all.

Jim leaned over the radio, straining to follow a conversation coming from the ground through the garbled static.

"Whoever you are, you'd better bring my plane back right this instant!" a voice insisted. Jim concluded it was the skinny guy who had finally let go. Obviously it was not in his best interest to answer. He heard the clink of a microphone being tossed down, but the radio connection was still open.

"I'm calling the FAA to report a stolen airplane," the craft's rightful owner informed someone.

A voice answered him. "What happened?"

He said, "Someone stole the plane."

She said, "Land o' Goshen!"

He said, "Where're my glasses?"

She said, "Where they always are."

He said, "Get me the phone book."

A flurry of activity in the background was all bumps and garbled sounds as the two of them apparently managed to get in each other's way. Finally, Jim heard a rotary dial phone clicking. In the background was what he thought was a doorbell.

The clicking stopped. He said, "See who that is."

She said, "There's a black car parked out front."

He said, "I don't have the time to talk to any pesticide salesman now. Tell him to come back later."

More static.

She yelled, "I think you better come here!"

He said, "Not now. I'm busy."

She yelled again, "I think you'd better come here, right now!"

"Oh, okay, okay!" A bang. Static. "What is it now?" Pause. "Wait a minute!" The radio went dead.

Dr. Miller, finally beginning to focus on his new surroundings, asked, "What was all that?"

Jim said, "Uh…nothing, just random aviation jabber. Nothing important."

Dr. Miller was satisfied with the answer.

They flew on east.

❖

COUNTDOWN: **9** HOURS (**3:00** P.M.). They flew east, above the Interstate.

The takeoff had been precarious at best. And at first, Jim was barely able to steady the plane in its flight path. This made Dr. Miller a little airsick. Gradually, Jim got a feel for the stick and smoothed out the ride.

Dr. Miller started to get his air legs.

Dr. Miller said, "James?"

Jim said, "Yeah, Chief?"

"Isn't this stealing?"

"What?"

Dr. Miller's decibel level increased. "Isn't this stealing?"

"What do you mean?"

"Well, the plane and all, you know, stealing."

"I prefer to think of it as appropriating."

There were a few beats. "I can live with that," Dr. Miller said. "Good job, James."

"Thanks, Chief."

Jim dropped a bit in altitude and continued east.

❖

COUNTDOWN: **8** HOURS (**4:00** P.M.). Dr. Miller started to feel proud, having survived the ordeal. A newfound self-satisfaction and calm justifiably encouraged him.

"How fast are we going, James?" Dr. Miller shouted over the wind.

"About eighty miles an hour, but we've got a pretty good tailwind," Jim shouted back.

Dr. Miller looked down at the highway and then observed, "How come some of the cars down there are going faster than we are?"

Jim peeked over the side for a spell. "Umm, maybe this air speed gauge is busted." He tapped it with a knuckle. It did not budge.

Dr. Miller did some figuring. "It's going to be tight."

"What?"

"Getting to New York. It's going to be tight."

"I know."

They headed east under an overcast sky.

❖

COUNTDOWN: 7 HOURS (5:00 P.M.). Dr. Miller felt around in the cockpit area to discover an untouched day-old lunch: two baloney sandwiches and a couple of Hostess Twinkies. Dr. Miller said, "Would you like something to eat?"

"What?"

"Would you like a baloney sandwich and a Twinkie?"

"I'm not sure I'm up for any food. I lost my appetite after the soy-curd sandwiches."

"The what?"

"Never mind, I'll just take the Twinkie."

"What?"

"I'll take a Twinkie."

Jim reached back and Dr. Miller reached forward to pass the plastic-wrapped Twinkie. Dr. Miller ate both a sandwich and a Twinkie. He eyed the other sandwich.

They flew on.

❖

COUNTDOWN: 6 HOURS (6:00 P.M.). Jim said, "Sorry about the 'baboon' crack back there in the office, Chief."

Dr. Miller said, "What?"

"I said I'm sorry about calling you a baboon back there in the office a couple of days ago."

"Oh, forget it."

Jim turned on the communication radio and listened for a while. Jim said, "I'm not hearing anything about a stolen plane on the radio."

Dr. Miller said, "What?"

Jim repeated with more volume, "I said, I'm not hearing anything on the radio about a stolen plane."

Dr. Miller asked, "Is that good or bad?"

Jim said, "I don't know."

Across Indiana and over Ohio, they pressed on.

✢

COUNTDOWN: 5 HOURS (7:00 P.M.). Jim said, "Sorry about slapping you on the head like that back there in the office, Chief."

Dr. Miller couldn't hear. "What?"

"I said, I'm sorry about hitting you on the head a couple of days ago."

"Oh, that's all right, I think I needed that."

Over Ohio and into Pennsylvania airspace, they pressed on.

✢

COUNTDOWN: 4 HOURS (8:00 P.M.). Night was coming on, and Jim started to get a bit apprehensive. He lowered the plane and stuck closely to the highway lights as he moved east.

Dr. Miller said, "Aren't you flying a little low?"

Jim said, "I'm staying under the radar."

Dr. Miller said, "Oh." A beat. "James?"

"What, Chief?"

"Can you land this thing?"

"What?"

"Can you land this plane?"

"One way or another."

Dr. Miller noticed Jim looking anxiously over the edge of the wings, which didn't exactly comfort him. Jim tapped the fuel gauge to test its accuracy. What it reflected was unfortunately accurate.

They flew on eastward.

✢

CHAPTER 27

Boxcars & Cabbies

COUNTDOWN: **3 HOURS** (9:00 P.M.). "I'm going to have to put her down, Chief."

"What?" Dr. Miller asked.

Jim said, "We're going to have to land."

"So soon?"

"I couldn't get you on this plane, and now I can't get you off."

"What?"

"Never mind."

"Where are we?"

"Somewhere over eastern Pennsylvania."

"Let's keep going."

"We're running out of gas."

"That's bad."

"Yes, it is. I'd prefer to select my own landing site rather than have one forced upon me."

Dr. Miller thought for a beat. "I agree."

"Then it's unanimous."

"What?"

"Never mind."

The gas gauge was now on empty. Jim knew with a car there's always a few more miles when the needle hits the *E.* He wasn't so sure how it was with a plane. He didn't mention this fact to Dr. Miller, but he did run through a silent prayer in his mind. He figured that if there was a God, it couldn't hurt to pray.

Jim noticed up ahead a large, lighted area not too far from the Interstate. As he lowered the crop duster, he could see hundreds of railroad box cars sitting in disuse. It was a train yard. Right beside the large freight train staging area, there appeared to be a long, straight, lighted service road that looked unused. He aimed for it.

"What are you doing, James?"

"Trying not to kill us."

"That's good."

The shifting breeze was now in their favor as a slight headwind eased the plane down into a glide path that looked favorable for landing. The service road appeared to be good for the purpose of landing a light plane. Things looked good.

It suddenly got quiet. The two men could hear nothing but a gentle zephyr blowing in their ears. The engine stopped. No more gas.

"What are you doing, James?" Dr. Miller asked again.

"Trying not to kill us," Jim repeated.

"That's good," Dr. Miller said. "I'm glad you know what you're doing."

"Me, too."

Unbeknownst to Jim, he had taken the perfect approach for an unpowered landing. His trim was good, and his speed was good. He was petrified. Fearing the worst, he screamed out, "Hold on!"

Jim, clutching the stick like it was his first solo landing (which it was, sort of, except for the Marrakech landing experience, when he landed the plane in a big sand dune outside the city and almost killed himself and a camel). He closed one eye, shot up another request, and delivered a perfect three-point landing.

The plane came to a rolling stop. Dr. Miller jumped out. Dr. Miller said, "Nice landing, James. I knew you could do it."

As Dr. Miller was looking around, Jim sat motionless, unable to pry his own hands from the stick.

"Let's go, James. Time's a wasting."

Jim slowly evacuated the machine and tested the ground he walked on. He was glad to be alive.

"Oh, no, wait." Dr. Miller stopped.

A recovering Jim rose from kissing the pavement. "Now what?"

"The plane! It'll be reported as being stolen!"

"So what? Let's go!"

"No, no, it's just wrong. We'll be arrested and—"

Jim thought fast. "Okay, okay, I'll leave a note." James pulled out a notepad and pen from the cockpit. He started to write out a quick message.

Dr. Miller dictated, "Good. Tell them I will take full financial responsibility for the plane and the gasoline. Leave my name and address and tell the owner that I'm sorry for any inconvenience. Faithfully yours, Dr. Gustov Miller, et cetera."

Jim finished up and dropped the correspondence onto the front seat of the biplane. "Okay, Chief, I think that's it."

"Good."

What the note actually said was: *To Whom It May Concern; someone is standing right here and I am trying to make him think I am writing down the information about who took your plane and why, but I'm not. Sincerely, Bruno Walters, Sarasota, Florida.*

Dr. Miller asked as he looked around, "What's that?" Through a gate in the fence, Dr. Miller noticed a freight train picking up speed and moving east. "Follow me, James."

Dr. Miller raced through the gate and with surprising spryness hopped through the open door and into a vacant boxcar. Amazed at Dr. Miller's athleticism, Jim tagged along, running to catch up. Jim ran alongside the boxcar, and Dr. Miller offered his hand. Jim grabbed hold, and Dr. Miller swung him in.

Dr. Miller said, "There, now, that wasn't so bad, was it?"

Jim said nothing. He just laid back and attempted slow, regular breaths.

The train picked up speed, and they shot out of eastern Pennsylvania and into New Jersey.

❖

COUNTDOWN: 2 HOURS (10:00 P.M.). The empty boxcar in which they found themselves was relatively commodious.

They lay down in the front of the car and permitted a light sleep to come upon them. This desire for rest was enhanced by the syncopated click-clacking and nonstop swaying of the freight train. As they surrendered to their drowsiness, visions of Bea bounced rhythmically through their minds. They wondered what the next two hours would be like. Would they make it in time? Was Bea safe?

✦

COUNTDOWN: 1 HOUR (11:00 P.M.). The grinding air brakes of the freight train coupled with imagined scenarios surrounding the fate of Beatrix Peeters jarred the travelers awake.

The train came to a halt. They skittered out. When they hit the ground, they took in the panorama, having no idea where they were.

A shrill voice said, "Hey!"

A rail yard security guard was running toward them.

They scurried under the car in which they had traveled and ran away from the approaching guard, lickety-split. They jumped a small fence and found themselves at the rear of a passenger train depot. The weather had been slowly easing up and, for the first time since they had started their arduous journey, the sky was clear.

Dr. Miller stopped in his tracks and looked up. "Look at all those stars—millions and billions of stars. Infinity. Look, James, there's Orion, stalking his prey, and the Pleiades. That moon, it's so big. Amazing, absolutely amazing."

"Chief, do you really think this is the time for stargazing?" Jim asked, prodding Dr. Miller at the elbow.

"What a magnificent realm is nature," Dr. Miller waxed on, oblivious to the urgency consuming Jim. "Those stars have been looking down on us humans for all this time, yet they appear brand new and pristine. I somehow feel as if I am the first person seeing them for the first time." Memories of the starlit African night waved through Dr. Miller's mind. He had stood under the Southern Cross with his parents.

"Chief, we don't have a lot of time."

Dr. Miller, still entranced with the night sky that he had not seen in so many years said, "Too long…it has been too long. Look at what I have missed all these years."

"It's been quite a while, uh, Chief, since you've been out."

"James, look at those trees, the landscape, the shrubs, everything, the colors so vibrant, even in the moonlight. Look at the grass and the dirt. It smells so good. I could even eat it." Dr. Miller got down on his knees.

Jim grabbed him by the coat to pull him up. "Hey, Chief, don't eat the dirt. Let's not get carried away. Remember why we're here."

He gasped, and his eyes darted around. "Yes, yes, of course. Beatrix."

"Focus, Chief, focus." James took Dr. Miller by the elbow to point him in the right direction. "Let's get moving."

The two men ran around to the front of the depot and found the place to be nearly deserted. Out front on the street, one taxi cab optimistically waited for a fare that would seem to be hard to come by at this time of night and in this location. The cab driver had the overhead light on and was perusing the newspaper.

The men ran around to the driver's side door and frantically tapped on the window. The cabbie was a flat-faced fellow with a toothpick extending from the corner of his mouth. He was wearing a New York Yankees cap. He cautiously rolled down the window and drank them in. The cabbie said, "Yeah?"

Jim asked, "Where are we?"

The cabbie said, "On duh moon, where do you tink yous are."

Dr. Miller said, "No, no, seriously where are we?"

"Yous nuts? North Jersey!"

Jim said, "We've got to get to New York, Central Park, and pronto."

The cabbie gave them both another shrewd once-over and, laying aside his newspaper, said, "Hop in."

The fellows did just that. The cabbie reached for the meter.

Dr. Miller said, "Oh, and I am sorry to inform you that we don't have any money."

Jim winced and nudged Dr. Miller with his elbow.

The cabbie stopped in mid-action and commanded, "Out!"

Jim said, "Look, it's a matter of life and death!"

"Out!"

Dr. Miller said, "Please, I can pay you later when I can get some money."

"Den yous can get a ride later. Out!"

Dr. Miller said, "I can pay you double, later, when I have a chance to wire for the money, but please, we need to get to Central Park now."

"Out, duh both of yous!"

Jim had an idea. Jim said, "Have you ever read the story of the valiant prince that rescues the fair maiden?"

"Out!"

Dr. Miller jumped in. "The hero has to slay the dragon, fight off the evil villain, destroy the wicked witch, and climb the foreboding tower against all odds to save the beautiful princess!"

"Out!"

Jim added, "The hero saves the day—"

"Out!"

"He marries the princess and lives happily ever after."

The cabbie pondered. "I do like dat story."

"I like it too," Jim agreed.

Dr. Miller said, "We have to get to Central Park by midnight to rescue a coworker from a fate worse than death!"

"Woise dan death?"

Jim said in a solemn tone, "There are things worse than death, you know."

The men could see the cab driver working through the conundrum.

Dr. Miller said, "She's been kidnapped, and we've come all the way from St. Louis in the last two days, and it's absolutely essential that we leave the cops out of this and meet the kidnapper in Central Park at midnight tonight!"

The cabbie scanned the two guys in the back seat with continued skepticism. "Is yous guys on the lam?"

"No," they said together.

Jim remembered the ransom note in his pocket. He pulled it out. It was still wet, so he carefully unfolded it and gingerly handed it to the cabbie.

The cab driver carefully examined the document. The cabbie asked, "Is yous guy really on de up and up?"

"Yes!" they said together.

The cab driver eyed the two men again and handed back the ransom note.

Jim and Gus both had their hands on the back of the front bench seat, ready to plead further. They also both had their chins nestled on top of their hands, as if to accent their need. They looked like a couple of manipulating kids imploring their parents for an ice cream cone, a new toy boat, and a trip to Disneyland, all in one sad puppy-dog pose.

The cab driver reluctantly glanced at his wristwatch and took another survey of the adventurers. He relented.

"I don't knows why, but I believe you." Without another word, the cabbie started the car and they were off into the darkness. He did not start the meter.

The cab driver wove his way through the city streets with cunning agility. Mr. Idaja would be impressed. This way and that they advanced, making it impossible for the two passengers to be able to recreate the route taken.

Finally the cab jetted through a cave marked *Lincoln Tunnel.* On they went, twisting and turning unencumbered through the backstreets of New York City, Manhattan Island.

Screech! They came to rest at the edge of a citified forest.

The cabbie announced, "Central Park."

Jim asked, "What time is it?"

"Ten minutes to twelve."

Dr. Miller said, "What's your name, so I can pay you back?"

"Forget about it! Get out! You'll miss your date wit' destiny."

The two travelers got out of the vehicle and slammed the door shut as the cab immediately disappeared into the graveyard shift with a rumble of New York disinterest.

❖

CHAPTER 28

Look, a map!" Dr. Miller stooped and picked up a pamphlet from the ground. Somehow it had survived the damp weather. "It's a map of the park."

"Does it show the baseball diamonds?" Jim asked urgently.

Dr. Miller held the paper up under a street light. "Right here."

Even though the night was cloudless, the park was nonetheless dark and dreary except for the overhead lights that threw pools of illumination at irregular intervals. The moon was also full, which helped.

"It should be over here, James," Dr. Miller said, as he wove his way along the pathways. Jim followed warily.

"I've heard Central Park can be pretty rough after dark."

"Nothing we can't handle, James, compared to what we've been through."

They treaded in what they hoped was the right direction.

"It should be right around the next turn, if I read this map correctly." Dr. Miller was right. They turned the next little bend in the walkway to reveal an open space. It was a baseball diamond, suffused with the ambient city lights and the full moon. They took it all in, getting their bearings.

"There's home plate…the mound." Dr. Miller freely walked around the diamond, soaking up the memories and basking in the night air. He strode over to the batter's box, adjusted the soggy cap on his head, and pantomimed an at-bat. "If you want to know the heart and mind of America, learn baseball." Once upon a time, Dr. Miller had wanted nothing else but to play baseball. He patted his jacket pocket to reassure himself the baseball that had come through his window two days ago was still there.

Jim closely followed his boss around the field while his eyes darted into the darkness looking for the next event to unfold. "Chief, I like a good game as much as the next guy, but Bea's in trouble and we've got to keep our wits."

"You know, James, I was quite a little baseball player when I was a youngster. Infielder. I didn't have the arm for going into the hole, so they usually put me at second base."

"Chief?"

"Scoop 'em up and nip 'em at first. I didn't have much throwing power, but I was a pesky line-drive hitter. Not as fleet of foot as most, however; not like Lou Brock."

"Uh…excuse me, Babe, if I could encourage you to finish up your reminiscing for a sec', I would like to respectfully remind you why we are here…to save a certain someone from danger."

"Huh?"

"I'll get your autograph later, Mr. DiMaggio, but right now, to the business at hand?"

"Oh, yes, yes, of course, sorry, the entire ambiance, all of this stimulus is most distracting."

"I gathered," Jim said. He then moved squarely in front of his boss and gently put Dr. Miller's head between both of his hands and looked directly into his eyes. "Are you all right, Chief?"

"Yes, fine, thank you, James. What time is it?"

"I'm sure it's just past twelve," Jim said, looking up to the moonlit sky.

Dr. Miller shifted gears rapidly with a deliberate inhale and a subsequent firm exhale. "To the task at hand. Well, we seem to be at our appointed time and our appointed place. Let us look around and acquaint ourselves with the terrain. Do you see anything unusual?"

Jim imitated his boss by scanning the landscape. "No. What am I looking for?"

"Anything that would make us believe that we have happened into an ambush, anything suspicious, anything that would suggest foul play, or perhaps someone preceding us here to set a trap, who knows? Someone could very easily be watching us right now from the bushes in order to calculate his next move."

"Anything suspicious…" Jim scrunched up his eyes and slunk down to offer a wary scrutiny of intensity as he panned the horizon.

As they both looked about, Dr. Miller spoke, "By the way, James, I appreciate your concern for me, as well as your concern for Beatrix."

"Don't mention it."

All of a sudden, Dr. Miller found something on the ground. "Ahh…," he gasped as he hoisted a leaf into the air.

"What have you got?" Jim wanted to know.

"Um…very interesting." Dr. Miller mused.

"What is it?"

"A leaf."

"A leaf?"

"Yes," Dr. Miller said, entranced.

"Just a leaf?"

"A *pittosporum tobira* leaf, to be exact."

"Oh." Jim peered at the thing with concentrated effort. He asked, "What do you make of it?"

"Well, it is a deciduous shrub and they usually don't shed their leaves this early in the year."

"Wow," Jim said reverently.

"Quite. I find it fascinating. Don't you?"

"Yeah, Chief, a real brain puzzler. How does it help us find Beatrix? Let's just keep looking around, okay?"

Dr. Miller dropped the leaf and then refocused as he continued his investigation of the immediate area. "Yes, James," Dr. Miller ventured, "you were very impressive on our journey here. Do you always comport yourself so admirably in the field?"

"Never failed yet."

There was a pause.

"You know, James, I don't want to embarrass you, but really I must admit that I marvel at your courage—and your desire to get the job done and your concern for your fellow human beings. That is a quality that is most enviable."

"Thanks, Chief."

"To what do you attribute this quality?"

"I don't know."

"Is it because of your upbringing or your acquired beliefs?"

"Maybe so, Chief." Jim regarded his boss, thought for a second, and then confessed, "I guess I gotta feel like there's a right way to do things and a wrong way. You know, like there's such a thing as justice and purpose, and people are important and stuff. And, you know, Bea is a very special person and I'd do anything to make sure that she's okay."

"Yes, I know what you mean. I'd do as much for her." Dr. Miller continued after a moment of guileless introspection, "I am a proud person, James, and this whole experience of the last couple of days has made me…," Dr. Miller ambled off vocally.

"Made you what?"

"I don't know, humble, I suppose."

"I hear you," Jim concurred. He then amended, "As long as we're confessing our deepest, darkest secrets, I gotta admit that I'm a pretty proud guy as well. I depend pretty much on my own abilities, and sometimes I fall flat on my face. Every once and a while, you need something like a failure to motivate you to improve."

"Don't we all."

"But not by crawling around on my hands and knees like this, out here in the middle of the night. For crying out loud, Chief, I can't find anything," Jim confessed as he stood up to put his hands on his hips.

"Yes, for the most part the natural vegetation looks rather undisturbed, and the tracks in the dirt could have been made by the dozens of players who no doubt passed through the diamond today. "

"What'll we do now?"

"Wait."

"I hate waiting."

"That's the tough part."

They both stood there, marking time. A slight breeze blew through the night as the expanse of the whole universe came to rest like a huge burden of failure and helplessness on the shoulders of the two fellows who existed alone together in Central Park, New York.

"Do the swallows really come back to Capistrano every year at the same time?" Jim asked out into the black sky.

"I think they really do, James."

"Weird."

"Whoever or whatever we are waiting for is definitely late."

And then, as if on cue, a rustle in the bushes caused Jim and Dr. Miller to turn and face the noise. Dr. Miller sucked in air as if he was going to speak out loud. Jim quickly put his finger to his lips and motioned to Dr. Miller to follow him into the third base dugout that was below grade and dark enough to conceal their location. They hastily and silently skulked their way there and remained motionless.

❖

CHAPTER 29

Central Park at Midnight

Soon the source of the noise was apparent. Bruno Walters entered through the shrubbery, brushing himself off and muttering at the mess the bushes had made of his immaculate wardrobe.

"What the hay!" Bruno Walters said to himself out loud. "I'm gonna have to stop by the cleaners now."

Bruno stopped fussing over his clothes and started casing the joint. He was mumbling to himself as he ranged around. He sounded as if he was going over his spiel.

Bruno circled the infield a couple of times, gesturing and whispering to himself. He subsequently lifted and lowered his shoulders and gave a concerted sweeping gaze onto his immediate environment. It appeared he wanted to verify the direction and force of the gentle breeze that had come up because he wet the forefinger of his left hand and held it up in the air as if to confirm his suspicion. Satisfied, he moved in a desultory fashion, continuing his muffled monologue until he stopped with his back to the dugout containing Jim and Dr. Miller.

Dr. Miller whispered in the ear of Jim, "Wait here." While Jim sat on the bench silent and still, Dr. Miller hesitated for half a minute before he stated in a loud voice, "Hello, Mr. Walters."

Bruno jumped about two feet straight up into the night. He turned abruptly, stepped back a couple of paces and, grabbing his chest, gaped into the dark recess.

Dr. Miller emerged from the dugout.

217

"Oh, man, don't scare me like that. I almost wet my pants. I'm going to have to take these things into the laundry as it is." Bruno seemed to regain his composure. "You really know how to rattle a guy."

The one man stood glaring at Bruno.

Bruno smirked, "Top of the morning to you, Miller." Bruno peered at his watch and strained to make out the time. "It is morning now, isn't it? Let me be the first one to wish you a new day." Bruno flipped his right forefingers from the proximity of his forehead in the general direction of the Chief.

"Where are your buddies?" Dr. Miller spoke up.

"Where're yours?"

No answer.

"I don't know what you're talking about, Miller. I fly solo."

"Somehow I am not at all surprised to see you here, Mr. Walters."

"Well, I'm surprised. After your little buddy told me about this here appointment, I didn't think you had it in you, bright boy, to come all the way out here by yourself and expose yourself to all of this nasty old outside air."

"What would give you the impression that I would balk at the opportunity of meeting you here, Mr. Walters?"

Bruno smiled a big smile. "A little birdie told me."

"Oh?"

"Yeah, I know a lot more about you than you think I do."

"Oh, really, like what?"

"If you think I'm going to spill the beans yet, Miller, you got another thing coming. Where's the parchment?"

"Oh, that's what this is about, eh?"

"Yeah, that's what this is about."

Dr. Miller interjected, "Where's Beatrix?"

"Who's Beatrix?"

"As if you don't know. Where is she?"

"I asked you first." Bruno moved toward Dr. Miller in a menacing fashion with one fist flat against the palm of his other hand. Dr. Miller did not budge. Bruno then reached his right hand into his coat pocket and, as before, keeping it there, made a gesture as if he were wielding a pistol from within that compartment.

He blustered, "Now where's the parchment? Come on, talk!"

Suddenly inspiration and initiative hit Dr. Miller. He put his own hand into his coat pocket. Clutching the baseball in his fist, he poked a couple of fingers forward as if he had a handgun as well. "No, you talk! Where's Beatrix?"

This caught Bruno off guard. "Hey, come on now, I had the drop on you. Fair is fair."

"You come on, you weasel! Where is she?" Dr. Miller spewed, as he deliberately backed down Bruno. This was a different feeling for Dr. Miller. Wherever this assertion was coming from, Dr. Miller liked it.

Bruno held out his free hand flat to the ground as he casually retreated, keeping an equal distance from Dr. Miller. "Hey, hey now, you'd better be careful there. I could shoot you, you know."

"Oh? I could shoot you, too, you know."

"Now, now, wait just a minute here, now, uh, how do I know that's a real gun you got there?" Bruno stammered, continuing to keep his distance and pointing nervously with his free hand to the general area of Dr. Miller's occupied coat pocket.

"How do I know that's a real gun you have there?" Dr. Miller retorted. "You don't think I would have come unarmed after what you put me through, do you?" Dr. Miller said, mocking his adversary's finger motion.

"A bright guy like you answering one question with another, is that up to your high standards as a PhD of whatever it is you're a PhD of?"

"I don't know how many times I've told you, Walters, never end your sentences with a preposition."

"A what?"

"Never mind, Walters, suffice it to say I think I just might be sinking to your low level."

"Was that an insult?"

"Yes, I guess it was."

"Because I think I know when I've been insulted."

Neither man blinked during a long stare-down. Finally, Bruno swallowed and blinked his eyes first. That was all that Dr. Miller needed to advance.

"Let's see that gun of yours, Walters."

"Aren't you gonna take my word for it?"

"Certainly not."

"Well, if you shoot, I shoot."

"Good, at least I'll have the pleasure of taking you with me."

"Uh, now...wait a minute," Bruno said, taking his hand out of his pocket. "See, nothing, just a finger. Good gag, huh?"

"Yes, very clever. Now, talk. Where is she?"

"What?"

"You know what I'm talking about. Where's Beatrix?"

"Who?"

"Bea, you bully."

"Bea?"

"The one you kidnapped."

"Hey, I didn't kidnap no one."

"Liar!"

"No, honest Injun!" Bruno pantomimed an X over his heart with a set of crossed fingers in order to validate his comment.

"Come on, you louse, talk!"

"Wait a second now, let us not get trigger happy here. Let us negotiate. Where's you little friend?" Bruno said, looking around.

"What little friend?"

"Jimmy, James, whatever his name is."

"You deal with me. So you want to negotiate, eh?"

"Yeah, negotiate."

"What happened to your usual modus operandi?"

"My what?"

"Tearing the place apart? Slapping others around? Throwing people out of trains?" Dr. Miller prodded Bruno. Bruno did not answer. "If you don't have Beatrix, why are you here?"

"What?"

"How did you know to meet here at midnight?"

"Uh, that Jimmy guy, James...yammered his yap on the phone. He blurted out something about a meeting here in Central Park tonight. I just didn't wanna be left out of the mix."

Dr. Miller hesitated. "Uh, well then, if you do not have Beatrix, with what do you intend to negotiate?"

"All right! Okay, good. First of all, let's set some ground rules."

"I've got the upper hand. I make the rules." Still clutching the baseball, Dr. Miller brandished his non-gun. Dr. Miller thought again. "Sit down."

"What?"

"Sit."

"Where?"

"Right where you are. Sit!"

"I'll get my suit all dirty."

"Sit!"

"This is a five-hundred-dollar Italian!"

"Sit!" Dr. Miller reiterated with authority.

Bruno sat down right on the dirt infield.

"Fine. What do you want, Walters?"

"Uh…"

"The parchment?"

"Yeah. What do you want?"

"Beatrix."

"I don't get it. What is all this talk about this Beatrix broad?"

"Are you sure you don't know where she is?"

"I already told you, I don't know any Beatrix."

"You didn't kidnap anyone, right?"

"Kidnap? Me? That's a felony!"

"All right, if you insist you don't know where she is, play your cards. What do you have to negotiate with?"

"Do you have the parchment?"

"Another question?"

"It's catching."

"Suppose I do have the parchment. What do you have to offer?"

"I knew it!"

"What do you have, Walters?"

Bruno, in his crossed-legged sitting position, slowly raised and lowered his eyebrows temptingly. "Money."

"How much?"

"Thousands," Bruno lured. Dr. Miller didn't move. Bruno raised, "Tens of thousands."

"I am not that easily bought."

"Name your price."

"I want Beatrix."

"Here we go again. I told you I don't know any Beatrix. Are you a broken record or something?"

"I'm not sure I believe you."

Just then, from out of the shadows, another figure emerged. "I have an answer for you, Dr. Miller," said a female voice with an Eastern European accent.

Dr. Miller turned to see the notorious Rita. She was holding a gun in plain sight.

❖

CHAPTER 30

The Scroll for Your Life

She was dressed all in black—a black hat with a black fishnet veil, black gloves, black shoes, black evening bag in her left hand. She looked like the widow at her recently departed spouse's graveside service. The pistol in her right hand was also black, in keeping with the ensemble.

Dr. Miller said calmly, "Well, if it isn't the infamous Rita, or Madame X, or whatever your real name is." Dr. Miller looked at his watch. It still wasn't working. "A little bit behind your time, aren't you?"

"I believe I am exquisitely on time."

"Bruno Walters, allow me to introduce to you Ms. Rita, also known as Madame X."

Bruno, without standing up, reached forth his right hand and held it out as if he were expecting a reciprocated gesture. None was in the offing. He spoke, "How do you do, Rita…uh…X." He turned to Dr. Miller. "'Madame X sounds like a fake name to me. What do you think, Dr. Miller?"

"You think so, Bruno? Surprisingly perceptive on your part."

"Rita, eh?" Bruno regarded the lady.

Dr. Miller added, "Your competition."

"Competition!" Bruno exclaimed.

Rita backed away slightly.

Dr. Miller turned his attention to the lady. "So, I have no doubt that you overheard our conversation, Rita?"

"Every word."

After a beat, Dr. Miller said, "Well, here we are, together again at last. What shall we talk about?"

Rita looked at Dr. Miller and said, "You may take your empty hand out of your pocket now, Dr. Miller. I know you have no gun."

"How do you know that?" Dr. Miller inquired. He squeezed the baseball in his pocket.

"You would never even own a gun, much less carry one with you. I know more about you than you think I do, Gustov Miller."

"Everyone seems to tonight," Dr. Miller confessed as he pulled his hand from his pocket.

Bruno sat up, "Yous mean to say that you never had a gun?"

Dr. Miller shrugged his shoulders.

Bruno shook his head and said out loud to himself, "Jeeminy Christmas! Never trust a college graduate. Lies, lies, nothing but lies."

Rita picked up the thread of conversation, "I have the upper hand now, don't I?"

Dr. Miller admitted, "It would seem."

"I want the scroll."

"I want Beatrix." Upper hand or not, Dr. Miller was unmoved.

Bruno couldn't stand being left out. "Hey, hey, what about me?"

"You could be left out in the cold on this one, Walters."

Her eyes fixed on Dr. Miller, Rita pressed, "Where is it?"

"Where's Bea?" Dr. Miller topped.

"Give me the scroll, and I'll lead you to Miss Peeters."

"No dice. I see Beatrix first and make sure she's all right. Then the scroll."

"Do you have it with you?"

"No."

"I think you do."

Dr. Miller slowly unbuttoned his coat, showing his inside pockets, and then systematically patted or pulled out pocket linings to reveal nothing except the base-ball. "Perhaps this looks familiar to you," he said.

If Rita recognized the baseball, she gave no clue.

"I can get the scroll in rather short order," Dr. Miller said, "provided I see Miss Peeters first."

Bruno perked up, "Hey, this ain't bad."

"Stay out of this, Walters," Dr. Miller spat out.

Bruno spat back, "Why should I?" Bruno rolled his head to look at Rita. "Listen, sister, how do you plan on getting rid of the merchandise once you got it?"

Rita returned Bruno's look, "What do you mean?"

"What are you gonna do with the scroll? Sell it? Paper your dining room with it? What?"

"I fail to see how that is any business of yours," Rita said coolly.

Bruno looked down in disgust. He sighed, "Amateurs." Picking his head up he enticed, "I'm willing to pay for it. I'm willing to pay hefty for it. You want cash?"

"How much?"

"Hundreds, thousands, name your price!"

Dr. Miller corrected Bruno, "I thought you said thousands, tens of thousands."

Bruno confessed to Rita, "Thousands, tens of thousands."

Rita gave no answer but continued to hold the gun as she thought.

"I'm offering you a quick cash solution to your disposal problem, sister."

"She hasn't got it yet, Walters," Dr. Miller noted.

"Relax, Miller, take a pill or something. I'm merely a legitimate businessman offering alternatives to the young lady."

Rita asked Dr. Miller again, "Where is it?"

Dr. Miller again responded, "Where's Beatrix?"

"There she is!" Bruno shouted, pointing off into the night.

❖

CHAPTER 31

The Exchange

mmediately and involuntarily, Dr. Miller and Rita looked in the direction that Bruno was pointing. By this time, Bruno had moved close enough to Rita to lunge at her, and with a quick upward motion of his already outstretched right hand he deftly flipped the pistol out of her hand, grabbed it mid-air, and bounded up directly in front of her, all in one smooth motion.

"That's right, people, nobody move." Bruno strutted triumphantly, waving his free hand and displaying the gun in his other. "Well, now, boys and girls, guess who's in the cat-bird seat once again. The terms for negotiating have shifted in my direction...Miller...X."

Dr. Miller recovered first. "I'm still not going to tell you where the scroll is, Walters."

"You're in a rut, Miller."

"No deal."

"Okay, I'll play your silly game. You'll give it to me if I can hand over this Beatrice dame?"

"Beatrix," Dr. Miller corrected him.

"Beatrix...Beatrice...whatever. You'll give it to me, won't you?"

Dr. Miller paused.

Rita blurted, "I'm not telling you anything!"

Bruno turned his attention to Rita. "Oh? I think you will." Glancing back at Dr. Miller and then chuckling out loud, Bruno faced Rita, moved in on her and said threateningly, "You see, Miller here is too polite, but I know how to get information out of resistant females. You'll sing like a little Baltimore oriole when I'm done with you."

Rita slid away from the thug as Bruno slowly followed her winding retreat. Walking backwards, she circled around Dr. Miller on the third baseline as Bruno closed in. Dr. Miller stood in place and, with a gaping mouth, rotated like a planet, keeping his face to the other two. Skirting the opening of the dugout, Rita edged out toward the infield while Bruno faithfully followed.

At that moment in time when Bruno's back was to the dugout mouth, James Morrison sprang into uncompromising action. From out of the dark recess of the third base dugout, Jim lunged and with one sweeping move clouted Bruno on the back of the neck. Jim's ambush was a total success. Bruno fell hard to the dirt with a dull thud as the pistol flew from his hand. Quickly Dr. Miller collected the gun and halted Madame X in her impulse to flee.

"Don't leave us just yet, Rita," Dr. Miller said. She stood still.

Jim let out a delayed scream of pain, grabbing his right hand with his left. "Aaaiiiyyyooowwwch...my hand!"

"James, are you all right?" Dr. Miller sputtered.

"I think I broke something!"

Dr. Miller checked Bruno and came up with some information, "You knocked him out, James, good job!"

Jim said, "The guy's a brick wall."

Keeping a sly eye on Rita, Dr. Miller went to James and said, "Here, let me see."

Jim held out his hand for inspection. "I'm glad now I didn't waste all that money my foster mom gave me for violin lessons on learning how to actually play the thing; if I did know how to play the violin I wouldn't be able to play it now."

"I didn't know you took violin lessons."

"I didn't."

"What did you spend the money on?"

"Comic books and those little white candy cigarettes with the red tips. Ouch!"

"I don't think anything is broken, but you'll have quite a contusion there tomorrow." With a mix of rebuke and admiration, Dr. Miller asked, "James, why did you do that?"

"I was mad!"

"That was a rash thing to do—but very brave. Let us take advantage of the situation. Rifle Mr. Walters' pockets and see what you can find."

Jim leaned over the slumbering body and gave it a frisk, favoring his injured hand. "You're not going to believe this," Jim whistled.

"Nothing would surprise me tonight. Let me see."

Jim handed Dr. Miller a passport that he had extracted from Bruno's possession.

Dr. Miller perused the thing and said not a word but shuddered with open-mouthed wonder. He then walked over to the unconscious Bruno and thoughtfully compared the picture in the passport with the real-life version lying face up on the dirt.

As Dr. Miller examined the fellow, he uttered, "Martin Samuel. I didn't recognize him without his beard."

"So this is the infamous Damascus Butcher on the ground here," Jim said, astonished. "He's sprawled out like a brown bear rug. Who'da thunk it?"

"That's him, a puffed-up albino ape, finally taking some uninvited time off from doing whatever it is that such creatures do with their time." Gus mulled things over. "I've never seen him before, I mean face to face, that is."

"He doesn't look so tough, now, does he?"

Dr. Miller stood upright and regarded Rita. "I am going to have a little talk with the mysterious Rita, here." Dr. Miller regarded the lady and stated, "You can have the stupid parchment, I don't care about it any more. I just want to make sure Beatrix is safe."

Rita responded, "Do you have it close at hand?"

"Jim?"

"Right here, Chief." Jim removed the parchment scroll from his pocket and wiggled it in the air triumphantly.

"All right, I'll take you to her," Rita relented.

"Good. Let's go."

A figure moved out from the shadows.

"No need to do that, Buzz," a voice said. "Bea's a lot closer than you think."

❖

CHAPTER 32

Voice from the Shadows

The voice at first seemed to be omnidirectional, as if emanating from the ether. It halted Dr. Miller quite fixedly because it was a strangely familiar voice, a voice that was ancient and long ago, but sounded upon its recent arrival as if it had never really departed. It might have been a voice that Gustov Miller toyed with unconsciously daily for the past so many years, a voice that hammered his soul and his memory softly and barely noticeably, unless he was actively looking for it.

"Over here," the voice said. "Right at hand, as a matter of fact."

Dr. Miller was not frightened as he considered the shadow moving in his direction; he was rather intrigued.

The figure wore a coat with the collar turned up and a baseball cap pulled down over the face.

"Who are you?" Jim demanded.

"Ask your boss," came the answer.

"Who is it, Chief?"

As the moment of realization took hold and the urge for denial was quenched, Dr. Miller murmured with an expression of stunned doubt, "You called me Buzz."

"Go ahead, Gus, tell him who it is." There was a mutual pause before the shadow spoke again, "Surely you recognize the voice, the method, the modus operandi."

Dr. Miller instantly assumed the exact same stance of the shadow as if a mocking bookend. He turned up his collar, pulled down his Cardinals cap, and hunched over. "James, I believe the last piece of the puzzle has fallen into place."

The two figures faced each other and circled. The shadow mimicked a beggar's voice, "Have you got any change to spare, buddy?"

"Spare change?" Gus smiled through. "So, it is spare change that you want, now, eh? You've sunken to begging. What on earth do you need money for, anyway?"

The figure flew into the reveal mode by offing his cap and throwing back his collar to expose his face, "Gus, baby!"

"Andy, baby!"

The Miller brothers fell into each other's arms and then separated to engage in a series of elaborate handshaking moves that were well coordinated between them but would totally baffle the uninitiated passerby. After the elaborate routine of corresponding gestures and coordinated body movements, they paused and looked at each other for a long time.

"Andy, you took ten years off my life these last two days," Gus said.

"How long has it been?" Andrew Miller asked.

"Too long, brother," Gus retorted, "entirely too long. Fourteen, fifteen years."

"Hold it! Wait a minute! Time out!" Jim was shouting. "Halt! Cease and desist! Stop and don't say another word! Would someone please tell me where Bea is and what is going on here?"

"Relax, James, everything is fine," Gus said. "Beatrix should, no doubt, be within earshot."

"You're right, Gus," Andy said.

Gus looked to Andy, "Would you like me to make the introductions, or do you want to do the honors?"

"Go ahead, knock yourself out. I'll feel free to interject along the way."

"James, I would like to introduce to you Andrew Miller, my long lost brother."

"Which one of us is long lost, brother?"

"This, Andy, is my more-than-competent assistant, James Morrison."

"Ah, yes, Jim," Andy said. "I've heard so much about you I feel as if I've known you forever."

"How?"

"From Bea. She can't stop talking about you."

"Do you know where she is?"

"Gus was right. She is very close at hand. Beatrix," Andy waved his hand like a magician about to reveal his vanished assistant, "come forth."

From the same bushes, Bea sprang out. "Jim, Chief!" and then she said with meaning, "Jim."

"Bea!" Jim shouted.

"Beatrix!" Gus said.

Both men ran toward her, but Jim got there first. He hugged her. Gus stopped short and hung back, realizing the fervor of the embrace in front of him.

The release that Gustov Miller realized at the slackening pace of emotion summarily brought him back down to earth. He froze in place as his two employees enjoyed what was quite evidently a bona fide, passionate, unfeigned embrace.

Jim swung Bea around like a sailor handling a USO girl in Times Square on VE day. Jim was ecstatic, and Bea was rapturous.

Gus watched the two with mixed emotions—the utter joy at knowing Beatrix was safe and sound, and the disillusionment at knowing her heart belonged to another. His prayer was answered, but not in the way he had dreamed. He pushed back tears generated by a combination of despondency and fulfillment.

"Cripes, Bea," Jim said, "am I ever glad to see you!"

Bea did not even try to hide the teary look that overcame her. "Me too, Jim."

Gus smiled, quickly recovered, and then said cavalierly, "Beatrix, let me tell you, the instant I realized you were all right I felt like Atlas must have if the weight of the heavens was lifted from his shoulders. What a relief this is."

"Thanks, Chief. Thank you, Jim." Bea paused, as if she could keep the secret no longer. "But it was Andy's idea."

Gus squeezed his expression a bit and said, "I have no doubt. It was brilliant! A great concept and flawlessly executed."

"You liked it?" Andy asked.

"I have never been audience to such characterizations, split-second timing— a masterpiece. Why didn't I see it coming?"

"You were distracted and tired—and a bit pompous, too," Andy added.

After an admiring beat, Gus spewed, "My, but that was good!"

Andy beamed.

Jim pointed to himself. "Hello. Would somebody fill the kid in, here, please."

Gus said, "Most, if not all, of the events of this seemingly chaotic last forty-eight hours have been very well orchestrated by this man here—my brother, Mr. Andrew Carvin Miller. I should have suspected immediately that something was amiss the instant that your photograph arrived some three days ago. And then that baseball that came through the window. Stupid, utterly sophomoric of me."

"Long before that," Andy assured.

"Before that?" Gus echoed.

"This thing has been in the works for quite a while, brother. Angie, would you care to fill in the blank?" Andy smirked and with his hand ushered Rita into the conversation.

Rita said, "I knew Bea from an acting class we took together back at college. And I knew Andy from a short-term mission trip we took, so I introduced them to each other."

Andy said, "Go on."

"Andy concocted this whole thing months ago. He decided he needed an inside operative close to the Lost and Found International family."

Bea interjected, "Me."

Gus and Jim went slack-jawed.

Andy said, pointing to his brother, "I finagled your previous assistant."

Gus supplied, "Mrs. Sycamore?"

Andy said, "That's right. Mrs. Sycamore felt compelled to leave LFI because for some reason she had come to suspect that perhaps you were being investigated by the FBI for gunrunning or drug smuggling or some such thing—"

Gus said, "That's why she quit so suddenly."

Andy said, "Then I hustled Bea in there with an irresistible resume, and you hired her on the spot."

Gus shook his head, regarded Bea and then said, "The inside woman."

Bea lifted her eyebrows and smiled a big smile.

Jim was astounded.

Andy said, "She got the lay of the land inside LFI and even helped set up the scheme."

Bea dragged a toe through the dirt sheepishly and said, "Ah, shucks, it was nothing."

Gus was boggled.

Andy said, "That's not all."

Gus said, "There's more?"

Andy assumed the physical manner of a familiar character—familiar to Gus and Jim, that is. Andy launched into his compelling reenactment of Indian civility incarnate. In a thick Indian rendering, Andy pointed to himself and said, "Allow me to reintroduce to you, your friend Mr. Idaja, administrative secretary to the Raja and Rani, who recently fell into possession of the so-called Amulet of Zoroaster. You no doubt recall enjoying a sumptuous repast with myself and the royal family but a few nights ago?"

Gus and Jim were speechless.

Andy gestured toward Rita, who bowed with a dramatic flair as Andy politely applauded. "The role of Madame X, a.k.a. the mysterious Rita, was elegantly portrayed by the smoky Angie Swanson. Her depth of character brought forth a subtle yet smoldering force not seen since the great Uta Hagen graced the stage."

"Oh, please, stop!" Angie piped up in false humility. "I cannot take all the credit. I owe so much of the success of my magnificent performance to my tireless, brilliant director, Mr. Andrew Miller." She flung her hand out toward Andy and slumped in exaggerated exhaustion, as if spent. They shared a laugh and applause.

Jim said, "You mean to say that this whole thing was a fake? The kidnapping, the note tied around the baseball, the Amulet of Zoroaster, the mysterious Rita—everything was just a big setup, a practical joke?"

Gus said, "I have perhaps neglected to mention my brother's proclivity for elaborate practical jokes."

Jim responded, "I'm not sure what you just said, but I think you've neglected to mention a lot of things."

"Unbelievable! I am flabbergasted," Gus stated flatly.

"I am stunned too," Jim seconded.

Andy, caught up on the wave of success, said, "You wouldn't believe what I had to go through to set this whole thing up. I had to call in some favors from some acquaintances in exotic places—Achmed, Mohammad, the villagers, the royal party, everything. I had to make it look real."

"How long have you been planning this thing?" Gus wanted to know, shaking his head in disbelief.

"For months and months, now. And by the way, don't try to cash that check Idaja gave you. It'll bounce higher than the Taj Majal."

Gus turned to Angie. "You were magnificent."

"Thanks. I love receiving favorable notices." Angie blushed unashamedly. She then turned to Andy and said, "I like him, Andy. Got any more brothers?"

"What about him?" Gus pointed to Martin Samuel, conked out on the dirt infield. "Who is he? Was he in on it? Bruno, or Samuel, or whatever his name is."

"I've never seen him before tonight," Andy said simply.

❖

CHAPTER 33

The Plot Revealed

Y ou don't know him?" Gus exclaimed.

"No," Andy crossed over to the limp body and knelt beside it. "He just happened along and nearly got in the way of things. Who is he?"

They all looked at the peaceful figure resting on the ground.

Jim gasped a response, "That's really him. That's Martin Samuel!"

"Who is he? What did he want?" Andrew inquired.

"Well, he is a ruthless archeologist with a dubious reputation," Gus explained. "He wanted what I wanted, the Scroll of Nablus. But I'm fairly certain he's also wanted on several outstanding warrants related to the way he does business."

Jim came alongside Martin Samuel and placed his fingers on the neck of the hulk. "He's okay, just a little unconscious at the moment. What are we going to do with him, Chief?"

"I don't know." Pointing to the supine Martin Samuel, Gus looked at Andy. "You weren't expecting him, were you?"

"No, I had no idea."

"He must have thrown a monkey wrench into the works. You no doubt had to think fast to maneuver around him."

Andy pointed to the sky. "What could I do? I shot up a quick prayer and kept moving forward." Andy shrugged his shoulders.

Gus said, "Not very exact, Andy. Not as fast on the fly as you used to be."

"It worked out," Andy asserted.

"What about the parchment or scroll or whatever it is. Is it real?" Jim asked.

Andy looked at his brother and asked, "What do you think, brother?"

"It's a fake, isn't it?" Gus said. His brother smiled and nodded. Gus smirked, "But a first class one, I'll grant you that."

"I spent a lot of time on it," Andy said.

"It's good work," Gus assured.

"I had to think of something intriguing enough to whet the old appetite...something you were currently working on, something that you really wanted to be authentic. My only concern was that you would figure out that it was a fake too soon. So I had to keep you off balance, occupied, bombarded with stuff happening—telephone calls, a kidnapping, a midnight rendezvous—all to keep your mind on things other than the scroll."

"The special delivery, your picture?" Jim asked.

"My calling card. It was a little personal touch. I couldn't resist." Andy turned to Gus, "What did you think when you saw my photograph?"

"I didn't know what to think. Not enough data. And the baseball was a touch of genius. I never knew what happened to the ball you gave me all those years ago. It looks like you put it to some use. You had me on the ropes the whole time, brother." Gus shook his head in admiration.

"When did you figure it all out, Chief?" Jim asked.

"Not until I recognized his voice." Gus regarded his brother, "You had me completely snowed."

Jim said, "How in the world did you get Bea to agree to all of this?"

"Hey, I was all for it!" Bea affirmed.

"I had no trouble at all. Bea was very cooperative. We got together a few months ago and worked out the details, everything—Mr. Idaja, Mohammad, Achmed, and Rita. I had spent some time in the Middle East and India, and there were a lot of folks just happy to do me the favor." Andy turned to Jim. "How did you like my buddies, Mohammad the guide and Hassan the Egyptian outfitter?"

"The whole thing was a setup, huh?"

Andy said, "Yep."

Jim was still incredulous. "The parchment? The amulet? The tomb of Zoroaster?"

"Phony, phony, phony," Andy said.

"The Raja? The ransom note? The kidnapping?"

"Phony, phony, phony."

"The midnight rendezvous? The forty-eight-hour chase? The Arab thugs?"

"Phony, phony, phony."

Gus said, "But good ones."

"They had to be. I was up against the best," Andy said.

Jim was still flabbergasted. "But the journey across the desert, the quest for the amulet, the raven providing yucky food, how did you do that?"

"The raven is a very trainable bird. It was actually Angie's idea. She has a friend who is a professional animal trainer. That bird is actually part of Bret Braven's circus act, Braven's Ravens. Perhaps you've heard of them?"

"No."

"How'd you like the grubs?"

"Yech!"

"We sent you the best-tasting ones we could find."

"How many grubs have you taste-tested?" Jim wanted to know.

Andy laughed and said, "I took other people's word for it."

"But everything was so real and difficult. I could have died out there."

"I would never have let that happen. But it had to seem real. Otherwise you wouldn't have been convinced."

"How were you sure I'd make it through and bring back the amulet?"

"I asked the same question, but Bea told me you are very resourceful in the field."

"Ah," Jim tilted his head and smiled at Bea, "you told him that?"

"It's the truth. Resourceful." Bea smiled back.

Gus said, "What about the crop duster plane we stole? You couldn't have planted that, could you?"

Andy said, "No, I had to think pretty fast. Since I was nearby and dressed up as Idaja, I had to come up with something. I rented the thing for almost all the cash I had on me so the owner wouldn't report the plane as missing."

Jim said, "Unbelievable."

Andy said, "Standing on the back porch of the owner's house, I improvised. I made up some cock-and-bull story about an international medical crisis—having to fly the Indian ambassador's daughter to the hospital for an emergency appendectomy. I told him the ambassador's family was on the train when the emergency stop lever was pulled and the ambassador demanded immediate transportation to the best hospital in America, or some such thing. Anyhow, it was just outrageous enough to be true, so the owner gladly took the cash and didn't report it, I guess."

"Where's the plane now?"

"Probably where you left it. I'm sure he'll eventually recover it. I assure you, I more than compensated him for his trouble."

Gus was speechless.

Jim confessed, "We've been had, Chief."

"We sure have, James, and by the best."

"You were pretty good too, Beatrix." Jim winked at her.

She winked back, "Thanks."

Gus thought for a bit and then leveled Jim. "James, you weren't part of this conspiracy, were you?"

"No way, Chief. I've been had, just like you."

Gus moved toward Jim suspiciously. "Either you were very good at your performance or very innocent. Which was it?"

"No, honest, Chief, really."

Bea spoke up, "He had no idea."

Andy continued the thought, "Jim was ignorant of our little scheme, and among his other attributes, his concern for Bea was a useful lever in getting you out here to me."

"What about Milo?" Gus wanted to know.

"Who's Milo?"

"Rookie Detective Toole, the policeman?"

"Oh, I had to outrun him."

"You threw the ball through the window?"

"No one else."

"So, Milo wasn't involved?"

"No."

"Are you sure?"

"Of course."

"Forgive me, but somehow I can't help suspecting everyone."

Just then a moan was heard in the background, becoming more distinct as Martin Samuel moved toward consciousness.

Quickly Jim uttered, "Chief, what'll we do?"

Beatrix volunteered, "We should go!"

Andy showed a impish expression, "No, wait."

Gus immediately recognized that old familiar look on his brother's countenance and quickly said, "No, Andy, maybe Beatrix is right. Maybe we had just better leave."

"No," Andy insisted, "give me the gun, quick."

"No way! What are you going to do?" Gus captured Andy's rhythm. "You wouldn't."

Andy clicked off the trigger to produce a metallic snap. There was no loud report. "It's a stage gun."

Andy put the harmless weapon into the hand of the semiconscious Martin Samuel.

"Oh, my head!" The lumbering oaf rolled onto his side as he started to regain some composure. "Yes, on behalf of the university, I would be humbled to accept this monetary reward." With a bit more groaning, the light in Martin Samuel's noggin continued to swell. "What happened? My head…where am I…wait a minute?"

While Samuel continued to come to, Andy directed traffic in order to present a chorus line of the present company directly behind the staggering Samuel.

"What are we doing?" Gus wanted to find out.

"Follow my lead," Andy stated.

Andy raised his hands and feigned a frightened expression. The others picked up the cue and stamped on similar looks as they finalized their postures to resemble a straight lineup of cowering victims along the third base line.

Samuel slowly wobbled to his feet with the lineup to his back. He shook his head back and forth as if to test the connection it had to the neck and then he said, "Wha…happened?"

Andy leaned into his brother and asked, "Who is he?"

"Martin Sam—" Gus corrected himself, "I mean Bruno, Bruno Walters."

Andy piped up, "Okay, Bruno, you got the drop on us. Now, what do you want?"

Samuel turned in place to face the voice coming at him through the dark. "Huh?"

"You got us where you want us now, so make your demands."

It took Samuel a little while to drink in the group. "What?"

"What do you want?"

"I want to know why you people can't stand still," Samuel murmured. Just then he realized he was holding a pistol in his right hand. "What's this?" He shifted it to his left.

"You know perfectly well what it is, Walters."

"I do?" Samuel repeated, "I do."

"Let's rush him!" Andy said.

"No, no, stay back, or I'll shoot. I mean it!" Samuel brandished the weapon. The others froze. "What happened?" Samuel quizzed.

"Okay, you got the gun, now what do you want?"

"Some aspirin…"

"Come on, Walters, don't toy with us."

"No, no, that's not it…de…uh…"

"The what?"

"De…"

"The parch…" Andy said leadingly.

"The parch?" Samuel squinted.

"The parchment, Bruno," Gus said.

Samuel thought for a second, then the light finally reached its full intensity. "Yeah, yeah, that's it, the parchment! Aha! Thought you could pull the wool over me."

Jim contributed, "No way, Bruno. You're too smart for us by half a mile."

"And don't forget it, Sport. You have to get up pretty early in the morning to fool old…what'd you call me?"

"Bruno, Bruno Walters."

"Yeah, Bruno, Bruno Walters. Now, come on now, cough it up!"

"What?" Andy asked.

Samuel tilted his head. "Who are you?"

"He's my brother," Gus conceded.

Samuel looked back at Andy. "My condolences. Now where is the parchment?"

No answer.

"Cough up the scroll!"

Gus finally shook his head in mock surrender and relented, "You better give it to him. The man's desperate."

Jim added, "Okay, Chief, but I don't like it."

"You don't have to like it, Sonny, just give it here."

Jim handed over the fake scroll to Samuel as the latter gloated audibly. "Here you go, pip-squeak, nothing to it." Samuel pierced Jim with a scowl. "You're probably a college graduate too, huh?" Before Jim could respond, Samuel laughed giddily. "Well," he proceeded, "it has been really nice doing business with you, Miller."

Samuel started to leave, but Gus stopped him. "Excuse me, Walters, but I can't help noticing something."

"What's dat?"

"You seemed to have acquired a thug dialect."

"My what?"

"A cheap two-bit phony gangster accent."

"Oh, yeah?" he smirked, "What are you talkin' about? Doo-doo-head! Dis is real! And it ain't cheap, and it ain't phony! But before I leave, I want to let you in on a little secret. Tings are not as dey seem."

"Oh?" Gus said innocently.

"No, I am not who I appear to be."

"Who are you?"

"No, bright boy, my name isn't Bruno Walters."

"It isn't?"

"No, you nit, it is not." Samuel paused for dramatic effect. "I am none other dan Martin Samuel!"

The entourage assembled on the third baseline gave a collective gasp.

"Dat's right, Miller. It's me, Martin Samuel, or as some like to call me, de Damascus Butcher."

"I don't believe it!" Gus topped himself.

"Well, believe it, pal. Martin Samuel, dat's me, de guy you've been lambasting in duh papers lately, huh? How's it feel now, Dr. Miller, to be duh fool, duh laughingstock, huh?"

Jim faked an impulse to advance on Samuel, "Why you—"

"Easy, Junior."

Jim stopped.

"Had you all conned, didn't I? Made you look like idiots, didn't I?"

"I'll get even with you, Samuel!" Gus snarled.

"You can try, Miller. But really, I should hope you'd have learned your lesson by now, little Mister PhD" Samuel squared his shoulders in self-satisfaction as he started to amble away. "You can't mess with Martin Samuel, no siree, duh man of a hundred disguises, duh Damascus Butcher, Bruno Walters. I got to be going now, and don't bother to follow me, nimrod, or you could get hurt." Samuel looked directly at Jim. "So long, suckers." With that parting salvo, Martin Samuel vanished into Central Park, chortling in self-content as he went.

After a protracted silence, as the Damascus Butcher was allowed to skulk into the night, everyone exhaled and the laughing began.

Amid the uproar Jim mocked, "'Don't bother to follow me, nimrod?' What does that mean?"

"So long, suckers!" They laughed again to the point of tears.

Gus said, "That was good, Andy, very good. Somehow that makes the last two days worthwhile."

"The look on his face when he saw the gun in his hand—" Bea added.

"—was priceless," Jim finished the sentence.

"Can you believe that guy? What a buffoon!"

"He had it coming."

Another pause as the laughing wound down.

"Well, I don't have any more questions," Jim said.

"I do." Gus whirled on his brother. "Why?"

"Why?"

"Yes, why? Why all these elaborate histrionics? Why all of this manipulation? Why all the plots and characters? Why not just write me a letter telling me you will be visiting me for a weekend and show up at the front door a few days later like a normal person. Why all this maneuvering?"

"There are two reasons," Andrew said. "The first one is because I wanted to see you, to talk about old times, see what you're up to, and let you know that I'm still going strong."

"And the second reason?"

"The second reason is for you, brother, and you alone. So, everybody—away. Go. Leave us alone. I want to talk to my one and only brother."

Jim protested, "Wait, I want to hear what—"

"Come on, Jim." Beatrix started to lead Jim away.

"But—"

"Go on," Andy reiterated.

The Miller brothers were left alone on the third baseline.

❖

CHAPTER 34

Reflection & Relief

As the others left with some reluctance, the gravity of the scene shifted. The moon swept the large night sky from east to west. An exceptionally large meteor streaked a convincing trail across the dark canopy to celebrate with a natural fireworks display.

I looked at my brother whom I had not seen in fifteen years and who had just pulled off an elaborate—and expensive—hoax to get my attention. Now that we were alone, I hardly knew what to say.

Andy finally spoke. "So, Gus, how are you?"

"Well, tired," I admitted. "But for the most part…good. It's good to see you. I firmly believed that I would never lay my eyes on you again."

"Why did you believe that?"

"I don't know…why didn't you try to…keep in touch?"

Andy shrugged, "I just got tired of being rejected."

I said, "You're right, of course. I'm sorry…I guess, well, for the longest time I didn't want to see anyone…anyone who would make me think…think of Mom and Dad."

"I'm sorry, too. I should have been more persistent, but my time is not always my own." Andy reached out and embraced me again. I had missed that sensation more than I'd wanted to admit over the years.

"Andy," I said, "this little plot of yours here, with the kidnapping and the intrigue, this was good, real good. You have not lost your moves."

Andy said, "Better than that time in community college? When you helped me with that practical joke?"

"Which one?"

"There weren't that many! I'm thinking of the pre-vet major."

"Vicki Harris," I supplied. I never forgot a name.

"Right. I told her about this big job opportunity in an animal hospital in Hollywood or something. You know, being a doctor to the pet stars or some such line—and she bought it!"

"Yes, and you even rented that office space and pretended to be the leading animal doctor on the West Coast. What was it? You were on a nationwide tour to interview prospective vets. I think you took care of Lassie, Rin Tin Tin, and Flicka, or some such thing."

Andy said, "We kept calling her back for interviews. I even promised her a movie career through a prominent producer friend of mine."

I said, "You led that poor girl on for weeks."

"It was mean."

"Yes. It was kind of funny, though. But I remember when she found out it was all a hoax, she just smiled and laughed the whole thing off. She couldn't believe she'd fallen for it."

We stood in silence for a moment. Then Andy asked, "What did you do with all those letters I wrote?"

"Tossed them," I admitted, wishing now that I had saved every one of them. I pretended not to notice that my brother flinched at the truth.

After a while, I had to ask, "Why did you do all this, Andy? What is the second reason for this elaborate charade? Go on, level with me." After everything I'd been through, I could take it.

"Well, I had to effectively invade your space. I had to get inside your ivory tower and talk to you with your guard down. So, I came in as a client, Idaja. It had to be something good, something right up your alley, to make the deception work. It had to be believable for both you and Jim."

I slowly moved my head from side to side.

"I had to rattle your cage," Andy continued, "to the point where you'd be forced to leave that prison of yours."

"Prison?"

"Yeah, that self-imposed jail cell you call a home."

"I feel safe there," I said simply.

"Gus, you don't need safe."

"I don't?"

"No. Safe is stifling, safe is suffocating."

Where is he going with this? I wondered. "Seems like a lot of trouble to go through—for the results, I mean."

Andy said, "It was worth it. You needed to step out of your comfort zone."

The last thing I wanted was to admit he was right. But he was. I sighed and took the baseball out of my pocket. "That's why you used this as your messenger?"

Andy nodded. "You loved baseball."

"Still do," I murmured.

"Gus, when's the last time you saw the Cardinals play in the stadium?"

I hated to admit it. "1959."

Andy stood up. "Let's play catch."

"It's a regulation league ball. You always complained that it hurt your hand to catch without a glove."

"So don't throw hard. We'll just toss it."

I stood up and walked a few paces away from him, then tossed the ball. We tossed it back and forth, gently for the most part, as we continued to talk.

"I actually do feel pretty good out here," I said. "A baseball diamond was a stroke of genius. Or compassion."

"You made it, and you survived," Andy said as he lobbed the ball high.

I said, "Yes, I did, didn't I?" I caught his lob and returned one of my own. "Besides hoaxing me at my own expense, what are you up to these days?"

"Well, for one thing, I'm following in Dad's footsteps. I sort of took over the family business, you might say." There was a moment. "I'm a missionary."

"I thought as much." I shook my head. "Ever married?"

"Nah."

"So what exactly do you do?"

"I've circled the globe looking after his best interests—China, India, Australia, Africa, Europe, and even behind the Iron Curtain."

"You always were the adventurous sort. What do you do in these exotic places?"

"Whatever needs to be done: preaching in the Philippines, building a hospital in Africa, flying in South America. My boss has given me very little spare time in the last few years."

"What do you get out of it?"

"Next to nothing. That's not the point."

I looked at my sibling and quietly said, "I'm sorry, Andy, but I could never understand why Mom and Dad did it, either. What a waste of talent. There they were, in the bush in Africa, supposedly called by God, wasting their time on people who didn't want them there in the first place."

"What makes you think their lives were wasted?"

No answer.

Andy added, "'All things work together for good to them…'"

I caught the ball and turned away. "Please don't quote Scripture to me."

Andy persisted, "Mom and Dad were invited over there, and they helped a great many people."

"That's stretching the truth, but I know they really believed that, too. But just imagine the good that they could have done with their full lifetimes."

"Why think in terms of a lifetime, why not eternity?"

I shook my head. "As I suspected, here it comes, a sermon about some pie-in-the-sky heavenly eternity some day." I threw the ball back to Andy a little too hard.

Andy caught the ball and lobbed it back without speaking. I think he knew he didn't really have to deliver the whole sermon. I already knew, so it was as good as said.

We had resumed an amiable rhythm with the baseball. I didn't want a sermon, but I did want to talk to my brother. After all, he was the only person on the planet who could understand. "When Mom and Dad died, I was decimated, completely crushed…there was nothing left of me. I don't even remember the trip home from Africa. I just recall waking up, back in the States, in a strange bed, back at Uncle Eugene and Aunt Constance's place in St. Louis."

I could feel myself fumbling for words. "You know, now that I think about it, I'm not really sure I've ever even told myself this before. I was detached—and yet I was there." I shook my head. What good would come from where Andy was trying to take me?

"Keep going," Andy prodded.

Despite my silent protests, my mind continued to wander into the past. And then I was, all of a sudden, confronted with a vivid recollection of the scene. There were the bodies of my folks hanging down from the acacia tree, stripped of their skin. Piles of their flesh with gooey blood dripping down. I could see it in front of me. I felt a humid, hot blast of equatorial Africa. I smelled the odor of death. I heard the flies buzzing torridly, and I involuntarily recoiled at the pawing of the villagers. It was a brief, shivering, sensory reliving of the most horrid moment of my life. I swatted at the air to rid the area of flies.

Andy just watched me.

I forced myself to gather my wits. "I used to have a nightmare," I said. Now that I had started, it was all coming out. "I saw them there outside, hanging upside down in the early dawn, mutilated, not even recognizable. Then I was straining to keep up with the light. The sun moved too fast for me. I would look over my shoulder at the darkness, afraid now that it was going to catch me. And it always did. And the bodies were always there. I would dread that vision, the outside and the terror of the darkness, but I couldn't stop it. I was all alone. It was strange, though. I hated being alone, and I loved it at the same time."

Andy held onto the ball for a moment. "Gus, you're not alone in all this. Don't forget, I was there with you. For months after Mom and Dad were killed, I imagined that I had the power to live that day and the day before over again, and that I was a hero in saving Mom and Dad. That I warned them, and we fled together to a safe place. I tried to reinvent the past."

Gus said, "I promised God I would give up playing baseball if he would bring back our folks. I would do anything he wanted if they would just not be dead."

"I tried to convince myself that Uncle Eugene and Aunt Constance were my real parents," Andy said. "That way my parents wouldn't be dead."

"They were innocent, decent people, helping others. God let this happen!"

"I know."

"And you want me to believe in this God!" Well, I wouldn't, even if my brother had done what he'd done to get through to me. "Where was the justice?"

The image in my mind of the deathly scene persisted as it drove me to grope my way through my own maze of feelings.

"When I was older," Andy said, "I fantasized that the whole village where we were staying rose up and caught that witch doctor and took him and hanged him by the neck—put him on display for all to see the justice that was done."

"But that didn't happen."

"Gus, I realized that the notion of vengeance, that desire for what I thought to be just retribution, was poisoning me. It was crippling me. Holding onto that desire for blood was the worst thing I could do for myself."

"Now you're going to talk about forgiveness," I predicted. "God should be asking for my forgiveness for taking my parents."

Andy said, "We don't like it but it, happens. Sometimes systems fail, and the bad guys get away for a while. What do you do when that happens?"

"I don't know," I admitted.

"You do know, Gus, you do…you forgive."

"No!" I saw the lifeless bodies of my mom and dad, hung like sides of beef as if in a meat locker.

"Anyone who goes through monumental loss, like we did, has to face forgiveness. You've got to decide whether you are going to be forever held a prisoner by a tragic past or you are going to choose to be released by forgiveness."

"How can I forgive and forget? That would be a betrayal of the memory of my parents!" I felt the perspiration as it rolled down my face just as it had done that dreadful morning so long ago. Salt water got in my eyes. I blinked at the irritation.

"They're my parents, too," Andy said. "I'm not saying to forget, just forgive."

I hesitated, then spoke, shaking my head, "I have so much bitterness against them—against God, who allowed this, when he could have done something."

Andy paused and then admitted, "I felt just like you did, Gus, but eventually I realized it would be a process, a desperately needed process—and a step of faith, I guess you'd call it. So I took the first step."

I had no answer. I heard the thuds as the ties were cut and the gory corpses pounded to the muddy dirt. I flinched.

"When Jesus was hanging on the cross about to die, he asked his Father in heaven to forgive his murderers. He gave up his rights for us. Are you somehow better than Jesus?"

Again, no answer. I stood by the crude graves quickly dug on the Masai Mara. I saw the mounded dirt, packed down hard and final.

With a casual toss, Andy interjected a new thought, "What did Mom and Dad tell us so often when we got scared or felt danger? They said 'We are ready to die; we already have eternity in our hearts, but the people we are ministering to are lost and need the message we bring.' The process of forgiveness starts when I realize that justice or revenge cannot alter the past. That God is in charge. And in our case, we know where Mom and Dad are right now, in a much better place."

"I hate the thought of it," I insisted. "Even if that is true, it still doesn't seem to help much. It's too abstract."

"Not really. Suffering and loss force us to ask him good, hard, honest questions." Andy looked up. "Are you a good God? Sovereign? Can we trust you?"

I sighed. "I've asked him those questions and he gave me no answers!" I pounded my own thigh with a closed fist.

"Maybe you didn't want to listen. Maybe God had something to say through your suffering."

"How so?" I asked, although I was pretty sure what Andy was going to say.

"Heartaches act as a loudspeaker to wake us up. Instead of keeping God at arm's length, when we suffer we realize we need him.

I was thinking, my mind churning with disparate thoughts. I was grateful for the simple task of throwing the ball back and forth in the moonlight.

Finally I blurted, "When I was a kid, I prayed for Mom and Dad, Andy. Every night, I prayed for them. They died. For years I woke up every morning asking why. After years of no answers, I gave up. I'm just empty, Andy."

"I've got to make a choice to offer you comfort, brother. But you have to make a choice to receive it."

In a rollercoaster of rage, I slammed the baseball into the dirt as hard as I could. "No, no, it's too easy. I will not have it be that easy!" I stomped around on the ground like an angry grape-crusher, mad at the fruit and angry at the God who caused it to grow. But after my flailing rant, I crumpled into the dirt myself, next to my baseball. I started to shake uncontrollably, keening at my pent-up loss.

Andy grabbed hold of me and rocked back and forth with me. "It's all right, Gus...it's okay...I'm here." Andy wasn't going to let me go, of that I was sure.

"It can't be," I screamed into the night. "They can't be dead!" I wailed bitterly, but Andy held on.

"Mom, Dad, I love you! And I hate you both! I hate to lose you! I'm sorry, I'm so sorry. I don't hate you—I love you!"I groaned, squalled, and lamented uncontrollably, an enormous bawl that was years in the making. Andy just held on.

"What am I going to do?" I sat up and looked my brother in the face. "Andy, all I have is you, and I've pushed you away." I hugged my brother.

Andy held on.

"I'm sick," I said urgently.

"You'll be okay," Andy said as he held on.

"No, no, I'm sick to my stomach." I pushed away from Andy and leaned my head over and vomited onto the ground. Andy reached for me again.

I vomited again.

"What am I going to do?" I finally said, wiping my mouth.

"Let go, Gus, let go of the grief." Andy held on.

"I can't let go; I've got to keep them alive."

"You can't do that, brother. You've got to let them go. Just say goodbye."

"It's too painful!"

"Let go, Gus. Say goodbye to them."

"Goodbye…goodbye, Mom and Dad. I love you."

Finally, at last, I said a deep-seated goodbye to my parents and my angry grief. Andy held me, his grip as strong as ever.

Slowing the wrenching tears gave way to joy and release. My breathing settled into a regular rhythm, and Andy began to loosen his grip.

"What do I do now?" I asked.

"Jesus," Andy said simply.

"What about him?"

"Do you have a problem with Jesus?"

"No…I guess not."

"Jesus forgives," Andy said. "You need forgiveness. You can't compare yourself with someone else. It doesn't matter if you miss being perfect by an inch or a light year. 'All have sinned and come short of the glory of God.' A miss is as good as a mile, brother. Everyone needs Jesus. You know the drill," Andy prompted me. "You don't have to make a big scene and bring Jesus down from the cross to you. You can do it right where you are. Just speak your heart and be honest with God. Say that you want to go his way. He knows your heart, you can't fool him."

"I've got so many questions…"

"So do I. Who doesn't? In India, they tell a story about a soldier getting shot by an enemy arrow. His comrades hurry to him while on the field of battle in order to bind his wounds and to save him. He stops them short to ask, 'Who shot the arrow?' After they answer him, they try to patch him up and take him off to safety. He says, 'Wait, what is the arrow made off?' They answer. He stops them again. 'Wait, what was the trajectory? How many feathers on the shaft? How was it made?' On and on, he asks questions without yielding to the treatment he needs. In short, he bleeds to death asking superfluous questions."

"What do I say?" I asked.

"Just speak your heart."

I gulped hard, then cast my gaze downward. "I tell you, Andy, I'm guilty."

"Of what?"

"I'm guilty of resenting Mom and Dad for loving God more than me. For staying bitter at God for not preventing their deaths."

"Don't do it, brother. Don't hang onto that guilt. Allow for forgiveness just as you have already been forgiven. God is willing to do that."

There was a solemn silence after which I requested, "Could I be alone for a while, please, Andy?"

"Sure. I've got to go soon anyway. I'm headed for Germany in a few hours."

"Germany? What are you doing in Germany?"

"Some friends of mine are transporting some sensitive religious materials into East Germany." Andy thought. "Why not come with us? We could use a good man like you. You're smart and pretty quick on your feet, you know, for a bookworm."

I didn't answer right away, so Andy said, "I'll tell you what, I'll be right over there waiting. Come on, Gus, time is wasting and eternity is waiting." Andy stood up, picked up the baseball, and tossed it back to me. With that, Andy walked back into the shadows he'd come from.

With the ball in my hand, I stood up and wandered over to the pitcher's mound and paused there alone, looking up at the night sky.

"Well, God," I said out loud, "Jesus…before I start, I want you to know I have a lot of questions, and you aren't going to have a very smooth sailing with me. I admit I've got this stupid pride. I'm not a very easy-to-know person. In fact, most of the time I'm downright petrified. I would never tell anyone else that, but you, of course. Uh, and to be totally candid, I'm still angry at losing Mom and Dad, but I guess you know what's best. I guess I really don't want to give in to you…but I suppose you know what's best for me, so I'm willing to be made willing to want you…whatever…you get my drift? I'm sorry, Jesus, I'm sorry. I apologize to you for turning my back all these years. It's not right. Please, Jesus, let me go your way."

At one instant within my heart of hearts, there was a swirl of fresh essence—a beautiful, intuitive, soulful gust. All of my guile and determination melted before me, like an opaque fabric being suddenly removed from the object of the revelation. It was not of my doing. It was extremely substantial, yet ethereal at the same time. I was vividly aware of my own inadequacies and that I was somehow doomed and so, so forlorn. The inner aches of my being were unusually transparent and obvious to me, as if I were naked to myself and also to the Creator of the cosmos for the very first time. It was monumentally humbling to me.

I stood there, motionless, looking at the stars. "There," I voiced upward, "is that what you've been waiting for all these years? For me to say that and come full circle to you?" There was no answer. "Well, I'm glad to be home, Father."

I didn't expect to feel what I felt inside. A three-ton weight was hoisted off my soul, and I felt like a newborn baby would feel, with a new life in front of him, new skin, and a proud and doting Dad to watch over him—all that mushy feely stuff.

You know, at this point, I could readily make a case for the following principle: the greatest emotion that could possibly be experienced by the human heart is not love, or joy, or confidence, or success, or satisfaction, or pleasure, or any of those things; I would eagerly confess that the greatest emotion anyone could experience is relief—there is nothing like it! And yet, not just encountered by one's emotion or will, but sensed by the very motivational center within. Relief. Forgiveness.

I smiled a big smile and said under my breath, "Ollie ollie oxen free. Free!"

✤

CHAPTER 35

The Parting

Gus savored his new freedom for a few beats. Then his attention was drawn to movement on the first baseline. Beatrix Peeters and James Morrison, holding hands, emerged from the shadows. The shimmer about them was indisputable. Even the casual observer would have seen the steam of infatuation wafting off their necks and lips. They were unashamedly flushed with a recent unambiguous caressing, cuddling contact.

Gus smiled a huge smile at them, and they returned a huge smile back at him. Jim and Beatrix had an unmistakable glow of love about them.

"Hi, Chief," Bea said.

"Beatrix, James," Gus returned.

"Everything okay, Chief?" Jim queried.

"Great, just great, couldn't be better. How are you?"

Jim looked at Bea and then back to his boss and said, "Great, great. You?"

"Fine, James, fine, thank you. And thank you!" Gus hesitatingly pointed upward.

A little befuddled, Jim said, "Oh, good, good. That's good."

Beatrix Peeters smiled an even bigger smile, if that were possible.

Jim started to tear up. "I love you, Chief." He moved to Gus and reached out to invite an embrace from his boss.

"I love you too, James." Gus reciprocated with a hearty hug of his own.

"I love you too, Beatrix," Gus ventured.

"Thanks, Chief, same here."

Gus went up to Bea and cornered her with his gaze. He said, "You were right, Beatrix. Right all along. This is just what I needed. Thanks for your prayers."

"I'm happy for you, Chief."

"I'm happy for you, too, and James—for the both of you." And he was. "I've got to catch up with my brother."

Jim spoke, "Wait, Chief, where are you going?"

"God only knows."

"But what are you going to do?"

"God only knows."

"How long are you going to be gone?"

"God only knows."

Jim was dumfounded, but finally put some words in his mouth. "You can't leave everything like this." Jim looked at Bea, "Can he?"

Beatrix shrugged her shoulders.

Jim asked, "What are we going to do?"

"I don't know, James. Why don't the two of you get married and have some kids?"

"What?"

"As long as one of them is a boy and you name him Gustov."

"Chief, ix-nay on the arriage-may…"

Bea inserted, "I would never saddle a kid with a name like that, but I do like James Junior."

"I don't know if I'm ready to plunge into…you know…"

"Go back to St. Louis and think about it. That's my last official advice as your boss."

"Last official advice?"

"You can have it all."

"All?"

"Yes, the house, the books, the business, the car, everything. " Gus took some keys out of his pocket and handed them to Beatrix. "Here."

Bea said, "What'll we do with all this?"

"Whatever you want. Sell it, live in it. It's yours, all of it. Consider it a gift from your dad."

Jim said, "I never had a dad."

"I know. You do now."

"What about your equipment, your artifacts—"

"It's yours."

As Gus moved off into the night, he shot over his shoulder, "The only thing I am going to need is God, my dad. That should suffice."

Gus waved his right hand in the air as he stopped and turned to speak directly to Jim. "Oh, and by the way, James, you can put that Lou Brock card, which is no doubt in your pocket, back in the display case behind the desk, where it belongs, please."

"Doggone it! How did you know that?" Jim sputtered, as he just then remembered the thing being exactly where Gus said it was.

"I didn't until just now. So long, and God bless the both of you—and thank you!"

Gus whirled and ran off resolutely into the future, out there somewhere.

The night sky reflectively beamed back the cool, clear presence of God.

"Isn't it a glorious night?" Gus emphasized as he exited and flowed into the oncoming tomorrow.

Beatrix waited and then observed, "And conventional wisdom says that lives can't change."

"Amazing, who would have thought it?" Jim finally yelled into the blackness after Gus, "Good luck to you, too, Chief, wherever you go."

Jim offered Bea his arm and she took it as they snuggled closely and started to amble off in the opposite direction.

"What are we gonna do with all his stuff?" James asked, holding up the keys.

"He seems to think we should get married and move into the house," Beatrix ventured.

"Well, yeah, you know, me and you…"

"Yes?" she said hopefully, turning her face up.

"You know…us, Mr. and Mrs. James Morrison, husband and wife…"

Beatrix halted. "Is that your idea of a proposal?"

Slowly Jim shook his head. "No, well…yeah, Bea, I guess so."

Bea looked out into the darkness as the wheels turned in her brain. She had hoped he would change. After all, Dr. Miller had.

"I can't marry you," she finally said, "if you're not a Christian."

"I don't really understand what just happened with the Chief," Jim said, "but that's not me, as much as you want it to be."

Bea said, "I love you, Jim."

James looked at her eyes, deep into those beautiful eyes. He let go of her arm and walked away some twenty paces, where he plumbed his soul. He thought about a lot of things in very little time. He thought about his own childhood without a mom or a dad. He thought about Lost and Found International and how much he liked it, how it was like a family to him. He thought about Dr. Gustov Miller, his newly former boss. He thought about his coworkers. He thought about one coworker in particular, standing twenty paces from him. He thought about her and how much he didn't want to lose her. She said she loved him. He didn't want to lose her. He did love her, or so he thought, but he did not want to deceive her. He liked the idea of being in love with her, but he did not like the consequence. He turned and walked back to her.

"Bea," he stood looking with searching depth into her lovely eyes, "I love you, too, and I don't want to lose you. But I can't do what you want me to do. But I can love you my way and my way only…"

Bea looked at Jim, pleading, her heart bursting.

"And if that's not good enough, I'm sorry."

Bea did some soul-searching herself, and within that examination she discovered Jim's resistant answer mixed with a bitterness and self-determination that was not mated to her spirit. She heard a phantom in his remarks that was foreign to her. She said, "I can't accept that offer."

"Then it's done?" asked Jim.

"Yeah, I guess so." She offered a hand. "Shake on it."

They did. She leaned forward and kissed him.

The long, lingering, open-mouthed kiss was, indeed, more of a sentence-ending period than a comma. She halted the kiss and then stepped back.

"What was that for?" Jim asked.

Bea hesitated, "Goodbye."

"Goodbye?"

She nodded. It was goodbye.

James Morrison and Beatrix Peeters separately weighed the present juncture of duration as they observed the passage of time drifting into the early morning awakening of the city.

Gustov Miller was on his way to his great adventure, not knowing exactly his destination. But he was content to know the Father, God, and his Son, Jesus Christ, the Knower of the way.

On the other hand, Jim and Bea, also not knowing where they were going, remained unsure and discontented with the vagueness of their future. Both of them stood there, physically an arm's length apart, but in other ways miles disconnected.

They slowly and wordlessly repelled each other like two discordant ends of magnetized iron bars.

She walked south and he walked north, both ambling along listlessly.

Unbeknownst to her, he looked desperately over his shoulder; seeing her pressing southward, he returned his gaze northward and continued his pace. She did not dare to look at him for fear of her own desire. She already regretted her decision, but she was resolved. She was humble. He was proud.

As she walked away, tears pooled up and streamed down her face.

As he walked in the opposite direction, tears puddled in his eyes as well and flooded his hidden countenance.

They kept moving their separate ways on Central Park West.

❖

CHAPTER 36

The Final Meeting

I found Andy in the shadows, and we went back to the hotel room that he had booked for us months ago. We stayed up most of the night talking—after all, we had a lot to catch up on. Andy's plane was out of JFK Airport about midmorning. Not having been out of the country since 1947, I would have to resolve the mundane matter of a passport before I could join him as speedily as possible.

About breakfast time, we went down to the lobby with Andy's luggage. I spotted Bea across the lobby, alone. I surmised that Angie must still be up in their room. Then I detected that Bea was wearing the same ensemble she'd had on in the park, hours ago. I didn't think she'd been to bed at all. I saw no sign of Jim, which saddened me. I had hoped they would work things out. She looked so forlorn sitting there alone, and she barely seemed to notice me. While Andy went to the desk to settle the bill, I meandered to the seating arrangement where Bea sat. I took the chair opposite her.

Finally, she looked up at me. "Good morning, Chief. How are you?"

"Well, Beatrix, I am doing quite well. I seem to have come full circle. I have come home to the Lord."

Tears gleamed in her eyes. "I'm so happy for you. I've prayed so long for you and Jim."

"You took it to heart to put aside your plans in order to invade my little world for a purpose not of your making," I reminded her.

She smiled weakly. "I was on the mission field all along, wasn't I? Now I'm just waiting to see where the Lord wants me next."

"I can't tell you how grateful I am for your persistence." I scanned the lobby, hesitant to ask what was on my mind. "Where is James?"

Bea looked at me, and her eyes immediately welled up. She started to speak, but her voice choked on the first syllable.

"What is it, Beatrix?"

After a bit, she said, "Chief, I'm so torn. I love him so much…I had such hope. But I couldn't go any further with him. He's not ready to believe."

"I knew as much. I could readily see how he felt toward you and I certainly sensed the attraction you two shared." I looked at the oriental rug under my wingtips.

Bea sat up straight and regarded me with an awkward anticipation. She collected her words as if getting ready to lead the witness. "Chief, I wasn't sure until a few days ago that you…had feelings for me."

I took in some air, about to speak, but Bea held out her hand flatly to me. She continued, "I want you to know that I am truly sorry for this. I did, honestly, notice the way you kind of drooped when you saw Jim and me embracing in the park last night. I could feel your disappointment. I should have known, but I'm really sorry that I just didn't get it until then. I'm so sorry."

I waved away her concerns. "It's all right, Beatrix. It's not your fault. I suppose I find it strange that I am so overjoyed with finding the one who loves me with boundless love—the God of the cosmos did not give up on me, and that produces at my very core an incomprehensible happiness—yet I am so dreadfully disappointed at the same time. I made this trip in order to rescue you and to prove to you the worthiness of my love."

It was Bea's turn to look at the carpet. "I think it's amazing that the Lord would not let me see your interest in me. I suppose if I knew how you felt about me, I wouldn't have gone through with the whole thing. I was so blind not to see it, and yet to be so awkwardly smitten by Jim Morrison."

I paused for thought. "You see, Beatrix, I do believe that a great love can only be replaced by a greater one. I had thought, all along, that God was my enemy; that he somehow had it in for me. But in reality, he is and always has been my greatest friend and ally. He was patient with me. I now fully understand that it was I who built the barrier between us, not him. Let me quote to you the verse in the Bible that I wouldn't allow Andy to quote to me last night: 'All things work together for good to them that love God, to them who are called according to his purpose.' Man devises his plan, but it is God who directs his path. I suppose I, too, am glad that you had no clue; otherwise, this whole strategy never would have unfolded. Thanks be to God."

Beatrix started to cry. I put my arm around her. Through those tears mixed with laughter she said, "Here you are and here I am, the former atheist and the longtime Christian." She directed her gestures to accompany her words. "You, so clear on the workings of God, and me, so clueless and so inadequate when it comes to being able to figure out how immature it was to fix all my hope on Jim and all along not having the least notion of your interest in me."

I removed my arm as Bea dried her eyes.

Finally I said, "So what's next?"

"Good question. Where are you going, Chief?"

"I don't know, but I do know the Knower of the way. I will follow Andy as he follows the Lord."

Andy must have subliminally heard his name because at this point, he appeared next to us and pointed to his watch. I stood up to walk my brother to his waiting cab. Then I would go into the city and find a passport office.

"Goodbye, Miss Beatrix Peeters," I said, "and may God richly bless you."

"Goodbye, Dr. Gustov Miller, you too. Keep in touch. What should I do with LFI?"

"Like I said last night, it's up to you."

"It's really up to God."

"That's right."

With that, I smiled and walked through the lobby doors. The future was beckoning me. Forgetting what was behind, I pressed on to what lay ahead.

✤

Epilogue

Beatrix Peeters went back to St. Louis. She buttoned up Dr. Miller's house and put the business on hold. LFI was on hiatus. She did not know where Gus had gone; she received no word from him for some time.

The apathetic Jim Morrison was waiting—for what, he couldn't say. He, too, went back to St. Louis. Maybe he was killing time, waiting for life to rain down upon him significance and joy. He was alone and aimless for a short time, then on a restless whim he joined the Army Rangers. He felt invincible.

In the middle of the night, Jim just stood there stoically in front of Bea's apartment for over an hour. He left a short note in her mailbox. It read, *Bea: I've joined the Army. I report tomorrow. Wish me luck, Jim.*

The next day, Bea wrote in her diary, *I cannot stop thinking about Jim. I can only assume that this decision on his part to join the Army is rash and uncalculated. Did I make the right choice by turning him down? I do think I really love him. The thought has occurred to me that perhaps I should have said yes to him and trusted in the Holy Spirit to change his heart in time. Maybe I could help Jim to realize his need for salvation. He just doesn't see it right now. Part of me wants to belong to Jim Morrison in marriage and another part knows the problems associated with being unequally yoked. I am getting no clear answers from God. I guess I have to wait. I hate waiting.*

Prayer Journal: Lord, I pray for Jim and his well-being. I pray that you will keep him safe and out of danger. Lord, please be with him. And let him know of your presence with him and your care for him. I cannot bring myself to pray for disaster to befall him. That's too frightening. Jesus, I want you to keep him safe. But I do know that very often people have to be put in rock-bottom situations that cause them to stop trusting in their own abilities and start leaning on you. My father used to tell me, "There are no atheists in foxholes." Whatever it takes, Jesus, for you to bring Jim around, I pray that you will do it. I still love him, Lord, and I love you. Please give him the desire of his heart. And give that to me, as well.

I pray for the Chief and Andy, both. Keep them in the palm of your hand. Thank you for giving the Chief purpose and meaning in his life. He has such incredible abilities that you have given him. Wherever you lead him and Andy, protect them by your Spirit, and may they realize fruit and joy because of their labors. All this, of course, by your will and for your glory, Jesus.

Give me clear direction as to what I should do. I would really appreciate clarity for me and for your purposes. In your name, Jesus, I pray. Amen.

Bea, sometime later, read the information on the official transcript:

```
Name: James Mitchell Morrison
Home: St. Louis, Mo.
Birth Date: 7-24-47—Joplin, Mo.
Sex: Male
Religion: Christian
Race: Caucasian
Citizen: USA
Service: U.S. Army
Rank: PFC
Casualty Date: 4-18-72
Casualty Type: Missing In Action—MIA
Reason: Helicopter Down, Soc Trang Province, Near Thanh Tri—Vietnam
```

Beatrix Peeters wept that day. She made no entry in her diary or prayer journal.

After a while, Bea grew despondent over the fate of Jim, so she gave up her apartment and deposited herself in the vacant Miller mansion. She got a job at the drugstore to make ends meet, and at night she took library science classes at the local community college. She lived alone in that big house and waited. She didn't know what she was waiting for, but she waited. She hoped, she waited, she prayed, and she experienced regret.

The brothers Miller were finally faithful to the family business. God was good to them. He gave them meaning and purpose and some good return on their investment. Bountiful and quick was the harvest gleaned.

✤ ✤ ✤

ABOUT THE AUTHOR

L. Frank James Jr. was born into a Christian home in Pasadena, California. Having a rich Christian family heritage, he was raised in the church and was taught the Gospel of Jesus Christ from an early age.

Drama and theater attracted Frank during both his high school and college years. At Pasadena City College, he was a drama major and graduated from Cal State L.A. with a bachelor's degree in Theater. While in Southern California, Frank earned a master of fne arts degree in Theater from UCLA.

Frank and his family moved to Northern California in 1989 to help plant Valley Spring, Presbyterian Church in Roseville, California. He held the position of Drama Director under David George, Senior Pastor, and is now the Pastoral Care provider.

He taught high school drama and has a long list of acting and directing credits in community as well as professional theater.

AWARDS, ACTIVITIES, AND RECOGNITION

Robert Reed acting award UCLA—*Hamlet*

Birdsal acting award—*Remember Me*

Elly acting award—*The Dining Room*

Bank of America award—Best actor

Published author: Plastow Publications—Church format sketches for Sunday morning worship events

Publishing awards: *Best Book of 2006* (USA Book News) in religious fiction for his novel, *An Opened Grave: Sherlock Holmes Investigates His Ultimate Case*

Performed and directed with various touring companies, worked with FACE (Fellowship of Artists for Cultural Exchange), and mounted and toured with two shows for ELIC (English Language Institute in China) to Mainland China

Performed and directed with "Last Minute Productions"

Participated in worldwide mission trips to China, Kenya, Tanzania, Philippines, and Mexico

Participated in theater—Paris, France—Theatre Du Terte

On the eve of this book going to press, Frank died an untimely death in a car accident on his way to church Sunday morning, September 2, 2007. Please see the inside back cover for a short tribute to Frank's life.

Praise for Frank's First Novel

An Opened Grave: Sherlock Holmes Investigates His Ultimate Case

Winner: Best Religion Fiction Book of 2006
— USA BOOK NEWS —

"Fans will appreciate this well written, entertaining and unique spin."
—MIDWEST BOOK REVIEW

"Mr. James does an admirable job…. Overall, it's an impressive accomplishment. Recommended."
—CHRISTIAN FICTION REVIEWS

"A brilliant weaving of good detective fiction with profound issues of faith. A great accomplishment!"
—JOHN ELDREDGE, author of *Captivating*

"Frank James is one of the most creative and engaging writers I have ever met."
—HUGH ROSS,President of REASONS TO BELIEVE and author of *The Creator & The Cosmos*

1934080-00-4   US $14.95
Trade paper: 240 pg
Fiction / Suspense / Christian

"Like G.K. Chesterton and C.S. Lewis, Frank James is a fine storyteller and a notable Christian apologist. Unusually well done; captures the Doyle-Watson style."
—THE SHERLOCK HOLMES SOCIETY OF LONDON

"Anyone who loves Sherlock Holmes stories or who would like to share a sharp intellect's grappling with the profoundest of religious mysteries will enjoy and learn from this book."
—FOREWORD MAGAZINE, Alan J. Couture

"The fictional vehicle allows the reader to examine assertions about Christ and the Bible in a more entertaining, though none less accurate, method than examining the same premises in a non-fiction format. I enjoyed the journey.
—AUTHOR'S CHOICE REVIEWS, Carolyn R. Scheidies

To comment on Frank's books or to participate in on-line discussions about literature, writing, theater, the arts, or ministry, go to www.lfrankjames.com.

PUBLISHER CONTACT: For publicity materials, bulk institutional purchases, or to purchase other books by L. Frank James, call The Salt Works at 916.784.0500.